The Unforgotten

Shaune Lafferty Webb

Book 3 of the
Safe Harbour Chronicle

THE UNFORGOTTEN

Book 3 of *The Safe Harbour Chronicle*

The moral rights of Shaune Lafferty Webb to be identified as the author of this work have been asserted.

Copyright 2019 Hague Publishing

Hague Publishing
PO Box 451
Bassendean, Western AUSTRALIA 6934
Email: contact@haguepublishing.com
Web: www.haguepublishing.com

ISBN 978-0-6485714-1-4

Cover: The Unforgotten by Jade Zivanovic
http://www.steampowerstudios.com.au/

Typeset Garamond 12/14

Acknowledgements

As the Safe Harbour Chronicle draws to a close, there are a few people I would like to single out for their continued support through the years: my husband Gregory Webb, brother Lee Lafferty and sister-in-law Lesley Lafferty, cousins Mitchell and Alison Warner, and long-time colleague Danielle de Valera.

As always, my sincere thanks go to Andrew Harvey, principal of Hague Publishing, and cover artist Jade Zivanovic of Steam Power Studios. Your patience hasn't gone unappreciated.

To my readers,
I'm sorry to be parting company with you on this particular journey,
but perhaps you'll be kind enough to join me on another …

Chapter 1

WHEN the horn sounded, shrill and urgent, Rab peered over the side of the steep-walled ravine, looking for Cloud. As soon as he had lowered her down on the rope, she had waded across the shallow stream to harvest from the opposite bank. Although the banks on both sides of the stream were seeded each season, for some reason *ungtilis* always thrived best on the far side. Some time ago Cloud had completely disappeared among the lushly growing stand. She'd be on her hands and knees now, snipping the tall blades close to the base where most of the flavour was concentrated. Her head surfaced at the second blast of the horn. Rab covered his ears with his hands. Seeing him, Cloud just smiled and slowly began shaking her head.

She wasn't going to play along. He'd more or less expected that she wouldn't. Cloud was halfway across the calf-deep stream, having threaded her way through the remaining *ungtilis* crop, when the horn sounded for the third time.

Rab stepped away from the edge of the ravine and walked back to the sturdy boulder where he'd tied off the rope to check that the knot was still secure. Below him, Cloud would be putting on her boots. He made it back to the edge just in time to grab the rope as Cloud began her ascent. It wasn't so long ago that there had only been a sprinkling of thorny urse clinging to the cracks and crevices in the ravine walls. Urse was the name Feathers gave to any plant they didn't cultivate or exploit and, like the *ungtilis* on the stream bank, this particular type of urse had begun to thrive in the warmer weather, posing an additional hazard to Cloud's climb. Qworkas didn't favour the thorny urse, so before she went harvesting again, he'd have to descend the wall himself and slash the bushes back. No harm done. It was kind of ironic really because, a decade ago, he would never have believed the day would come when the vegetation on this planet needed pruning.

Rab might have smiled at that thought had the horn not sounded again. Someday he'd convince Cloud to ignore it. What's the worst that could happen? Cloud had never been prepared to find out – yet.

He felt a sideways pull on the rope and glanced down into the ravine, looking for her among the urse. She was hanging off the rope in a clear spot to the left. No question – the urse would have to be thinned out before she scrambled down into the ravine again.

When Cloud drew close to the top, Rab dropped to his knees, ready to offer his hand to haul her the last of the way up. She really didn't need his help but accepted it just the same. The Qworka-skin bag slung across her back was bulging. The harvest had been good this year.

"Any idea what this is about?" Cloud asked. She shrugged the bag from her back and passed it to Rab. Before she'd descended into the ravine, her dark hair had been bundled tidily into one long braid. Now the braid was coming unravelled at the edges and the odd urse thorn was caught up in the loose strands.

"Not a clue," Rab replied, slinging the bag across his back.

Cloud started pulling the rope up the side of the ravine, making loop on loop in her hands.

"Four short blasts," she said, glancing at Rab as she began to make her way back to the boulder where he'd secured the end of the rope, coiling as she went. "Can't be all that important."

"Precisely why I suggested we ignore it," Rab said, trailing after her.

Cloud shrugged as she bent and started on Rab's knot. "You knot like a Feather. Next time, would you consider making them easier to untie?"

"Want to fall down the ravine?" Rab countered.

"Not especially," she replied, smiling up at him over her shoulder. "You're curious," she said, turning back to the troublesome knot. "You're always curious. You just don't want to admit it." The knot finally came free.

"Not especially," Rab told her and, raising his boot, tapped her gently on the leg.

She rose, coiling the last of the rope. "I swear the older you get, the more you remind me of Fin," she said with a gentle punch to his shoulder before starting out ahead of him towards home.

***

Alone, Rab and Cloud made their way through the gate in the outermost wall ringing their settlement. Once inside they veered left, located the gate in the second wall and passed through it. Weaving right, they backtracked for some distance until they came upon the gate in the third and innermost wall and entered the settlement itself. Theirs was the largest of the Feather settlements, being the seat of government, and the only settlement with a substantial population of tunnel-people – the doq'iri, a Feather word that Rab had soon learned meant 'thin-skin people'. In their push north, the Feathers had gone only so far. It was as though some physical barrier had stopped them. Perhaps it was simply a matter of proximity to the life-giving river. The mine was the only settlement of any kind north – jit – of the main colony. Rab had always found it curious that the Feathers used the same word for north and backward and, almost as strange, that the only other settlements were small and, for the most part, scattered to the east – seyn.

While Rab had done time at the mine, neither he nor Cloud had ever seen any of the other settlements, so they relied on the word of the handful of tunnel-people who had travelled further afield. Apart from size and the number of tunnel-people living there, all settlements were apparently alike. Each was set out in the same kind of ring pattern with narrow lanes mirroring the circular outer wall and wider lanes, like spokes, connecting them. The Feathers' dwellings, too, were generally round and usually constructed of stone or, more rarely, brick. Feathers referred to their dwellings as ts'uns. At least that's the best the doq'iri' had ever come to pronouncing the word; Feather was a challenging language. The windows in ts'uns were either narrow or non-existent and their roofs sheathed in Qworka-skin or a thick rough cloth saturated with the boiled down fat of Qworkas to render it water-repellent. The ts'uns where the tunnel-people lived were constructed in a similar fashion, although they were considerably smaller and crowded closely together near the perimeter. For practical reasons, their walls were higher since even the shortest human stood a good head above the tallest featherwoman, who on the whole were of superior height to the males. Rab and Cloud's ts'un lay on the far side of the settlement, furthest from the outer gate.

There was no time to rush back to their ts'un and off-load the heavy coil of rope and the bag, which was stuffed almost full with Cloud's abbreviated gleanings. Instead they hurried down the wide lane leading to the core of the settlement, passing as they went an outer swath of simple ts'uns. The closer they drew to the core where the more affluent and influential of the Feathers lived, the more elaborate and colourfully decorated the ts'uns became. The Common, along with the palace that flanked it, dominated the centre of the settlement. Most days the Common served as a public thoroughfare but, save for an intricately carved stone throne, the raised semicircular platform at its heart usually stood empty, being reserved for the sole use of the Kun and his attendants, whether they happened to be occupying it at that particular time or not.

Now the Common hosted an eclectic gathering of Feathers and doq'iri, although the two rarely intermingled even when marshalled to Assembly. Feathers and doq'iri weren't exactly on equal footing and neither could readily communicate with the other in anything much but hand-signals and the odd featherword a few of the tunnel-people had eventually mastered. If it weren't for Lilly Benson, there'd be no understanding at all and the Feathers rise to ascendency might have been a bloodier but more obvious climb. Instead it had been a creeping, insidious thing that was done before the tunnel-people had even realised it. Sunny would have seen it coming. Even her old grandfather might have had wits enough to suspect the Feathers' intentions.

Rab hadn't and, like the rest of his kind, had simply let it happen. His grand and noble hope that Feathers and humans could live as equals had been as naïve and foolish a dream as the quest he'd once taken to find the ships that could carry them to safe harbour on some distant and more hospitable planet. Now he and the rest of his human companions were more like captives on this planet than the guests he had hoped they would be … no better than slaves who planted and harvested the masters' crops, labourers who built and repaired the rock-walls that ringed the masters' settlements, miners who dug and sifted dirt for their red metal, and unwilling soldiers who, bit by bit, hacked away at the Top-siders already declining numbers whenever their pitiful forces foolishly decided to attack. In some respects the tunnel-people functioned as currency, too, their labour traded off in allotments of time from one Feather owner to another in payment for a debt or anticipation of a favour. Although the Kun owned most of the humans himself, there were a few, a very few, Feathers who had been granted the special privilege of personal ownership of a human. Fin was one of those rare humans under personal ownership. Rab and Cloud belonged to the Kun.

This was not the kind of life Rab had hoped for when he and Gift had brought Pi'a'weh back to his people; not the kind of life Cloud and Fin had hoped for, either, when they'd abandoned the relative safety of Glint's Top-sider band to come looking for them. They could leave, of course.

Sneak out through the three-walled defences late at night. But to what? More scavenging? They'd done enough of that. To where? The desert where they could join up with the few surviving Top-siders? They'd simply be trading one side of the conflict for the other and that didn't make a lot of sense — not when here, with the Feathers, they had three meals a day, a roof over their heads when it rained, shelter when it grew cold, although at the cost of their freedom and pride. At least the children were safe. Well fed and safe — most of the time. Rab tried to keep telling himself that, even if he didn't fully believe it. And he'd never say anything of the kind to Gift. Her child, Sunny's namesake, was still out there with Glint and his people among the Top-siders … among the enemy … assuming Glint's people were even still alive.

Rab stepped up beside Cloud, falling into place at the rear of the assembled tunnel-people. Cloud dropped the rope she'd been carrying to the ground by her feet and, slipping the Qworka-skin bag from his shoulders, Rab placed it on top of the coil of rope. As he looked around, he noted, not for the first time, that their numbers, too, were slowly dwindling. The old ones he'd seen and met when Sunny had first brought him down into her tunnel city were nearly all gone now — even Ruby, the woman who had nursed Fin's brother back to health and then seen to his burial ten years later. Of all the tunnel-people who had gone, Rab missed Ruby the most. At least she'd been spared the long journey and hadn't been among the large group of tunnel-dwellers the Feathers had force-marched across the rugged land to this once desolate place, where now life was beginning to blossom once again.

A decade and more ago, while Rab had only wondered if the climate was shifting and could only hope that the subtle warming he had noticed year after year wasn't an aberration, somehow the Feathers had *known* it wasn't. Whatever had given them that knowledge had also prompted them to commence their long migration north from their distant southern asylum. How many times and across how many generations they had made that journey south when the weather began to chill, then north again when it began to warm, even the Feathers probably couldn't answer. But migrate they did, each time taking away and bringing back the Qworkas along with the cages that penned the hairless but otherwise cat-like Juarox no human could stomach, their seeds and their ancient skills to both husband and exploit the healing surface. Only this time they'd stumbled upon the tunnel city and collected a ready source of labour on their way. And they'd stumbled upon something else equally unexpected: a relentless though deplorably outnumbered enemy in the nomadic Top-siders.

When Cloud nudged his elbow, Rab glanced to his left and spotted a frowning Fin walking towards them, little Tickie perched on his back. For an instant, Rab was transported back in time. That's just the way he had carried Fin's brother in the cold and the mist and the snow for day after endless day until they had come upon Sunny. So much time had passed. Stitch had been dead these many years and Fin had a young child of his own now.

Tickie's little face broke into an enormous smile the moment he noticed Cloud.

"Kood," he squealed, the high pitch prompting Rab to cringe.

Kood was the closest Tickie ever came to pronouncing Cloud's name.

"Tickie," Cloud chimed back and, reaching out, took the willing child from his father's shoulders.

Over the nine years they'd been with the Feathers, Cloud had developed an affinity with children – other people's children. But she'd stitched too many wounds, set too many splintered bones, failed and prevailed over too many fevers only to send the young survivors into a future of endless servitude to ever want any children of her own. It had been an easy agreement for Rab. Even if not by blood, he'd already had two sons and a daughter – lost one boy in death and the girl to a broken spirit.

"Do you know why we've been called?" Cloud asked Fin as she settled Tickie comfortably onto her hip.

"A couple of scouts returned early this morning while you were both gone," Fin replied, ruffling his son's fair hair. "I'm guessing there's some news."

"Top-siders?" Rab enquired.

"Could be."

"Where's Neila?" Cloud asked, glancing around in search of Fin's wife.

Rab, too, had noticed her absence among the softly-talking clutch of tunnel-people.

"She was rostered to the mine just after you left this morning," Fin replied. "Guess she's about halfway there already."

Now Fin's dour mood made sense. Fin invariably became edgy and anxious whenever Neila worked the mine. It wasn't hard to understand why. The mine was a dangerous place. Rab had spent three years coming and going from that dusty open hole in the ground. It was hard labour. Even the Feathers seemed to appreciate that and, as strange as it always seemed to Rab, weren't disposed to work the miners to death. Cloud had never been rostered out to the mine, her obvious and natural skill with the planet's native flora apparently being viewed as too valuable a gift to squander by having her dig for red metal.

Rab was about to ask who else had been placed on the roster when Tickie raised his tiny arm, waving and pointing it close to Rab's face. Rab looked and saw Lilly Benson, one of the few, rare survivors from her generation, shuffling in her distinctive bent kind of way across the Common. As usual, Button dutifully plodded along beside her. One of Button's hands was cupped beneath Lilly's elbow to steady the elderly woman. In the other hand, she carried the stool that Lilly would sit on when she took her place on the left corner of the platform.

"Looks like we're included this time," Rab said, nodding in Lilly's direction.

Lilly didn't attend every Assembly and, when she did, it generally meant the Kun had something particular to convey to the tunnel-people as well. Rab was usually heartened to see Lilly arrive. Her presence signified that they wouldn't be forced to stand in the Common, impotent and ignorant, while the Kun rasped and clicked his way through some long and incomprehensible message to his people. Today there was something about the expression on Lilly's face that unsettled him. She looked tired, worried. Then again Lilly often looked tired and worried, he supposed. She was an old woman. She'd left most of her friends behind in the tunnels and seen those who had been forced on the long journey with her buried here on the surface. Without the Feathers' devoted attention, Rab suspected Lilly, too, would have gone to her grave long ago. Still, despite her pampered treatment, Rab had the suspicion that Lilly would have much preferred to be standing among the jumble of pots and pans in her stall back home in the tunnel city than to be seated by the side of the Kun, translating for her people whenever the Kun felt disposed to permit it.

What would they do, Feathers and doq'iri, when their translator was dead? Of all the tunnel-people, it had been a perverse stroke of luck that the distracted and frequently vague Lilly had been gifted with the ability to pick up feathertalk. Although some of the surface-born tunnel-children were slowly developing a modest familiarity with the harsh sounds and terminal clicks, none so far had remotely approached Lilly's proficiency.

Of course, most of the Feathers hadn't bothered to reciprocate, clearly regarding tunneltalk as little but inconsequential gibberish. Only Pi'a'weh had mastered a little of their language, although it had taken considerable effort and a great deal of time to do so.

Cloud grasped Rab's arm and, with some concern, he noticed a cloaked featherman, one of the Kun's regular attendants, bearing down on them. Cloud's hand slipped from Rab's sleeve as the Feather began to lead her away towards the front of the gathered tunnel-people. Grabbing the Qworka-skin bag and the coil of rope, Rab hurried after her, slinging both bag and rope over his shoulder as he pushed his way through the crowd. He could sense Fin close behind. When Tickie raised his arms, clearly growing distressed, Rab snatched him from Cloud's hip and passed the young boy back to his father. A young human learned early that, as far as Feathers were concerned, it was better to be invisible.

It was no use calling to the Feather who had a hold of Cloud. Even if he could have understood what Rab said, he wouldn't respond. All Rab could do was stay close. He'd been too focused on Cloud to notice until then that the platform at the head of the Common was no longer deserted. Not only had Lilly been settled into her allotted place, Button standing sentinel-like at her back, but most of the Kun's attendants had already filed through the narrow channel down which the Kun, himself, would slowly wind his way. The Feather who had been leading Cloud left her among her kind in the front row directly in front of Lilly. He'd displayed as much interest as someone discarding an empty pack. Turning, he started up the ten broad steps to the platform where he stationed himself to the side of the Kun's throne.

"This can't be good," Fin whispered at Rab's back. "Seems the Kun's got a message for Abby."

Rab didn't need – or want – to hear it. He glanced sidelong at Cloud, who Fin still called by her tunnel name. On catching his eye, she gave a quick shake of her head. Well, at least Rab was satisfied that she hadn't been keeping something from him. She appeared to know as little as he did.

When Tickie began to tug on the loose end of the rope, Rab flung the coil back towards Fin, hoping to keep the boy distracted. The bag he kept on his shoulder.

A shuffle of heavily-shod feet and the swish of feathers up on the platform signalled the Kun was nearing the exit of the channel and would soon emerge into the open. Most Feathers had abandoned their fine feather cloaks, donning them only during the perceptibly colder snow times. Otherwise the tightly-woven cloth garments covering the thick rind of their skin provided adequate protection. The Kun and his attendants were the exception. Rab had never seen them without their elaborate feather cloaks and the Kun's cloak with its row upon row of intense and various colours was, not surprisingly, the most splendid of all. It had taken a long time and his first breath-taking sight of an arc of colour in the sky for Rab to realise that the feathers of the Kun's cloak had been dyed to mimic a rainbow, something he'd only seen before in pictures in the books down in the tunnel city library. The Feathers paid homage to nature in almost every aspect of their lives, and that was probably one of the things about them that Rab most readily understood. They, like his kind, had been deprived of colour and variation for so long that where they couldn't find it, they created it. For the Feathers, life and art went hand in hand. The brick and stone walls of their ts'uns were always decorated using pigments that, now, were sought out and collected for them by the enslaved tunnel-people. A Feather might ornament the exterior of his or her ts'un with the figure of an animal – sometimes a Qworka – sometimes some other animal that was either imagined or perhaps remembered from their ancestral past.

Sometimes Rab could make no sense at all of a decoration that just looked like lines or nested circles and squares to him. Clearly there was some significance to the pattern because the drawings were always executed with exacting precision and often repeated from ts'un to ts'un. But the Feathers didn't limit their art to their ts'uns or to items of special value. Even the simplest and most mundane utensil was usually adorned in some form. Rab hadn't seen a pick handle, a cooking pot, the legs of a table or even the back of a spoon that wasn't inscribed in some fashion. But the Kun's throne, with its deeply incised carvings on the front, sides and, as rumour had it, even the seat, was unarguably the most resplendent. The animals and plants that decorated the natural surface of the stone throne appeared to have been snatched out of a moment in time, beasts at the very point of springing, plants caught as they answered some ancient, played-out wind. Now both were locked together forever, unchanged and unchanging, stilled by the experienced and knowing hand of the Feather who had snared them. The throne, along with everything else the Feathers could carry or drive, like the Qworka flocks, had been brought up from the south. Rab had watched the constant progression of the vast migration in both fascination and awe while he and Gift had journeyed northward with the Feathers. It had taken ten of the strongest and biggest feathermen and women to haul the enormous six-wheeled cart in which the Kun's throne had been securely tied down with straps that Rab later discovered had been made from the tough sinew of slaughtered Qworkas. It had been those same ten strong feathermen and women who had lifted the throne from the cart and set it in its temporary location until the Kun's palace and the semicircular platform in front of it had been completed. Although he didn't know for certain – it wasn't always easy to distinguish one Feather from another – Rab suspected it might have been those same ten who had lifted the throne once again onto the platform where it now rested, awaiting the Kun who had just emerged into the open, heralded by another brief shuffle and swish. It might have been his imagination, but it seemed to Rab that, just like the Kun's attendants, Lilly's back might have stiffened a little as she sat, waiting patiently on her stool at the far edge of the platform.

The Feathers, who made up a good three-quarters of the crowd, had fallen silent long before the Kun's rear touched the seat of his throne. It took Rab's fellows longer to respond and still, every now and then, Rab heard a muted cough or the soft mewling of an infant. Likely the Kun would not be pleased. It was usually impossible to glean much from looking at a Feather's face, the hard rind of skin limiting their means for expression, at least as far as human interpretation went, but, every so often, Rab swore he could detect some subtle change. Perhaps it was something different about their strange eyes that blinked sideways rather than up and down. Whatever it was, Rab felt certain that he'd seen a scowl momentarily distort the face of more than one of the Kun's attendants. It seemed that, in the Feathers' eyes, humans were just never going to measure up.

A shiver suddenly ran down Rab's spine, prompting him to glance away from the throne towards the opposite side of the Common. He knew it. Pi'a'weh was standing in the front row of Feathers and, even at a distance, Rab could tell that he was looking directly at Cloud. There was something odd about that Feather – more odd than usual anyway. From the first moment Cloud had begun to tend to his injuries, Pi'a'weh had developed an intense interest in her. It bothered Rab; it *more* than bothered him. Sometimes Rab got the feeling that there was something

Pi'a'weh wanted to say to her. He'd mastered a few words of their language and if it was thanks he was wanting to express, Pi'a'weh could certainly have done that by now. So it had to be something else.

A single blast of a horn snapped Rab's attention back to the platform. The Kun was ready to speak. The Kun never rose to address the Assembly and any personal message that was to be conveyed was done so by one of the Kun's attendants who would step down off the platform and seek out the recipient in the crowd. Usually the attendant charged with that duty was the same one who had blown that accursed horn: Big-Noise, Gift had quickly dubbed him. On the rare occasion a message was to be passed to one or all of Rab's people, it was generally accomplished through Lilly Benson.

Today it appeared that the message the Kun had for Cloud was not going to be of foremost importance because he immediately launched into what, from long experience, Rab suspected was going to be another tedious monologue delivered in typical staccato style with each second or third word terminated in a sound much like the click of a tongue or the snap of a dry stick. As the Kun clicked on, Rab shifted anxiously from foot to foot, sometimes glancing at Cloud, sometimes looking over his shoulder towards Fin, who seemed transfixed by the Kun's unintelligible address. Tickie was very obviously bored and Rab hoped Fin would think to keep the boy quiet. Teasing out the frayed ends of the rope wasn't going to keep him occupied for much longer but any disruption could only delay the Kun's speech.

Click – snap. Click – snap. At one point during the Kun's seemingly endless speech, a muffled sort of gasp bubbled up among the Feathers on the far side of the Common. Apart from that and a barely audible one word utterance from Fin, Rab noticed nothing else unusual. Matters were progressing much as they always had at every Assembly.

He didn't know how much more he could take. Along with his eyesight and his hearing, with age, Rab's capacity for patience had deteriorated. When the Kun turned to Big-Noise, Rab almost missed it. The Feather stepped down off the platform and Rab's immediate thought was that he was heading for Cloud. Instead, the Feather began a slow meander among the gathering of tunnel-people, stopping every so often to study someone in the crowd. Rab tried to follow his progress but continued to lose sight of Big-Noise until he singled out one of the older boys and, grasping him roughly by the upper arm, made to lead the youngster away. Immediately the woman standing beside the boy cried out and lunged to regain him. She had made a foolish mistake. With a casual swing of his free arm, Big-Noise caught the woman hard across the throat and dispatched her, crumpled, to the ground. There was one among the crowd with the courage to stoop to the woman's aid but Big-Noise, distracted by the resisting boy, failed to notice.

The crowd parted for Big-Noise after that and, when he set about selecting first a girl and then another two boys, no one dared interfere. The children were quickly shepherded away from the Assembly and passed to another of the Kun's attendants who escorted them into a narrow lane leading off from the Common. It happened sometimes, this mustering during Assembly, and since only that morning a contingent of workers had been sent off to the mines, it was clear the four children were destined for the quarry. While the mines demanded back-breaking labour, the quarry was a sentence to hell. From experience, the Feathers had learned to select only the sturdiest of humans for quarry-work, those nearing adulthood who could ensure them the most longevity. Unskilled as cutters, the girl and three boys would be assigned the job of hauling and haulers had the highest incidence of all human fatalities.

With the children gone, the Kun's interest shifted to Lilly and Rab began to listen more closely, hoping that he might be able to understand at least a word or two of the usually incomprehensible feathertalk. The mustering of the children had heightened his apprehension. It wasn't that he didn't trust Lilly's translation, but he'd known Lilly too long not to be wary. She wasn't what he'd call a particularly focused woman. In fact, among the tunnel-people, she had, for a long time, been regarded as tiresomely absent-minded.

As hard as he tried all Rab managed to make out was Lilly's name — *Yiri (click-snap)* — and what sounded like *tchusuk*, feathertalk for mushroom. But that didn't make a lot of sense. Why would the Kun be concerning himself with such a mundane thing as mushrooms? He felt Fin grip his arm, and when Rab glanced at Cloud, hoping to learn something from her expression, he realised from her frown that she, too, had understood something of the Kun's message to Lilly.

The Kun fell silent and Lilly turned her attention to the Assembly. Her eyes roamed the front row of humans and finally settled on Cloud.

"The Kun wishes you to return to the tunnels, Abby," Lilly said in that same clear, strong voice Rab had only heard since she'd been living among the Feathers. "The mushroom crop has developed some kind of disease and, so far, Dee has failed to find a cure. The Kun knows of your skills and he instructs you to repair the damage. Two scouts are to escort you and you will leave at first light tomorrow morning."

"No!"

The word was out before Rab realised it. Too late now. He stepped forward, aware of Cloud's hand, reaching out to drag him back.

"I won't allow my wife to travel alone with only two of the Kun's scouts for protection."

Even from a distance, he noticed Lilly blanch.

"Are you sure that's what you want Lilly to tell them?" someone whispered beside him.

Rab's head snapped around. He hadn't noticed Fin step up. Tickie wasn't in his arms any longer, but cradled against Cloud's chest.

Fin was right.

Rab turned his eyes to the ground for a moment, thinking.

"Lilly," he said, looking up. "Please ask the Kun if I may accompany Abby and his scouts. Tunnel-people had developed many skills in the past and much of their knowledge was written down in the books in the library. Abby can't read and if she fails to find something obviously wrong with the crop, she may need my help."

"*That's* all you've got?" Fin muttered under his breath.

"Those books won't help," Cloud whispered, inching up behind him.

"I know that," Rab whispered back. "But *they* don't."

Lilly remained silent for a long moment. Although the Feathers used symbols, they had no formal written language. How Lilly was going to convey the meaning of books and library, Rab couldn't even imagine. Still, when they'd broken into the underground city, the Feathers had seen both the books and the library that held them and Rab was counting on the Feathers having developed a description of sorts for such foreign things and for Lilly to be aware of it.

Finally Lilly began to speak and it never ceased to unsettle Rab to hear those click-and-snap sounds coming from the mouth of a human. The Kun listened in silence and, when Lilly was done, cast a brief glance of his disconcerting side-blinking eyes out towards the Assembly, catching Rab by surprise when they found him. Slowly the Kun's focus drifted back to Lilly. His nod to her was rigid, characteristically Feather. It seemed Rab had got what he wanted and all other audience for the day was concluded because the Kun was already on his feet. It was the usual way. Only on rare occasions had Rab witnessed a featherman or woman speak up from the Assembly. Either the Kun took counsel elsewhere or he took no counsel at all. And if the latter were true, then it was truly astounding that Rab's little ploy had been successful. He sighed silently in relief.

At the far side of the platform, Lilly was also on the move, the ever vigilant Button aiding her to her feet.

"So," Fin said, as he attempted to wrest the frayed ends of the rope from his son's insistent fingers, "seems you'll be seeing Gift again soon. That'll be interesting." He shook his head and smiled.

Cloud swung around, wearing a look of practiced indifference Rab recognised only too well. "Can't think what you could mean," she replied, deftly relieving Tickie of the end of the rope before passing him back to his father.

Rab snatched the coil from Fin's shoulder before Tickie could reclaim his prize. Until Fin had mentioned it, he hadn't even considered that Cloud's return to the tunnels would bring the two of them back into contact. Cloud and Gift never had taken to each other. Not since that night when he had agreed that Gift could go with him to return Pi'a'weh to his people but sent Cloud and Fin away to safety with Glint and his band. Cloud had resented Gift after that – resented her for having wounded Pi'a'weh, but probably more so for obliging, as she saw it, Rab to risk his life returning the injured featherman. Gift's resentment was more difficult for Rab to understand. Someday maybe he would make sense of it – someday.

"We'd better start packing," Cloud said, slipping the rope from Rab's hand.

The crowd was beginning to disperse. Just ahead of him, the woman Big-Noise had knocked to the ground was being assisted by two others who each had a hold her elbows. She staggered as she walked – and sobbed. The boy must have been her son. Of the parents of the girl and two other boys, Rab saw nothing; they had vanished into the crowd. Glancing back, he realised that even slow-moving Lilly and Button had gone. Resigned, he started off after Cloud who, with Fin beside her, was making her way towards their ts'un on the far side of the settlement. Every so often, Tickie leaned sideways in his father's arms, bent on reclaiming the end of the rope Cloud shouldered. He'd made quite a mess of it. When Fin lowered him to the ground, the little boy shot off into the shifting crowd, compelling his father to go chasing after him.

Cloud stopped walking and turned to Rab. "You could have chosen your words more carefully back there," she said. "You won't *allow* me to travel alone with the scouts!"

Rab knew he was going to pay for that mistake sooner or later. He'd hoped it would be later.

"It's all I could think of to say in a hurry."

"Next time," Cloud said, settling the coil of rope higher onto her shoulder, "take a little longer to think. I could manage out there by myself and you know it."

"Of course you could. That isn't why I said it."

"Well?" she pressed him.

"You were ordered *to* the tunnels, Cloud. No one said anything about bringing you back."

Cloud opened her mouth to speak but something, a remnant of his lost blindsight most likely, prompted Rab to spin around before she got a word out.

Pi'a'weh was standing behind him.

As a consequence of his old injuries, the little featherman was plagued not only by a limp but by a constant wheeze that accompanied him wherever he went. Today the noise of the crowd had masked his approach. His yellow eyes blinked quickly sideways – once – twice – before they settled on Cloud.

"Them say met'ah – *click!* – Qworka that p'ace. This say doq'iri eye good."

That's all Rab heard and evidently all Pi'a'weh had to say.

With a parting swift blink, he began to limp away, merging quickly with the crowd.

On the rare occasions when he had spoken to them in the past, Pi'a'weh's speech had been peppered with so many clicks and clucks, his message had been rendered largely incomprehensible. Today, although he was speaking very quietly, he was also speaking very deliberately. Still it had taken Rab a moment to work out that he had interjected the featherword for white, *met'ah,* into his little speech. It was one of the few featherwords Rab knew.

He turned towards Cloud, concluding very quickly that she, too, had been left just as puzzled by what sounded like some kind of warning.

Chapter 2

"THERE are metal Qworkas out there and we should be careful. That is what he meant, isn't it?" Cloud asked, staring after Pi'a'weh. "What a ridiculous thing to say."

Rab turned to her and frowned. "He said met-*ah*, Cloud, not met-*al*. White," he explained in a whisper.

"Oh, that makes so much more sense," she replied irritably.

This wasn't the place or time.

With a hand to her back, he hurried her on after Fin. They caught up quickly and walked with him through the thinning crowd of tunnel-people. Fin left them by the entrance to his ts'un. He looked even more uneasy than Rab felt, but promised to bring Tickie by in the morning to say goodbye.

"So," Cloud said as soon as they were alone inside their own ts'un, "why did you shush me back there?"

"Because of the things Pi'a'weh said," Rab replied, dumping the Qworka-skin bag inside the open doorway.

Cloud walked to a hook protruding from a side wall. "And?" she prompted, stowing the rope.

"I don't want Fin to know about it."

Cloud turned around, considered him for a long moment, then moved across the earthen floor of their modest ts'un to a table by the back wall. Pulling out one of the two mismatched woven urse chairs, she sat down.

"I see your point," she said at last. "What do you think Pi'a'weh was trying to tell us?" she asked, gaze following Rab as he headed towards the table. "I mean … white Qworkas? There's no such thing."

"Pi'a'weh thinks there is," Rab replied, drawing out the remaining chair. "Didn't you notice something odd happen while the Kun was speaking? Just for a moment."

"There was a kind of gasp," Cloud said, interrupting. "I heard that. Do you think that's what they were talking about? White Qworkas?"

Rab smiled half-heartedly. "Maybe. Whether it was that or not, Pi'a'weh seems to believe that these white Qworkas pose some sort of threat. And I'd feel a lot better if we knew what he meant exactly by 'that place'."

"The tunnels," Cloud suggested.

Rab waved a hand. "He could have meant anywhere."

"Or everywhere," Cloud added. "He did say we should 'eye good' after all. I wish Neila wasn't at the mine," she said after a brief silence. "If Fin finds out about this, he might —"

Rab cut her off. "Pi'a'weh isn't likely to tell Fin anything. I got the impression that he felt he was taking a chance just telling us."

"I guess," Cloud agreed with little enthusiasm. Her focus drifted towards the large old packs that were lying, almost forgotten, in the darkest recess of their simple ts'un. "Suppose we'd better start making preparations. I'll separate the *ungtilis* later, give half to Fin in the morning and the rest he'd better take to the markets. It'll only spoil if we leave it here." She shrugged and placed her hands, palms down, on the table in front of her. "You know I was almost looking forward to going back to the tunnels, but now …" She pushed off from the table and rose. "… I'm not so sure."

Rab followed her to the two old metal crates that stored the sum total of their possessions. Like most of their furniture and wares, the crates had been brought to the settlement from the tunnels a long time ago. They'd seen better days. The lids didn't close properly anymore and one of the crates was crushed to the point of puncture on one side.

"I guess we just need enough to get there," Cloud said and, dropping to her knees, flipped back the lid on the nearest crate.

"Take extra," Rab advised, slipping to the ground beside her. "We don't know what conditions are like in the tunnels now," he explained when she turned to him, looking puzzled. "Do you think you can do anything about the crop?"

"Depends," Cloud replied, returning to her sorting. "I think I'm more worried about what's going to happen if I can't."

What could he say to that?

Cloud began stacking their clothes and meagre supplies in a neat pile, Rab adding to it occasionally with items he felt Cloud had overlooked. She said nothing when he placed her cropping knife beside the battered canteens she had selected to take with them.

"What's that for?" Rab asked, when Cloud withdrew his old drawstring pouch from the bottom of the crate.

"Green-weed," she said and, getting to her feet, took it to the low bench where they kept their cooking and healing supplies. The bench was little but a battered piece of thin metal, propped on legs of broken brick, but it served them well enough and as improbable as it seemed, the samples of erratic plant life Cloud continued to amass were enough to warrant the bench's considerable size. From them, she made potions to reduce fever, potions to combat pain and infection, potions to ease the merciless coughing disease that fell on them during snow time, and potions that were quietly surrendered to both human and Feather when the prospect of bringing yet another child into their thinly balanced world became unthinkable.

"Green-weed doesn't work on us," Rab reminded her, rising to join her at the bench.

"No, it doesn't," she said, pulling a small and unobtrusive-looking canister from the very back row. She popped the lid, tipped the canister, and long strings of the familiar green plant along with some loose powder spilled onto the top of the bench.

Rab was surprised to discover that she still collected the stuff.

"But there'll be two Feather scouts with us," she told him as she began to stuff three or four of the long strings inside the pouch. "It works on them."

Rab cupped her chin in one hand and gave her head a gentle shake. "Someone should tell you you're too kind." Leaving Cloud to clean up the spilled powder, he went to collect their old packs.

***

Just as he'd promised, at first light, Fin brought Tickie to say goodbye. Neila was still away at the mines. When Cloud handed over the two bags containing the divided *ungtilis,* Fin looked down and his face crumpled into a frown.

"Something wrong?" she said. "I asked you if something is wrong?" she repeated when Fin failed to answer.

"Hmm?" Fin replied absently then lifted his gaze. "Oh ..." he said, stumbling over his words. "Nothing." He hefted one of the bags as if suddenly realising he was holding it. "What will happen if they find out about this?"

"Find out about what?" Rab said, bending to gather his full pack.

"Giving you food to feed your family? We could have eaten it ourselves, you know, and never told them a thing about it."

"Yes ... but ..." Fin hesitated again, then glanced at Tickie who, at that moment, was attempting to raise Cloud's heavy pack from the floor. "I suppose it'll be all right. Half of it's going to them."

"Without lifting a finger," Rab muttered to himself.

Sometimes he wished Fin had never come to this place. The old defiant boy was long gone and Rab missed him, something that would have struck him as unthinkable once. As he went to collect Fin's old spear from its resting place against the far wall, he wondered again if it might not be better for them to take their chances out in the open with the dwindling number of Top-siders.

"Oh no, not that!"

Cloud's bark snapped him out of his reverie.

"Why have you got to bring that?"

Rab just smiled back at her, as she stood beside Fin in the entrance. "Why have you got to bring the green-weed?"

From the first day Fin had made it, Cloud had started to develop an aversion to the spear. 'It's only good for killing things,' she'd insisted.

And so it was!

"Maybe he should take it," Fin said, surprising Rab.

When Cloud shot him a dark look, he added, "The Top-siders may be our kind but they're not our friends and they're still out there. Many things have changed since we've been in the settlement. You don't know what you might be walking into."

"And that's what the scouts are for," Cloud argued.

"Is it?" Rab asked, relieving Tickie of Cloud's pack. "More likely it's to make sure you don't go wandering off."

"Don't you mean 'we'?"

"No, I mean 'you'," Rab replied, passing Cloud her pack. Tickie came sprinting after him. "If I go over to the Top-siders ..." he shrugged, "... well, I'm just one more insignificant Top-sider. If you go, they'll lose someone skilled in agriculture. This planet's coming back to life but it's still fragile. They need you."

"Oh, thanks," Cloud said, slipping her pack onto her back. "Nice to be needed by someone." She bent to her knees and held out her arms to Tickie.

"Did I say they were the only ones?" Rab said, glancing down at her. He looked up when Fin put a hand to his shoulder.

"You're coming back, aren't you?"

"I don't think that's up to us, Fin, but we hope to. Why?"

"I thought …" Fin faltered. "…after what you just said …"

Rab shook his head. "The Top-siders are finished. There's no point."

Fin began to finger the ties on one of the Qworka-skin bags Cloud had given him. "Do you think Gift knows that?" he asked after a moment.

He was thinking about Sunny.

Rab didn't reply. Gift, perhaps best of all of them, knew the chances Top-siders took every day in the open.

When Cloud released Tickie and rose, Rab turned to the little boy.

"I expect you to take care of your father while we're gone," he said. "Can you do that?"

"Yes," Tickie declared with a solemn nod, then reached out for his father's hand.

"I'd walk with you to the gate but I have to find someone to mind Tickie," Fin said, towing his son into the lane.

"You'll watch the place?" Rab asked.

There wasn't much to watch and, when all was said and done, it wasn't necessary. What could happen to it?

Fin nodded. "If you promise to be careful."

Pi'a'weh's same warning!

With Tickie singing out a good bye, they started off down the lane.

"That was odd," Cloud said once they were out of earshot.

"What? Fin can't take Tickie with him to the forge."

"Not that," she said, shaking her head. "I meant him asking if we were coming back."

"He's worried. That's all. With Neila away at the mine …" Rab shrugged and didn't bother to finish.

"I know how that is," Cloud replied with a touch to Rab's back, then glanced briefly over her shoulder.

They wound their way through the maze of lanes past modest ts'uns and, here and there, the odd patch of dirt where someone was attempting to establish a food garden. Two Feathers were waiting for them just inside the outermost gate – the scouts assigned to escort them. Rab didn't think he knew either of them and it appeared that Cloud didn't, either.

The Feathers had donned their cloaks, evidently anticipating that the weather might turn bad before they reached the tunnels. Rab wasn't expecting to be given a thorough visual inspection but that's exactly what he received. The bigger of the scouts, a female, scanned him from the top of his head to his heavily-shod feet, paying particular attention to the spear he was carrying. Cloud was subjected to a similar review from the male. Whatever they were looking for, the scouts appeared to have found it. With a wave of her long hand, the female motioned them to follow her through the gate.

"What do you think that was about?" Cloud whispered, leaning closer to Rab as she walked, step for step, behind the second scout.

"Not sure. Maybe they weren't convinced we knew how to dress for the surface."

Cloud snorted. "What arrogance! I could walk those little creatures into the ground. And if the Top-siders had more weapons and larger numbers –"

When the female glanced over the shoulder of her feather cloak, Rab reached for Cloud's hand.

"I don't think I'd mention our people from the open anymore if I were you," he warned softly.

"Do you think they understood me?"

"Don't know, but I'm guessing they understood something."

They walked mostly in silence from then on with barely a word passing between the Feathers and none between Rab and Cloud. The scouts were setting a fast pace, so they should reach the roosts and the small outpost settlement that flanked it by the middle of the day. Rab heard the roosts long before he could see them. Qworka young created one hell of a racket, the main reason, Rab supposed, for founding the main settlement some distance away.

Cloud tapped Rab's shoulder, then raised her hand to tap her ear.

She'd heard it, too.

Evidently so had the scouts, who picked up the pace, bringing them quickly into the overwhelming noise, dust, and smell of the outpost settlement. Although he'd initially carried out some of the early repairs on the roosts, Rab hadn't been to this place in a very long time. What he saw just beyond the small and open settlement startled him. The roosts now stood fully intact – every one of them. There wasn't a damaged wall, roof or turret to be seen. It was as though they had suddenly become alive and, in some respects, Rab supposed they had. Qworka adults were swooping into and out of the pierced openings in every one of the soaring towers. The silent dun-coloured walls he'd remembered had turned a writhing, beating black. The sound of it was almost deafening. How could the tunnel-people and the few Feather breeders who worked this place bear it? Day in, day out, nothing but the choking dust whipped up by the Qworkas' large and powerful wings, the stench of their fertile droppings, and the noise – the endless noise. He'd never given much thought to it before but now Rab was beginning to suspect that the breeders who'd been stationed to guard the roosts and supervise the collection of their droppings might just be the least favoured of the Kun's subjects. Or they were completely deaf.

A breeder was approaching from the small, unprotected settlement. Rab had never heard of a Top-sider raid here but the place was so vulnerable, it wouldn't be too difficult to carry out. Perhaps it was the Qworkas and their deserved reputation for aggression that kept the Top-siders away. Cloud had barely avoided losing part of her scalp to a Qworka once. Had the beast swooped lower, she could easily have lost her head. But it had been Gift's husband who had made the most fatal mistake, underestimating the lethalness of the Qworka's scythe-like talons. He'd paid the ultimate price. It took a certain skill to toil among the Qworkas. The Feathers seemed to be born with it and those tunnel-people who had been sent to work alongside them in the roosts either acquired the skill or died trying. How many had been lost in those early days? Rab couldn't even remember anymore. There weren't near so many Qworkas when he had worked on the roosts, but he'd been among those who had acquired the appropriate skills quickly and had only carried away a few scars.

The female Feather scout raised the multi-jointed fingers of one hand and motioned for Rab and Cloud to stop.

"What?" Cloud snapped, turning to Rab. "Are we just supposed to wait out here in the dirt?"

"Seems so," Rab replied with a shrug when the two scouts proceeded to follow the breeder who had come up to greet them.

Rab watched as they headed into the settlement. While most humans were occupied over at the roosts, there were a few stragglers moving about the settlement; mostly women tending to young children. The Feathers liked to keep a breeding population of human workers even out in this woe-begotten place. Either the women and children were accustomed to Feather scouts coming and going from their settlement or they were schooled to ignore it – Rab didn't know. All went about their business as though nothing out of the ordinary was happening. If they'd noticed two human travellers on the perimeter of their settlement, they didn't show it.

Cloud dumped her pack and settled down on the ground beside it. Rab remained standing. It was easier to watch the scouts that way. He'd liked to have been able to hear them but the persistent noise of the Qworka young made that impossible. Not that he'd be able to understand much of what was said but sometimes even he could pick up on a particular tone in their speech. He'd like to have been able to talk to some of the human women, as well, but not one of them could have heard him even if he'd yelled at the top of his voice.

Evidently the Feathers who lived in the settlement were not deaf. Two others had come out to join the first and all three were involved in an animated discussion with their Feather scouts, heads bobbing rigidly as they talked. Something had them agitated.

Them say met'ah – click! – Qworkas that p'ace.

What place? And what exactly had Pi'a'weh meant by white Qworkas?

Rab would dearly love to have an answer to both questions, because his guess was that was exactly what the Feathers' current conversation was about.

He looked away and turned to Cloud.

"Something is going on out here?"

"Why do you say that?" she asked, glancing up. She was halfway through relacing her left boot.

"Look for yourself." He pointed towards the clutch of Feathers.

Cloud quickly finished with her boot and rose.

"Could be anything," she said after a moment studying them. "A problem in the roosts even."

Rab just shook his head. "The breeders here would deal with that themselves. Not discuss it with a couple of scouts who barely know one end of a Qworka from the other. Besides there's nothing wrong with the roosts. You can see that plainly from here."

Cloud fell silent for a while. "You think it's got something to do with what Pi'a'weh was trying to tell us," she said at last.

Their two Feather scouts had started back, leaving the breeders behind.

Cloud bent to retrieve her pack.

"Whatever it is," she whispered, "they don't look happy."

Rab smiled to himself. How Cloud ever managed to assess a Feather's mood, he couldn't fathom. She was usually right though, and he never failed to take notice.

"Thanks for the warning," Rab whispered. After one final glance towards the settlement, he fell back into step behind the scouts.

***

Rab had been keeping a careful account of the days. The Feathers were walking them quickly and, although the pace suited Rab – it meant they'd arrive at the tunnels in good time – he couldn't help but think there was more to their urgency than some trouble with the mushroom crop. It had been many years since Rab had taken this route south back to the tunnels, many more years still since he and Gift had journeyed north with Sunny and her old grandfather. But he remembered it well and wished he didn't. They wouldn't come across the grave of the old man or the skeleton of his beloved horse. The elements would have seen to that. But it was a certainty they would be obliged to cross the river. Rab always hated that part of the journey, fording waist and sometimes chest-deep in the fast-flowing stream. The first time he'd crossed the river, travelling north from the tunnels, Gift had been swept from his shoulders. If it hadn't been for Sunny, he'd have lost her then and there. And so it came as a surprise when he discovered that the Feathers, or more likely their human workers, had constructed a stone bridge across the narrowest part of the river. The bridge told him more about what the Feathers were doing top-side than he had learned inside the Kun's settlement. They were moving about, covering territory.

More surprising still was the condition of the territory itself. Sure the climate was changing – growing warmer. But he hadn't anticipated just how much the land would have responded during the time his every movement had been determined by the Kun. It hadn't exactly turned verdant, but it showed every promise that it might. There was urse everywhere and, in some places, the rare and pitiful head of a new and different vegetation peeked above the surface.

At night, Cloud lay in his arms and they counted stars. Of course, they could see stars from inside the Kun's settlement and, in some respects, had grown almost complacent about their presence in the night sky. But out on the surface, away from the haze of cooking fires, the tiny pin points of light looked so bright and seemed so distant, even Rab sometimes doubted what he knew to be absolutely true. A long time ago, some of his kind had ventured from one of those stars and settled here. Yet sometimes, most times, it seemed so impossible.

Although their scouts clearly didn't like it, during the day Cloud stopped at each new show of vegetation to sample and assess its value. Some she declared too bitter; others she deemed potentially poisonous, at least to humans. When she did come upon a likely food source, she angered the scouts even further by dawdling longer than they obviously considered wise to gather some of the leaves to add to her existing supply back at the settlement and, on one occasion, hurried away to snatch a tiny inconspicuous-looking flower that Rab had completely overlooked. She was amassing quite a collection, which she kept bundled inside one of her spare shirts at the very top of her pack. Undoubtedly she had it in her mind to exploit some of the plants someday. How she was going to manage that was a mystery to Rab. It was unlikely the Feathers would allow any human to travel this far afield alone. He didn't ask her about it. A long time ago he had learned not to query Cloud about things like that. Sooner or later she usually found a way and typically without his interference.

They arrived at the plateau above the tunnel city without incident. They hadn't encountered any of Pi'a'weh's white Qworkas. Nor had they come across any Top-siders. Rab was pleased about that – for the sake of the Top-siders anyway. Their numbers had been so reduced it was unlikely any small Top-sider party would have caused too much trouble for Rab, Cloud, and their two scouts. Those who still survived tended to raid the settlements not challenge lone travellers who usually carried too little of worth. It struck Rab as strange though that they had seen no evidence of Top-siders at all. He'd more or less expected to come upon something, maybe a ruined cart or a scatter of discarded rubbish, perhaps even a hastily-dug grave. Instead they saw nothing at all. It bothered him.

The first thing Rab noticed about the plateau above the tunnel city was the absence of smoke. Had it grown so warm underground that the tunnel-dwellers weren't using their fires anymore? Or had they simply run out of fuel? If the latter, then the tunnel city was facing a larger problem than trouble with the mushroom crop.

The two scouts stopped at the top of the rock-hewn stairs leading down to the platform and the entrance to the tunnel city. At first Rab wasn't sure what the scouts wanted until the female reached out and took his spear. Its loss had him wondering if he'd ever see it again. Still the scouts lingered and Rab finally realised that they meant for Cloud and him to precede them down the steps.

Not overly trusting souls, Rab thought to himself with a smile. Sure they'd been content to allow Cloud and him to trail them all the way from their settlement to the tunnels, but when it came to a confined climb down a set of stairs, where it would be all too easy to nudge them over the side, the scouts baulked. There were times when Rab feared of ever understanding these Feathers. It would have been just as easy to have attacked them from behind during their long journey, but it seemed they hadn't thought of that. Or perhaps it was the fact that they had come to the rare place where the Feathers themselves were actually outnumbered. But there had only ever been one instance of resistance and that had occurred in the first days when the Feathers had surged through every tunnel in the city.

The challenge from the city's inhabitants hadn't amounted to much. Some tunnel-dwellers dead, Cloud's birth father among them. More injured and left to Ruby's care. It had been the surprise that was largely responsible for the tunnel-dwellers' quick defeat. They simply weren't prepared. Even if they'd had warning, Rab suspected the outcome would have been the same. They weren't a fighting people. Hadn't been for a very long time. If Sunny had still been alive, perhaps things might have been different. Perhaps not. Even Sunny could only have done so much. Other than Sunny, Gift was the only other person Rab could think of who might have been both clear-headed and stubborn enough to rally a league of defenders. But Gift hadn't been raised in the tunnels. To the tunnel-dwellers, she was a Top-sider and, despite having a common adversary in the Feathers, tunnel-dwellers still bore a lingering distrust of Top-siders. They'd stolen the tunnel-dweller children, hadn't they? Gift was only tolerated now and the fact that she'd risen to a position of some authority had more to do with the Feathers than the tunnel-dwellers. That and her innate skills and capabilities. Even the tunnel-dwellers had recognised her value. But now, if she truly had failed in maintaining the health of the mushroom crop, then there'd be no place for her here as far as the tunnel-dwellers were concerned. What the Feathers intended to do about it was another matter entirely.

Rab trailed behind Cloud towards the entrance of the tunnels. Last time he was here the heavy metal gate was lying on the ground just inside the entrance. No one had bothered to move it since the Feathers had broken it down. It was gone now. He caught up with Cloud as she stepped through the now open chasm, trying to catch her eye. If she'd noticed the missing gate, she wasn't interested enough to mention it. She was the first to start down the upper tunnel and, despite the years she, too, had been away, didn't miss a step as she moved through the relative darkness. At the entrance to 'the house' that marked the entrance to the lower tunnels she stopped and waited for Rab.

'The house' had been entirely stripped and clusters of shimmerers now colonised walls that had once been barren. Even the metal canister that once held the wadded-up balls of paper they'd used to stuff beneath their clothes for insulation was gone. The hearth, too, was cold and gave every appearance of not having been used for years. Once Rab had required the light from the hearth to make his way to the lower tunnel, but now that the shimmerers thrived here in 'the house' as well, the two narrow open entrances on the left side of the hearth were obvious. Rab headed towards the opening closest to the hearth and began to make his way ahead of Cloud down the shimmerer-lit lower tunnel into the city.

Emerging from the tunnel, he entered Market Square, surprised, although he shouldn't have been, to find the place sparsely occupied by tunnel-dwellers who took little notice of their arrival. The stalls that had once lined both sides of the marketplace were now few in number and scattered randomly about the broad and open space. Overhead, the brightworms shone on, as though nothing had changed, and lit the floor below.

"It's even worse than I thought it would be," Cloud whispered, coming up behind him.

Although Cloud had returned to the tunnels not long after the Feathers had entered them, unlike Rab, she hadn't been back here since. He should have thought to prepare her for what they'd find, but, glancing around, taking in the austerity more fully, Rab realised that he hadn't even adequately prepared himself. It was the comparative silence that struck him the most. Once the place had buzzed with chatter and bartering, clanged and banged as goods changed hands, bustling with life. Now one of the big transport carts could be wheeled through the Square with absolute ease.

Rab looked past Cloud, seeking the scouts. They'd have to take Grocer's Alley to reach the mushroom fields, but Rab didn't know if he was permitted to accompany them that far.

When the female scout raised a hand and pointed, Rab started off through the Square towards the place where the smaller off-shoot tunnel connected with the large cavern that was Market Square. As he passed by some of the remaining stalls, a stall-holder would occasionally glance up, more hopeful than expectant, as Rab interpreted their expressions. He didn't linger but, from the brief glimpse he had, didn't recognise any of the stall-holders. *That* was no surprise. He hadn't got to know many of the tunnel-dwellers anyway, even when he'd lived on and off among them during the years he'd spent searching for Gift. They were probably acquainted with Cloud but she passed wordlessly by each stall as well. Either they had forgotten her, which Rab doubted, or like Cloud, the people who had been left in the tunnel city chose to guard their talk whenever a Feather was around.

Grocer's Alley was even more deserted than Market Square. In the past some of the entrances to the small niches that served as tunnel-dwellers' homes had been covered over with strips of cloth. Even when an entrance had been left open, it was considered impolite to glance inside. Now Rab didn't bother with the old courtesy. There didn't seem much point. Every other niche showed signs of abandonment and those that weren't abandoned looked stark. Gone were the glowing hearths, the pieces of furniture dotted here and there across the floor. Gone were the voices and the laughter. Gone was the life and the strength of the city.

Many times in the past Rab had marvelled at the tenacity and the resilience of the tunnel-dwellers. Many times he'd anticipated that the city, through a lack of food, resources and fuel, would wind its own quiet way down to extinction. Now it had finally happened and not at all the way he had expected. And if the mushroom crop could not be saved, then there was no place left here for *anyone*, not simply Gift.

They came to the end of Grocer's Alley and a broad sweeping turn into the wide access tunnel leading to the mushroom fields. To the left was the enormous warehouse where the harvested crops were stored, awaiting transport in smaller carts down Grocer's Alley to the food merchants in Market Square. Rab hadn't laboured with Fin and Stitch in the mushroom fields very often but every time he had taken this route in the past, the access tunnel had been throbbing with activity. Either overladen transport carts were being hauled along the tracks where croppers had gathered in preparation for offloading into the warehouse or emptied carts were being hauled back along the same track to the fields. Now the long track was empty and there were no croppers waiting at the entrance to the warehouse, which, for the first time Rab could remember, stood with its two massive doors firmly closed.

The track ran hard against the wall of the tunnel on one side and, as they crossed over the dual rails to the opposite side and a clearer path, Cloud stumbled and grabbed Rab's arm. Like him, she'd been looking back towards the sealed warehouse. Hands clutched, they walked abreast beside the track in silence, the scouts following closely behind. Towards the end of the access tunnel they came upon a transport cart that had been left abandoned on the tracks. Usually the croppers ran the carts in tandem: three carts coupled together with a complicated type of locking mechanism Rab never had bothered to study. But there was only one cart standing idle on the track and although when he passed it Rab did catch that distinctive earthy aroma of mushrooms, the cart was completely empty.

Behind him, Rab heard a brief spate of feathertalk clicks and snaps before the male scout stepped up, passed by them and took the lead. They were nearing the entrance to the enormous domed cavern and the fields of the ailing crop.

Rab glanced over at his wife, walking silently beside him. Cloud had saved the crop once before. Could she do it again? Even if her skills were up to the task of rescuing the crop, was it really worth the effort?

Maybe the tunnels simply weren't meant for their kind any longer.

Chapter 3

RAB was immediately struck by the intensity of the light and a distinctly sour smell. The large cave had always been a bright space, courtesy of the brightworms overheard, but now the place was almost glowing. There wasn't a single patch on the domed ceiling that hadn't been colonised. The light actually hurt his eyes. Sloughing out of his packs, he stripped off his outer coat, wiped his brow, and crawled into his packs again.

As for the smell, it had to be coming from the broad field of 'shrooms fanning out beyond the entrance to the tunnel, where six or so tunnel-dwellers were bent to their knees, hard at work. In days gone by there would have been perhaps forty or more croppers. Far off in the distance Rab thought he saw Gift. She wasn't on her knees like the rest. Instead she was standing and appeared to be examining something in her hands.

"This place stinks," Cloud said, stating the all too obvious.

She set off ahead of Rab in pursuit of the scouts who were weaving a tortuous route through the row upon row of delicate caps. The mushrooms were all of that smaller variety Cloud had intentionally cultivated many years ago when the standard and larger mushroom strain had begun to develop an insidious disease. Whatever was wrong with the crop this time, it couldn't have been any stray strain Gift had inadvertently introduced. Superficially nothing looked different. It had been the same last time. Only on closer inspection would the problem be noticeable.

Cloud stopped at the first full stand of 'shrooms. Bending, she cautiously stripped the upper layer of flesh from the top of the nearest cap with the tip of her cropping knife. The surface beneath looked abnormally wrinkled and dry. Plucking the cap from its stem, she swivelled around on her heel and passed the decapitated head to Rab.

"Ever seen anything like that in your travels?" she asked, rising.

Rab turned the cap over and over again in the palm of his hand. "Can't say I have. It looks …" he hesitated, "…it looks almost like it's got too close to a fire." He brought the severed cap close to his nose and sniffed. The offensive sourness was overwhelming.

"That's what I thought," Cloud replied, reaching out for the severed cap. Closing it inside her hand, she started out after the scouts. Halfway across the broad field she stopped, bent, and repeated the same procedure again: gently peeling back the flesh from the cap of a mushroom, studying it for a moment, then removing the cap from its stem.

"It's the same," she said, again passing the cap to Rab.

He glanced at the cap only briefly before handing it back to Cloud.

"What's wrong with them?"

She shook her head and, raising her hand, wiped at a trickle of sweat running down her temple. "I don't know. But if they're all like this …" She shrugged.

"And what do you think that's all about?" Rab pointed past the scouts towards a sectioned-off area of crop.

Although the isolated area wasn't particularly large, it was still a potentially valuable stand of the crop. Earth had been mounded up on all four sides of the thigh-high metal barrier and the area between the mounded up earth and the barrier was flooded with water. Rab couldn't understand why Gift would have done such a thing.

"I haven't a clue," Cloud replied and let the ruined cap fall from her hand. "And I don't know what that's all about, either." She pointed, drawing Rab's attention to the far reaches of the cave.

He hadn't noticed it when he'd entered but either the Feathers or the 'shroom croppers themselves had opened up a large cavity at the very end of the cave. A diffuse circle of light was spilling out across the floor there, bathing the 'shrooms in that area in what looked like wan sun-light.

"What is going *on* here? Come on." Cloud grasped Rab by the forearm. "We have to talk to Gift."

The scouts reached Gift ahead of them. She didn't move but glanced up, seemingly aware that she had company. Smiling faintly, she took a step forward and leaned in to kiss Rab's cheek. Though the same gesture was repeated on Cloud, it was made with noticeably less enthusiasm.

"I didn't know you were coming," she said and then flicked an indifferent look towards the scouts. "No one told me. Well, maybe they did and I just didn't understand. Doesn't matter." Her attention drifted back to Cloud. "I'm glad you're here."

To Rab, the declaration sounded genuine. And that gave concerned him.

"I suppose they sent you to look at the crop," Gift continued, then shifted her gaze towards Rab. "But what are you doing here?"

"Chaperone," Rab replied.

Gift lifted an eyebrow.

For a moment, Rab considered telling Gift the truth, admitting that he'd lied to gain the Kun's consent. But one glance at the scouts, lurking nearby, changed his mind. Who knew what they did or didn't understand?

"If Cloud can't find out what's wrong, I'm to see if I can find anything useful in the library."

Gift just went on staring at him. She always had been adept at working things out for herself.

"I see," she said at last, her voice tinged with amusement.

"Maybe you should go there now," Cloud suggested. "I want Gift to show me around the crop and to explain that." She jerked her head, indicating the cavity they'd just noticed at the far end of the cave. "You won't be much help to us. We'll meet you later back in your old space."

It wasn't the most subtle of Cloud's ploys; she was hoping to rid herself of the scouts.

"Good idea." Rab caught the eye of the male Feather. "Library," he said. "I'm going to the library. All right?"

The scout didn't respond, just blinked his oblong-shaped eyes sideways.

Rab shrugged, turned, and started back the way he had come. Neither scout moved to stop him. As he made his way back towards the tunnel entrance, he was aware he'd picked up two shadows. Glancing back, he saw the two Feathers trailing behind him and, back in the field, Gift squatting beside Cloud who, using the sharp blade of her cropping knife, was beginning to peel the top layer of skin off another mushroom cap. The shadows trailed him all the way back through the better-smelling air of Grocer's Alley to Market Square. He lost them the moment he started down the tunnel that would eventually lead him to the library. He didn't know where they'd gone and didn't care as long as it wasn't with him or back to the stinking 'shroom field. Rab didn't come across a single tunnel-dweller or Feather on his trek down the once familiar twists and turns of the old tunnels. The tunnel-dwellers would be off somewhere else, working to the Feathers' instructions. And the few Feathers who resided here permanently? Well, who knew where they were or what they were doing, other than Feather business. One thing was certain – they wouldn't be too far away.

Rab had a passing impulse to visit the hospital but there'd be no one there; no one who would recognise him or welcome his presence anyway. Ruby was gone and he didn't even know who was in charge there now.

It shouldn't have surprised him to find the entrance to the library open. Someone had removed the door. But his biggest surprise came when he stepped inside and discovered the shining walls. During the time he had been gone, shimmerers had made themselves at home on all but one wall of the room. Rab had often wondered just how large the library really was. He'd got an inkling of its size the first time he'd come down here with Gift and old John Braham. Watching the old man glide around in the darkness, shepherded by the guiding lights of the small lamps he'd carried, Rab had assumed the room must be large. He didn't need those lamps anymore and only now did he understand how grossly he'd under-estimated the extent of the library even then. And he still couldn't see the back wall where the shimmerers had failed to colonise. But there, on the right side of the room, was the ladder the old man had used to reach the uppermost shelves; there, towards the front, the table and chairs he and Gift had sat at. Rab tried counting the row on row of cases and shelves but soon gave up. It was too dispiriting an exercise once he realised how many now stood empty. Though he couldn't know how full the cases and shelves had been when the old man frequented this place, Rab knew, with absolute certainty, that they had been much fuller than this. Fuel. They'd been burning the books for fuel. The Feathers wouldn't care. They didn't write; they didn't read. Perhaps if they had a written language of their own, the books would have been better valued.

And now that he saw how badly the library had been savaged, it left him wondering why the Kun had agreed to him coming here. Perhaps the Kun didn't know, the destruction not even worth the effort of reporting. As he moved towards the table, Rab's thoughts were interrupted by a sound unfamiliar in the library. He had company.

On instinct, he glanced under the table and immediately found two scruffy-looking children. One was about six, he judged. The other perhaps two or three years older. The youngest was a boy; at least Rab thought he was. Crouching as he was in the shadows, it was hard to tell. The oldest was most definitely a girl; her head was capped in a mass of unruly brown hair although the soft features of her face were masked by a determination Rab was more accustomed to seeing among Top-sider children.

"You come out from there now," Rab said in what he hoped was a reassuring voice. "You're not in trouble."

"A lot you know!" the girl snapped back as she retreated further into the shadows, dragging the little boy with her.

Well, she was sharp. There was a lot he didn't know.

"All right," Rab said. Straightening, he drew out one of the chairs and sat down. "You're not in trouble *with me*. So why don't you come out and tell me what you're doing under there."

"Hiding. We thought you were a Feather."

The voice was tiny, hesitant, and Rab judged it to be the boy's, a guess confirmed when the girl spoke again.

"Shut up. He's not even tunnel. What are you talking to him for?"

"You did," the boy whined from underneath the table, making Rab smile.

"Well, I'm bigger. It's my job."

"And I'm bigger still," Rab replied and peeped under the table once more. "It's my job to find out what you're doing here. Come on." He thrust his hand out towards the little girl. "If you tell me your name, I'll tell you mine."

"You first," the girl said after a pause. "Then we'll see."

Rab sighed. He didn't remember tunnel kids ever being so cagey.

"Rab," he said. "My name is Rab."

It was dark there in the shadows but, thanks to the shimmerers, he could see well enough to know that the little girl's head had snapped around to look briefly at the boy.

"Dee's Rab?" she ventured, inching forward.

She'd used Gift's Top-sider name. And yes, he supposed he was Gift's Rab.

"That's right," he said, reaching further under the table. "Dee's Rab. I've come back for a little while."

"Who said you could?" the little girl asked. Her head was almost completely out from under the table, but still she refused Rab's hand.

"The Kun," Rab told her.

"Why?"

"To help fix the mushrooms."

"Huh! Nothing can fix them," she declared, inching out further.

"Who told you that?"

"My mother did."

"Did she? Well, that's why I'm here anyway. But you haven't told me *your* name yet."

"My name is Charlotte," she said and scooted the rest of the way out from under the table. "But I like Charlie better." Rising, she pointed under the table. "That's my brother, Patrick."

"And what does he like to be called?"

"Patrick," the boy replied in a tone that suggested he thought Rab might just be slightly crazy.

As the boy crawled forward, Rab took a hold of his outstretched hand and pulled him all the way out. But something was left behind on the floor. Once the boy, a mirror-image of his sister, was out of the way, Rab realised it was two books. He got up from the chair, bent to his knees and nudged the books out from under the table. Placing them on the table top, he sat back down and turned to the little girl: Charlie, as she 'liked better'.

"What were you going to do with these? Read them?"

The little girl's face erupted into a smile. "You're funny," she said and, pulling out a chair, plopped onto the seat. "If you're here to fix the mushrooms," she said, growing serious, "what are you doing in the library?"

"Could be I'm in the library for the same reason you are."

The little girl considered that possibility for a moment.

"Our mother sent us," she said at last, clearly suspicious. "Who sent you?"

"I sent myself."

"Then you'd better watch out for the Feathers. They don't like it when we take books."

"Is that so?" That hadn't been Rab's impression.

The little boy, Patrick, walked around the table and climbed onto the seat on the opposite side. "You'll get punished," he said solemnly.

"How?" Rab asked, shifting his attention to the boy. "How will I get punished?"

"You could get sent to the mines," the boy suggested. Glancing down, he grabbed one of the books Rab had retrieved from under the table and began to turn the pages.

"Been there already," Rab told him.

"Or the roosts," Charlie chimed in.

"Been there, too," Rab said, looking back at the girl.

Charlie shrugged. "Our father got sent to the mines."

"And where is your father now?"

Charlie just shrugged again.

"Mother says he's dead." The boy slammed the book shut and looked over at Rab. "But that's just what she says. I think Qworkas took him. Ouch!" His face contorted into a grimace. "What'd you kick me for?"

"Qworkas don't *take* people," Charlie scoffed. "They *eat* them. Every-one knows that."

"Well, that's not what Tommy says."

"Tommy knows nothing."

"Tommy's been top-side. He knows things."

"Yeah. Like how to fool little boys."

Charlie's brother leaped onto his seat and leaned menacingly over the table. "You watch who you call little!"

Rab raised his hand to ward off a pending scuffle. "Enough," he barked. "The library is no place for fighting. Why don't the Feathers like you taking books?" he asked of Charlie.

"They just don't. They yell at you if they catch you."

"Yell what?"

"I don't know. I don't talk Feather. You ask a lot of questions."

"Yeah," the boy piped up. He'd seated himself again. "Dee never said you ask a lot of questions."

"Sorry," Rab said, smiling. "Well, if the Feathers don't like you taking books, maybe you should just leave them here and go home."

"But —" the boy began until Charlie silenced him with another kick under table.

"All right," she agreed in a mumble as she rose from the table and started towards the open doorway.

After a moment, the little boy rose, too, and as he rounded the table, cast a troubled look at Rab.

"What do we tell mother?" he asked, catching up with his sister by the doorway.

He'd only spoken in a whisper, but Rab had heard him.

"Come back." Grabbing the books, Rab swivelled around in the chair. "Take them," he said, holding the two books out in his hands.

The girl hurried back, snatched the books and, turning, sped across the room and through the doorway, almost knocking her brother to the floor in the process.

Two more books burned. What did it matter anymore?

***

"So?" Rab said, leaning into the entrance of his old space. "What's wrong with the mushrooms?"

Cloud was seated on the bare floor but Gift was standing near the far wall. Rab had a suspicion he might have caught her pacing. Cloud got to her feet.

"Nothing. I could be wrong but I don't think the problem is with the mushrooms."

Rab stepped through the entrance into a barren space. No one was living in his old space anymore. He'd more or less expected it but still, seeing it this way, stripped completely bare, came as a shock.

"What then?" he asked.

"I think it's the cave itself," Cloud replied. "And that tunnel they've opened to the surface hasn't helped. It isn't cool enough anymore."

"Yes," Rab said. "I noticed." He'd been obliged to strip off his coat the moment he entered the cave. "Why the new tunnel?" he asked, directing the question at Gift.

The look she offered was almost identical to the look he'd received when he'd asked Patrick what he liked to be called.

"The Feathers regard our strain of mushrooms as a luxury food, Rab. It's highly valued. How do you think they've been getting them from here to the settlements?"

"I ..." Rab stammered.

He'd never really stopped to think about it before. He'd seen the carts arrive at the Kun's settlement, of course, but had never considered how they were loaded at the other end.

Gift waved a hand languidly. "At first we carried them up to the surface by way of 'the house'. But that was too inefficient for the Feathers. Now we haul the carts up the new tunnel."

Rab had difficulty imaging it. The tunnel had to be steep and even scaled down in size for transport across the surface, those carts would be heavy. "Are there tracks?" he asked. "I mean —"

Gift cut him off. "No tracks. Not yet. I think the Feathers might have had plans for us to lay them ..." she shook her head "... but now ..."

"Then you've decided the crop is finished."

Even he wasn't certain if he was asking for confirmation or making a statement.

"I'm afraid it is." Cloud looked over her shoulder, seeking Gift. "We don't know what to do. If we admit —"

"I don't think it's a matter of 'if'," Rab interrupted, "but 'how'. The Feathers have to be made to understand that there's not going to be any more food here."

"We have other food," Gift told him, stepping forward. "Qworka meat. And some of the plants that are harvested top-side are brought here." She looked at Cloud. "Probably some of the plants *you* grow and harvest for them. The Feathers transport them in every once in a while."

Rab shook his head. "It wouldn't be worth it … not without the mushrooms. They still provide the bulk of your food, don't they?"

"Yes," Gift replied and slumped to the floor. "What are we going to do?" Her voice sounded soft and distant.

"I don't think that's going to be your decision, Gift."

"What do you mean?" she asked, glancing up.

Rab crouched, balancing on the tips of his toes in front of her. "If the crop is finished, then this place is finished, too. There's no reason for the Feathers to keep it going if their crop is gone. You'll be moved somewhere else."

Gift's focus drifted briefly to Cloud before settling again on Rab. "Where?"

Something in her began to harden and Rab realised he'd never seen such an expression on her face before.

"I'm tired of moving somewhere else and then somewhere else again. The village. These tunnels. Top-side. The Kun's settlement. Then back to these tunnels again. Where next? There's nowhere left to go."

Rab held out his hand and, when she took it, eased her onto her feet again.

"You'll come with us."

He didn't need to see her to know that, out of view behind him, Cloud was about to remind him *that* wasn't *his* decision. But even the Kun wouldn't just allow the humans here to starve. He had to send them somewhere.

Gift smiled and patted his arm. "I'm sorry," she said. "I'm all right now. It's just that, well, I got frightened there for a moment. You're right. The Kun will just move us somewhere else and we'll be fine. We're good workers. The children are still strong. There'll be a place for us somewhere on the surface. I don't mind. Not really. But it'll be hard for the tunnel-dwellers to leave all this behind." She glanced about her and laughed lightly. "That was a stupid thing to say, wasn't it? There's really not much here," she said, splaying out her hands to take in the barrenness of Rab's old space. "I'm tired, that's all," she continued and then, running a hand through her tussled hair, began to brighten. "You must be hungry.

We'll go to my space and I'll get you both something to eat." She started towards the entrance and the lane beyond. "And you can tell me all about Fin."

She was talking far too fast.

"Fin has a wife and son now," Cloud said, hurrying after Gift.

Rab didn't listen for Gift's response. Instead he lingered in the entrance a while, saying a final farewell to the place that had once been his. It was easy to let go; easier than he thought it would be. After all, he'd vowed once before to leave and almost made it, too. This time there'd be no coming back. There'd be nothing worth coming back to.

He caught up with Gift and Cloud halfway down Braham Street. Cloud was telling Gift all about Tickie. Perhaps not such a wise thing to do. Though he doubted that Gift had ever forgotten about her own child, it probably wasn't the smartest thing to regale her with the charms of someone else's.

Gift was leading them into a sector of the tunnel city Rab had never visited before. He hadn't done a lot of exploring when he'd lived here – had never had the desire. Cloud seemed to know where she was going though, so he was content to fall in behind although he was mildly surprised to discover that Braham Street was a lot longer than he'd thought. On the way, they passed a couple of Feathers, neither of whom paid them any attention. Evidently they had been advised of his and Cloud's arrival.

Gift turned sharply to the right at the junction to a small off-shoot tunnel. The tunnel was narrow, hardly a tunnel at all really, and it was very short.

"Home," Gift said, ushering Rab and Cloud ahead of her through the only entrance in the wall.

To Rab's mind she sounded a bit distant.

Rab looked around and found a space that was reasonably well appointed. It wasn't a particularly large space, but comfortable, despite the lack of a covering of any kind to cushion the hard stone floor. A large table, battered and worn, occupied the centre of the floor and, around it, five equally weary chairs. Like the remaining table and chairs in the library, Gift's furniture represented some of the rare survivors. Without a fire it was difficult to see into the farthest reaches but there appeared to be a recess off to one side of the hearth, likely Gift's sleeping quarters. The rest of the space was dominated by an enormous stone bench that had been pushed hard up against the back wall on the opposite side of the hearth. The bench was overflowing. Pots and pans at one end. Canisters of all shapes and sizes at the other.

"It's not much to look at, I'm afraid," Gift said, following them inside. "I didn't bring anything with me and Ruby took most of Sunny's things a long time ago but she brought these few things back when I moved in here."

Sunny's things!

Was she saying that this had once been Sunny's space? Rab had never seen Sunny's space before. He hadn't been invited when she was alive and hadn't been inclined to visit after she was dead.

"I'm sorry," Gift said.

She must have noticed a change come over his face.

"I thought you knew. I'd take you somewhere else but –"

"There's no need for that," Rab told her. "Sunny's been dead a long time. If her ghost is roaming around in here, it can't be worse company than she was in life."

Rab was pleased to see a small smile surface above the lines of fatigue and worry on Gift's face.

"She wasn't all *that* bad."

"Well, maybe not," Rab conceded.

She *had* saved Gift from drowning after all.

"The way you two always talk about that woman," Cloud said, starting towards the table and its circle of chairs, "I'm sorry I didn't get to know her better."

"Don't be," Rab and Gift answered in unison, causing Cloud to hesitate when she was still only half-seated.

Finally Cloud smiled and Gift headed off towards the hearth. In no time at all she had a fire going and, after some clanging and banging around on the bench top, something bubbling away in the big pot on top of it. Rab watched her work, reminded of the efficiency she'd shown even when she'd been a small child under his inadequate care.

"I don't know how we're going to explain what's happened to the Feathers," she said, back turned. "No one here talks much Feather and the Feathers that live here rarely understand a thing we try to tell them. As long as the crop gets harvested and no one causes any trouble, they don't seem to care a lot about what we do."

"And the children?" Cloud asked, rising to collect three plates from the bench by the hearth.

Gift glanced over her shoulder. "The same," she replied. "Some are taken away when they're big enough. Others are left here to work the field."

Nothing had changed. But clearly it was about to.

Rab was making circles with the tip of one finger on the table. "We'll have to leave the explanation to Lilly," he said.

"Will they believe her?"

Rab looked up to find Gift standing beside him, pot in hand. From the opposite side of the table, Cloud distributed the plates.

"I guess I should have said will they believe *us*? We could be lying about the crop. Lilly wouldn't know." Using a large spoon, Gift began to fill the plates with bite-sized lumps of boiled meat Rab guessed to be Qworka. The meaty chunks were floating in a watery fluid that smelled distinctly of mushroom.

"They've seen the mushrooms, same as us," Cloud replied, seating herself. "Why would we lie?"

Gift returned the empty pot to the hearth. "To get out of here," she suggested at last as she returned to the table carrying a plate, larger than those Cloud had distributed, half-filled with shredded *ungtilis*. "A lot of the people here think life must be better on the surface now. A lot *want* to go."

"But not you?" Rab asked, turning his attention to the meal in front of him.

Gift returned to the table with three spoons: Feather spoons.

"Sometimes," she admitted, sitting down. "But it's like I said before. Just more moving around. This place. That place. None of it seems to get us anywhere. Oh, I don't know, maybe the people here are right. Maybe it would be better for us on the surface."

"I'm assuming you mean free?" Rab said, glancing up. "Not with us."

It had always baffled him why Gift had never attempted to escape this underground prison, tried to make it back to her daughter. Could be that's just what she had in mind now.

"With the Top-siders, you mean?" she asked soberly. "With Glint? He's gone. And so is every one of his people."

Rab was left in shock. Yes, many of the Top-siders had been killed during their raids on the Feathers' settlements. Some had died of natural causes on the surface. But there had been no word about the fate of Glint's band since Cloud and Fin had left them. They could still be alive — far to the west where they had fled. It wasn't like Gift to just give up.

"You can't know that," Rab said.

"We may be stuck down here in the tunnels, Rab, but we hear things. The people who bring supplies in also bring us news."

"Well, it must be better news than we get on the surface, Gift, because I've never heard anything about Glint's band of Top-siders."

Gift placed her spoon on the edge of her plate and, rising, went to the bench. When she returned, she placed a circle of string in the middle of the table. Randomly spaced along the string were ten or so little blue stones. Each stone was enclosed inside a miniature basket of knots that held them in place. Rab recognised it immediately. Cloud, too.

"This could be anyone's," Cloud said, gathering the string from the table. "Doesn't have to be Poppy's necklace."

"It's hers," Gift replied, reclaiming her spoon. "I found it in one of the stalls in the Market the first day they sent me back here. Prue told me it had come in from the surface."

Unlike Lilly, who'd also once run a pots and pans stall and wouldn't have remembered from one day to the next where or how she'd acquired something, Prue's memory was sharp. If she'd said it came in from the surface, then that's exactly where it came from. Besides, there were no little blue stones like those in the tunnels. Rab didn't know if Prue was still alive or not. Didn't matter really. If she was alive to be queried, she'd tell the same story.

Very likely the necklace had indeed once belonged to Poppy, Glint's wife and the grandmother of Gift's baby girl.

"She could have lost it, you know," Cloud suggested, returning the necklace to the table.

Gift just shook her head and continued eating.

Rab picked up the necklace and returned it to the bench by the hearth. As he made his way back to the table, he swore he saw something scurry underneath it, then shoot across the floor towards the entrance.

He pulled up suddenly with a hand on the rung of the chair.

"What?" Cloud asked, noticing his surprise.

"I'm seeing things," Rab replied. "Must be. But I'm certain something just ran from underneath the table."

Gift peeked briefly under the table. "Probably a Punn'tu," she said, motioning for Rab to sit down. "Gone now and they don't hurt you anyway."

"*What* is a Punn'tu?" Rab asked, reclaiming his chair.

"It's an animal," Cloud said before Gift could answer. "Remember that enclosure we saw in the mushroom field? It's a Punn'tu trap." She pointed with her spoon towards Gift. "Gift told me."

"Sometimes they get into the crop," Gift explained. "Eat the mushrooms."

"Then maybe that's what's happened," Rab suggested. "If we build more traps —"

Cloud shook her head. "They're not the problem. Although they haven't helped the yield. But we could kill every Punn'tu and it wouldn't make a bit of difference to the condition of the mushrooms."

"I've never heard of such a thing. Or seen one." Actually he hadn't really seen this one. All he could make of the thing, the Punn'tu, was a bit of brownish-coloured fuzz darting across the floor.

"Nor had we," Gift said, answering Rab, "until … oh … about two harvests ago, I guess. The Feathers didn't seem surprised when they started to appear, though. Guess the Punn'tus have been slowly following them north. The Feathers catch them and eat them sometimes."

Cloud dropped her spoon, garnering Gift's attention.

"What's the matter? Oh," she said, gesturing towards Cloud's plate with her own spoon upraised. "That's Qworka. Don't worry. Even an old boot would taste better than Punn'tu, cooked or otherwise."

"Can we talk about something else?" Despite years of being obliged to eat it, Cloud never had developed a fondness for meat.

"Is there someone named Tommy here?" Rab asked, certain that wasn't the 'something else' Cloud had in mind.

Gift looked at him curiously.

"We have two Tommys. Why?"

"Either of them Top-siders?"

"Depends on what you're calling a Top-sider. There's Tommy who used to be a bounty hunter, if that's who you mean."

One of the Pigeon Brothers? Surely not. Rab had never bothered to learn the given names of the two men who weren't actually brothers but whose demeanour was so alike as to have earned them that title from old John Braham. They'd been surface-roamers once. Roamers who, for a price, sought out tunnel-dweller girls who had been stolen by the Top-siders and then returned them to their home underground. Could they still be alive?

Clearly Cloud was thinking the same thing.

"*Pigeon Brother* Tommy?" she asked after a pause.

"What's a Pigeon Brother?" Gift asked.

"Did Tommy have a partner?"

"Oh, yes he used to. I think his name was Robert or Richard. Something like that. He died top-side. At least that's what Tommy said."

"Tommy didn't happen to say that Robert or Richard, or whatever his name was, got taken by a Qworka, did he? Maybe eaten?"

"Yes, he did," Gift replied, sounding surprised, "although I don't think he said anything about him being eaten exactly."

"Qworkas don't *eat* people," Cloud interjected. "Well, they don't. Do they?" she asked when both Gift and Rab turned to look at her.

"One nearly ate you once," Rab reminded her.

"It did not," she snapped back. "Just knocked me off my feet. That's all," she said, gesturing with her spoon in the air. "Anyway what's all this about? Why are you asking about a bounty hunter?"

"I came across two kids in the library. One insisted that Qworkas ate people. The other said they only took them and that it was someone named Tommy who said so."

"Two kids stealing books, I'll bet," Gift said.

"Charlie and Patrick," Rab told her.

"I'm not surprised it was them. Most of the kids are too scared to steal from the library. The Feathers don't allow it. We're not supposed to go in there at all really. Except since the door is gone …" she didn't bother to finish.

"That's the other thing I wanted to ask you about. Why do the Feathers care about the books?"

Gift shook her head indifferently. "I don't know, but they do. Sometimes they even go in there and look at the books themselves. At first they didn't care how many books were burned. At least that's what people here told me. Then they stopped it. All of a sudden. Well, at least they tried to stop it. Kids like Charlie still sneak in there when they think they can get away with it."

"What happens if they get caught?" Cloud asked.

"They get punished. Usually they're not allowed food for three or so days. Sometimes they are sent to work extra shifts in the fields. Sometimes …"

"… they just disappear?" Rab prompted.

"That isn't what I was going to say, but, yes, that did happen once," Gift replied after some hesitation. "How did you know that?"

"I didn't. Just guessed."

"It happened not too long ago." She reached towards the plate of *ungtilis*, grabbed a handful and began stirring it into the watery mass of Qworka meat.

It was a combination Rab had never tried. He snatched a handful of *ungtilis* for himself and Cloud quickly followed suit. It could only improve the flavour.

"There were three children, I think it was, who stole from the library," Gift took up. "The Feathers found out about it and the children were sent to the roosts to work. They never made it there."

"Surely they didn't go on their own," Cloud asked, stirring in so much *ungtilis* that the meal on her plate turned a bilious sort of green. "I mean when I was a kid, if someone had tried to send me out unescorted to some place I didn't want to go, I'd have taken off in some *other* direction."

Yes, she would. Rab would have, too. And so would Gift.

"A Feather scout took them. At least he was supposed to, but he never made it to the roosts, either."

"An accident?" Cloud suggested, tucking into her bilious green meal with renewed enthusiasm.

"Maybe. But no one's ever come across them since. Wouldn't you think someone would find their bones sooner or later?"

"What do you think happened to them?" Rab asked between mouthfuls.

"Me? Well, I don't know. Perhaps Top-siders took them."

"Or killed them," Cloud suggested. "It's possible," she said defensively, catching Rab's look of scepticism.

"Killed the children?" he pressed her.

"Yeah. Maybe not the children. But the scout."

"They may have." Rising, Gift walked back to the bench and returned with a loaf of 'shroom bread, which she placed in the centre of the table. "Sop up the rest with chunks of that," she suggested. "It isn't bad."

Tearing off a piece, Rab gave it a try. She was right.

"And what about Robert or Richard or whoever," he asked. "Has anyone ever come across his bones?"

"That wouldn't be very likely if a Qworka ate him," Gift answered with a small smile and seated herself again.

"I don't think you believe that story any more than I do."

"No," she said, taking a piece of the loaf for herself. "But Tommy is … well, not the most honest person I've ever met. It wouldn't surprise me if he, not a Qworka, killed his partner."

Rab shook his head. "I can't see that happening. They'd travelled together far too long already. Had to be something else. What were they doing top-side anyway? It's not like there were any captive girls to go hunting anymore. How did they evade the Feathers for so long?"

Gift was making circle after circle with a scrap of 'shroom loaf, mopping up the dregs from her plate. "I don't think you understand. They didn't evade the Feathers at all. The Feathers *let* them wander around on the surface. In fact, sometimes Tommy still goes top-side by himself."

"Why?"

"Why did the Feathers let them or why does Tommy still go?" she asked, glancing up briefly.

"Well … both, I guess."

"They scavenge."

It was a fair enough description of what they had *always* done. Only when he had known them, the Pigeon Brothers had scavenged for little captive girls – or at the very least ones they could pass off as little captive girls. He couldn't imagine what they scavenged for now. Gift seemed surprised by the question when he asked her.

"For Top-siders, of course. No one knows Top-siders like Tommy. Even other Top-siders don't know as much about the movements of other Top-sider bands. But Tommy does. At least he used to. Now it seems there aren't many to be found. They're nearly all gone. Dead, I suppose. Killed in the raids on the Feather settlements. Or pushed too far west where there's no food, no water –"

"You can't be certain of that, Gift. No one knows what's in the west. Not really. Even Fin and Cloud didn't travel far enough in that direction to know."

"He's right," Cloud interrupted. "Just because …"

When Gift rose from the table, plate in hand, Cloud stopped talking. Rab placed a hand over hers. The conversation had drifted places he had never intended.

"I doubt the Feathers will start back with you immediately," Gift said. "But since there's not much to be done about the crop, they probably won't let you stay too long. You'd better stay here tonight. I'll find some extra bedding for you down in the Market. But we should decide what to do, Cloud. And work out how we're going to tell the Feathers here about the crop. I could have had Tommy explain. He talks a little Feather, but he's gone top-side again."

"Let Lilly do the explaining to the Kun," Rab said.

"And what do I do about the crop until then?" Gift asked, reaching for his empty plate. "It will take you a while to get back to the Kun and for the scouts to return back here with his instructions."

"Salvage what you can," Cloud said, rising with her own empty plate. "It isn't all ruined yet. Harvest everything that's edible."

"Won't the Feathers here think that's strange?"

"I'm sure they will, but it's all you can do."

"All right," Gift agreed. "I'll try. But I think the Feathers are going to have something to say about it, whether I understand what that is or not."

"Do the best you can to explain, Gift. If you don't start now, the whole harvest might be lost instead of just part of it."

"There's something I don't understand," Rab said, only half listening to their talk. "Why would Tommy say his partner was taken by a Qworka?"

"Still!" Cloud grumped and dropped back down into her chair, plate in hand. "What does it matter what he said?"

"I was thinking about what Pi'a'weh told us."

"Pi'a'weh?" Gift asked. "Pi'a'weh speaks to you?" She sat back down, a look of disbelief on her face.

"Sometimes," Rab said until Cloud glanced at him admonishingly. "All right. Hardly ever. But just before we left he made a point of warning us about the Qworkas outside the settlement."

"So?" Gift said, returning the plates to the table. "Even roost Qworkas are dangerous."

She, better than anyone, knew that. Her husband had been killed by a Qworka … that, incidentally, had made no attempt to either take or eat him.

"He wasn't just warning us about any Qworka, Gift. He was warning us about white Qworkas."

Gift almost laughed. "White Qworkas. There's no such thing!"

"That's what I said," Cloud muttered.

"And Tommy never mentioned anything about a white Qworka killing his partner. Just that it was Qworkas."

"What exactly did Tommy say?" Rab asked. There was a small chunk of 'shroom loaf left and, since no one else seemed interested, he reached out and claimed it.

"Let me think." Absently Gift started to move loose crumbs around on her plate. "As I remember it, he said that they'd been tracking a small party of Top-siders." She waved the other hand. "The Feathers seemed to think the band was up to no good, I guess. Maybe planning a raid or something. Anyway, they'd tracked them too long and were running out of food. Robert – that's right – it was Robert, not Richard. Robert remembered seeing some wild Qworkas back the way they had come –"

"She said *wild*, not *white*," Cloud interrupted, tapping Rab's hand.

"Very funny." He turned back to Gift. She was smiling. "Go on."

"Yes, Tommy definitely did say wild. They agreed to split up. Robert was going to kill and bring back a Qworka and Tommy was to keep up with the Top-siders. Follow them, you know, leave signs for Robert so he could find him again. But Robert never came. Two days later, early in the morning, Tommy said he heard a lot of strange noises. He thought that they were coming from the sky but later he said that he couldn't be certain."

"What sort of noises?" Rab asked.

"He didn't explain them very well, I don't think. Or I've forgotten what he said. Just strange noises … back the way Robert had gone. He kept following the Top-siders for a while but said he couldn't stop thinking about those noises. And he'd expected Robert to have caught up with him by then. So he broke off following the Top-siders and started looking for Robert instead."

"And?" Cloud asked, inching forward.

Seemed she'd become caught up in Gift's story after all.

"He found him. What there was to find anyway. Just a pool of blood. It was pretty well dried by the time Tommy got there."

"Well, that could have been anything," Cloud said, reclining back in her chair.

"Could have been," Gift agreed. "But Tommy insisted it was Robert's blood. He found a lot of Qworka feathers around the site as well. Not a single bone though. But the ground was really disturbed all around. Like there had been a fight of some sort."

"Between Robert and a Qworka?" Rab suggested.

"That's what he thought."

"Oh, that can't be right," Cloud insisted. "There'd have to be bones left. Even if a Qworka did eat him, there'd have to be something left behind."

"Seems so to me," Gift agreed. "That's why I said it wouldn't surprise me if Tommy hadn't killed Robert himself and made up that story to explain why he never came back."

"Did Tommy say he *saw* any Qworkas himself?" Rab pressed her.

"That's the other part that never sounded right to me. He said he saw a lot of Qworkas. And they weren't just flying around the way they do – like they're intentionally going somewhere. He said they were flying in circles all kind of mixed up. Said some of them even banged into each other as though they were confused or frightened of something and that their behaviour scared him so much that he found some urse and hid in it for the rest of the day. Didn't come out until nightfall long after all the Qworkas had finally flown away."

"What's a Qworka got to be frightened of?" Cloud scoffed. "I think you're right, Gift. Tommy did it and made up some ridiculous story so he could get away with it."

Rab turned to Cloud. "The story's just a bit *too* ridiculous, don't you think? Wouldn't it have been easier to claim that Robert … oh, say fell and cracked his head open? No one would expect Tommy to bring his body back here to be buried. He'd simply bury him on the surface."

"Maybe Tommy's not that smart."

"Or maybe he's telling the truth," Rab countered. "It would make sense of what Pi'a'weh was trying to tell us."

"No it wouldn't," Cloud objected. "Pi'a'weh said *white* Qworkas, re-member."

"Tommy never said anything about the Qworkas being white," Gift said, recapturing Rab's attention.

"Well, Pi'a'weh said met'ah and met'ah means white."

"Yes, I think it does," Gift agreed.

"If Pi'a'weh wanted to warn us that there were Qworkas out here eat-ing people, he'd have said that, not just for us to watch out," Cloud said and stood up from the table. "I'm not going to worry about Qworkas, black or white, that do or don't eat people anymore. Tommy lied and Pi'a'weh doesn't know what he's talking about. It's as simple as that."

That would be the simple explanation, but still Rab wasn't convinced it was the right explanation. Of course, Tommy could have lied. But what possible reason could Pi'a'weh have to concoct some story about white Qworkas?

Chapter 4

FEATHERS were free to come and go from the settlement as they chose, but doq'iri weren't, so word of their return had somehow preceded them.

Tickie was waiting in the distance down the lane. Rab had expected Neila to still be away at the mines, so was surprised to see her standing in the lane beside her son. There was something about the boy's obvious impatience and the way he pulled on his mother's hand that brought Fin's younger brother to Rab's mind. Had he lived, Stitch might have had children of his own now, too. Or, perhaps like Rab, he'd have chosen not to.

Cloud pulled up just inside the inner gate and turned to the Feather scouts.

"We need to see Lilly immediately," she told them. "Yiri! Understand?"

Cloud had done her best to repeat her request in feathertalk. Perhaps the scouts took her meaning. Then again, when it came to Feathers, no one could ever be certain. The female scout launched into a flurry of feathertalk interspersed with the usual clicks and snaps, which, Rab assumed, was intended for her male companion. When the featherwoman was finished, the male took a light hold of Cloud's upper arm and began to speak. Rab hadn't understood a word of it. Seemed the Feather thought Cloud did, because he turned and began walking away in the company of the featherwoman.

Cloud looked at Rab and shrugged. "I –" she began but was robbed of the chance to say more when Tickie rushed at her, nearly knocking her off her feet.

"Kood's back!"

Rab was back, too, but that didn't seem to matter much to little Tickie. Cloud spoiled that child. She had the energy Neila lacked to play with him. Fin's wife was young but not strong and her recent roster to the mines had only weakened her further. Another mother would have been able to keep up with the young boy as he rushed down the road. Not Neila. And especially not today. She was limping badly. She should never have been sent to the mines. Perhaps, when they spoke to Lilly, if they got to speak to Lilly, Rab could ask her to use her influence to have Neila assigned to less demanding work. He had no doubt that Lilly would offer to try. The problem was, when the time came, would she *remember* to try?

"I'm sorry," Neila called as she hurried up the lane. Even from a distance, Rab could see the lines of fatigue on her face, lines that hadn't been quite so conspicuous when he'd last seen her. And when she reached out to drag Tickie away, he noticed a fresh scattering of raw wounds on her hands.

"I said we should wait outside your ts'un, but he wouldn't have it," Neila said, gathering the child into her arms. Immediately the boy began to pull at the thin brown strands of Neila's loosely tied hair.

"It's all right," Cloud replied. "We didn't expect anyone to come out and meet us. Are you hurt? You're limping?"

"Just a small accident at the mine. My leg will be fine in a little while and I get to spend some time with Tickie before they send me back."

Her leg wouldn't be fine in a little while. Not in a long while, either. And she wouldn't be going back to the mines … whether Lilly remembered to speak to the Kun or not. It would be obvious, even to the Feathers, that having Neila at the mines would be detrimental. But what use could they put her to now? She was good at sewing. Some of the more affluent Feathers had humans as their personal servants; perhaps Lilly could suggest that to the Kun.

"I wanted to talk to you as soon as you got back," Neila explained as she started limping down the lane between Rab and Cloud.

"Is something wrong?" Rab asked.

"Not wrong exactly. But someone went into your ts'un while you were gone. I don't know how it happened," she said, turning to Cloud with an apologetic expression that exaggerated the lines on her face. "Or when. But one morning not long after you had left, Fin found a canister of ground *ungtilis* lying in the lane outside your ts'un. When he checked inside, he discovered the whole place had been disturbed. And it seemed that some things were missing. Food stuff. And maybe some of your clothes. He tidied up a little but didn't –"

"Someone stole from us?" Cloud asked, cutting Neila off.

She sounded incredulous. With reason. No one in the settlement stole. Not the Feathers. Not the tunnel-people. Not even the few Top-siders who, over the years, had opted for the comparative safety of life inside the settlements.

"Were there thefts anywhere else?" Rab asked.

Neila shook her head as best she could with Tickie still pulling on her hair.

"Yours was the only one," she said. "They must have known you were gone. Fin thinks they might have even been watching you."

"I can't understand that at all," Cloud said. She sounded more angered than surprised now.

Rab was already angered. They all had very little but, if someone was in dire need, there was an informal understanding that all anyone had to do was ask. The tunnel culture was a sharing culture and nothing had changed top-side in that regard. One of the Top-sider newcomers must have stolen from them and, if so, then they'd just done a very stupid thing. The tunnel-people wouldn't tolerate it. And Rab had a sneaking suspicion that if the Feathers found out about it, they'd tolerate it even less. A divided and distrustful workforce made for an inefficient and ineffective workforce.

"Fin asked around," Neila was saying, "but no one saw or heard any-thing. Well, I suppose that isn't entirely true. He did find some tracks over by the inner wall. More like a scuffed-up place really, as though someone had jumped down off the wall. But that could mean anything and it might have nothing to do with the food being stolen from your ts'un."

Rab was inclined to think it did. It made more sense for the thief to have come from the *outside*. So it was a Top-sider thief after all, but not one who had relocated to the settlement. Unless they intended to raid, it was rare for a Top-sider to venture so close to the settlements. And Top-siders never entered a settlement to steal before a raid. It ruined the only advantage they had – surprise.

Neila was clearly struggling with Tickie, so Rab stripped off his pack and passed it to Cloud, leaving himself with only the spear that had been returned to him once they'd left the tunnel city.

"Let Tickie ride for a while," he said and stopped for the moment it took Tickie to climb from his mother's arms onto his shoulders.

Neila wasn't the only one waiting on their return. As they made their way past the outermost Feather ts'uns, Rab soon became aware that they were being watched. There were more Feathers out and about than usual and every one of them displayed a peculiarly unusual interest in two doq'iri returning from what should not have been a particularly notewor-thy mission. Among them was Pi'a'weh and his was the only interest Rab could understand. From the start, he'd expressed concern about Rab and Cloud venturing away from the settlement. Even after they'd passed him, Rab could feel Pi'a'weh's strange eyes follow their progress down the lane. What Pi'a'weh did, day in, day out, Rab didn't know. Sometimes the odd little featherman would be absent from the lanes and alleys for long stretches, then suddenly he'd be there again, hobbling around.

By the time they'd reached the far side of the settlement, Rab's skin was beginning to crawl from all the attention they were drawing.

Cloud went ahead of him through the open doorway into their ts'un. Neila remained outside. The place did look as though it had been looted. Fin had done a bit of tidying but, essentially, he'd left the ts'un as he'd found it.

The cans and canisters that Cloud usually kept neatly arranged on the bench against the far wall were all out of place. Some appeared to be missing. Quite a few, Rab realised, when after lowering Tickie to the floor, he went to inspect the disarray more closely.

Offloading both her pack and Rab's, Cloud hurried up to join him.

"They spilled a lot, too," Rab said, leaning his spear against the wall.

Cloud ran a finger along the bench, dragging a trail through a fine layer of powder. "Green-weed," she said, looking up at Rab. "What would they want with green-weed?"

What indeed!

"Suggests it wasn't Top-siders, doesn't it?" he said.

"Maybe not," Cloud answered after a brief hesitation. "They didn't take it. They tipped it over. Maybe intentionally."

Tickie made a lunge for the bench. He was just tall enough to get the tips of his fingers into the powder. Cloud scooped him up from the floor and, grabbing the nearest piece of cloth she could find, began wiping off his fingers. "You know better than that, Tickie," she scolded. "Never touch something if you don't know what it is."

Rab felt his face drift into a smile.

"Fine one to talk," he mumbled, remembering what Cloud had done the very first time they had come across green-weed – dug her fingers right into the stuff.

"Well, just because I'm stupid, doesn't mean Tickie should be," she told the little boy and, releasing his hands, gave him a quick swat to the rear and sent him back towards his mother.

"Will everything be all right?" Neila called to them from the lane.

"We'll be fine, Neila," Rab said, turning. "Don't worry about it. There wasn't anything you or Fin could do. We'll just tidy it up. But I guess we should all be more careful from now on."

"Do you think it was Top-siders?" Neila asked, gathering up her child.

"I do," Cloud said before Rab had a chance to say anything.

He did, too. He just wasn't prepared to say it – not yet – when it didn't make an awful lot of sense.

"When Fin gets back, I'll have him take you to the place he found the scuff marks," Neila said. "If you need anything before then, just come and get me."

Tickie waved over Neila's shoulder as she left.

"Now what?" Cloud asked. Abandoning the disorder on the bench, she pulled out a chair and sat down.

"We put it all back the way it was."

"That isn't what I mean and you know it. What's going on? First Pi'a'weh gives us some warning about white Qworkas. Then we find the 'shroom field in the tunnels ruined. Now this … Top-siders *sneaking* into the settlement when they've never done anything like that before."

Rab drew out the opposite chair and sat down. "Well, as I understood it, you thought Pi'a'weh was talking rubbish."

When Cloud made to answer, Rab hurried on.

"And the failure of the 'shroom crop has nothing to do with white Qworkas, whether white Qworkas exist or not. And the theft …" he glanced towards the wreckage of Cloud's food and healing supplies, "… maybe it's some new Top-sider tactic. There doesn't seem to be many of them left. Anyway, it's better if it is them and not one of us who stole."

"You're right," Cloud agreed. "Do you think we should tell Lilly about this? If there *are* Top-siders close enough to get into the settlement unobserved, shouldn't the Kun be made aware?"

It was a difficult question, one Rab couldn't immediately answer. After all the Top-siders were human like them.

"The Kun might already know," he suggested doubtfully.

If the Kun was aware that Top-siders were anywhere near his settlement, he'd have increased the security around its perimeter. And there wasn't any evidence of that.

"Yeah," Cloud said although it was clear she didn't believe it either. "And we may not even get to see Lilly. I couldn't tell if those scouts understood a word I said to them."

"They understood enough."

Rab jumped at the sound of the voice coming from the entrance to their ts'un. He swung around in his chair and discovered Button standing there.

How much had she heard?

They didn't see Button very often, usually only when she was on duty on the platform in front of the Kun's palace. And they never ever saw her without Lilly. It struck Rab how little she had changed. The Feathers were treating her well. She was still small, of course, but where others who had been brought here from the tunnels showed evidence of the years, Button looked as young and vital as she had the day he and Cloud had set out on their journey south. The skin of her face was free of the lines that marked Cloud's face and her light brown hair, hanging loose, showed no signs of greying.

"I'm sorry," Button said warmly, "I didn't mean to startle you. Lilly sent me. I'm to take you to see her now. Unless you're too tired from your journey." She made to step back a pace. "I can come back another time."

Rab was surprised how easily Button had found them. Seemed Lilly knew more about the comings and goings in the settlement than he realised. And how she kept it all in that sieve-like head of hers was even more surprising. When she'd lived in the tunnels, it was rare for Lilly to recall what she'd done or who she'd spoken to the day before.

"We're ready now," Cloud said, jumping up.

She sounded anxious, keen to take advantage of an opportunity to see Lilly. They might not get another. Rab doubted it was the business of the failing 'shroom crop alone that had Cloud so eager to go. She'd cared for Lilly for a long time and that kind of bond was hard to break, no matter how adamantly Cloud protested that she had indeed broken it.

"Rab, too," Button said when Rab remained in his chair.

That was a strange. Why would Lilly want to see him?

After a brief glance around, he decided that it was safe enough to leave their ts'un unattended and got to his feet. They'd been gone a while already and Neila had reported only the one incidence of theft. And she was on the lookout now.

He caught up with Button and Cloud out in the lane. Button had little to say as they made their way towards the Kun's palace. She hadn't changed in that regard, either; there had been a time when Rab thought she was mute. And that just got him wondering all the more. What was it about living under the Kun's protection that had so changed Lilly?

As they neared the palace, Button veered off into a narrow lane Rab had never taken much notice of before. He should have expected Lilly not to live in the palace proper. Doubtless there were matters the Kun preferred to keep solely among the Feathers, so it wouldn't do to have a doq'iri, one who understood every word that was spoken, wandering unchaperoned near his quarters.

"This way," Button said, leading them towards a small door set into the rough-hewn stone of a wall pressed hard up against the lane. Curiously, the door was wooden. Either the Feathers had carried it with them from the south or the door had once seen service down in the tunnel city.

Out of the corner of his eye, Rab caught the look of apprehension on Cloud's face. He was beginning to feel slightly unnerved himself. This was Lilly's space and Lilly was under the protection of the Kun. In essence, she belonged to him, more so than any other human really. Like most humans in and outside the settlements, Rab felt more comfortable when he was effectively invisible to the Feathers.

From the pocket of her loose skirt, Button produced something that looked like a large key. Rab only got a quick glimpse, but it appeared as though the head of the key had been shaped to resemble the head of a Qworka. Human ts'uns didn't have keys or locks; they didn't even have doors; and the entrances to most Feather ts'uns were swathed in either cloth or skin. The lock itself was a complicated affair. A long shaft was slotted through two protruding loops, one located on the far left of the door and the other bolted into the wall. The end of the shaft on the door side curved around and passed through a boxy-looking mechanism where the key would be slotted. Two smaller shafts extended out the other side of the mechanism, the top-most fused to a ring that encircled the long shaft on the far side of the opposite loop.

The strange lock tumbled and, accompanied by a tiny creak, the door swung open.

Rab had expected to enter directly into Lilly's ts'un. Instead he found himself in a wide open space. The ground beneath his feet was smoothly paved and in the middle of the space rose a tree. A tree! It was only a small tree with just a few thin branches, but its leaves were lush and plentiful and it was green. Green! The lush, green tree was surrounded by a low stone bench. To the left Rab spotted a well. Lilly had her own private water well! A cloth-covered walkway ran along all three sides of the enclosure and, in each of the four corners, raised garden beds were bursting with closely packed stands of healthy *ungtilis*. Two of the beds had also been planted with *pacha* and long trails of the rare vine had begun to spill over the sides of the low garden walls. Rab had tasted the *pacha's* small black berries only once. To a Feather, it was a delicacy; to a human, barely palatable. In the shade beneath the cloth overhang, Rab counted three centrally-set doors in the walls of the attached ts'uns. More plunder from the tunnel city?

Perhaps all of this didn't belong to Lilly after all and she was obliged to share this opulent space with others. Feathers? Surely not. Feathers and humans did not share living arrangements.

"That's my ts'un over there," Button said, partly settling the matter. She pointed towards the door past the well, then turned to relock the outer door. "Lilly lives in the middle section," she explained and began heading in that direction.

"Who lives on the other side?" Cloud asked as she trailed Button across the paved ground. Her heavy boots barely made a sound.

"The cook," Button replied over her shoulder.

Cloud nudged Rab so hard in the ribs, it actually hurt.

There was no key to Lilly's door and Button didn't even knock or call out to announce their arrival. Depressing a simple latch, she ushered Rab and Cloud ahead of her into Lilly's space.

"Perhaps she's resting," Button said on finding the room empty. "I'll go and get her," she added, hurrying around the corner.

Rab didn't mind the delay. It gave him time to take in their surroundings. Lilly might belong to the Kun but the Feather leader had certainly done his best to ensure her comfort. It felt warm inside Lilly's private domain. Warm, light and bright. Every home Rab had ever known had been cold, dark and oppressive. Even Feather ts'uns were gloomy inside. At least Rab had always assumed they would be on account of their thick outer walls. But Lilly's ts'un was constructed differently. It was hardly like a ts'un at all. At the juncture of the walls and ceiling were large open areas that allowed the light and air to seep in from the outside. It had something of the look of the roosts about it, although the holes in the walls of Lilly's space were larger, longer and, as a result, fewer. And unlike every other ts'un Rab had ever seen, unlike the roosts as well, Lilly's ts'un wasn't round. It boasted corners and fine straight edges where one wall abutted against another. An enormous centrally-placed hearth accounted for the warmth. Nowadays the humans in the Kun's settlements rarely used their hearths for anything besides cooking – until snow time came along, of course, when their cloth-roofed houses became bitterly cold inside. But snow time was a long way off and still Lilly was indulged and allowed to waste fuel that was still a precious commodity on the surface.

The warmth and light and brightness of Lilly's space weren't the only curiosities. There were pieces of furniture positioned about the room – actual furniture, not the scraps and scavenged relics Rab's people used. In some of the books in the tunnel library, Rab had seen pictures of furniture. Houses on Earth seemed to have been bursting at the seams with it – once anyway. Of course, the furnishings in Lilly's house looked nothing like those in the pictures. For one thing, the bits and pieces in Lilly's home had been designed for people of smaller stature and they were quite basic. Tables to eat at, chairs to sit on, and benches on which to store things. And Lilly's ts'un wasn't exactly bursting at its seams.

It had been those bits of furniture that had immediately captured Cloud's attention. She'd moved across the floor to inspect one of Lilly's long low seats while Rab had been looking up at the ceiling. Cloud was caressing – there was no other word for it – the smooth wood of what had to be a very old seat when he stepped up to join her. The seat was low and someone Rab's size would be obliged to sit either with their legs stretched out in front of them or knees pulled up towards their chest. The low seat wouldn't cause Lilly or Button any discomfort; neither were large women.

"Abby. You've come."

Rab spun around, startled by Lilly's voice.

She sounded just like the Lilly of old, not like the Lilly he'd grown accustomed to hearing – the one who sat high up on the platform, translating when she was instructed to do so, on the left hand side of the Kun.

Cloud rushed across the floor and embraced the little woman. Button stood slightly behind and to the side of Lilly, much the way she always did at Assembly.

"Oh, you haven't changed a bit," Cloud lied, edging back to hold Lilly's shoulders at arm's-length. "You look just the same."

"And you look worried," Lilly replied, though a broad smile further crimpled the lines of her face. "I was worried, too, that something might happen to you along the way."

She still thought Cloud was her daughter, Abby. No one had dispelled it – not Rab, who'd always known better and not Button, who must have suspected it for a very long time. It was kinder to let Lilly go on believing. Cloud had made the right decision. She'd taken care of the woman since she was a young girl, newly returned to the tunnels, until the day she, Fin and Rab had set out for the south. And if the Feathers had permitted it, she, not Button, would have been taking care of Lilly now.

"You shouldn't have worried like that. We had scouts with us. What could have happened?" Cloud said light-heartedly.

"Yes. Yes," Lilly replied. "Now sit," she said, gesturing towards the long old seat. "Button tells me that you have news and wanted to see me urgently."

Rab confessed to being a little stunned. Although there were times in the past when Lilly had managed to make a contorted sort of sense, times when she could remember things from one day to the next, more often her mind was completely distracted. Perhaps today was just one of her good days. Or perhaps life here among the Feathers had indeed transformed her for the better. If so, she was the fortunate exception.

Cloud took a hold of Lilly's arm and walked with her towards the seat. Rab followed behind with Button.

"So," Lilly said, seating herself, "I'm guessing it's about the crop. Is it as bad as they say? Can it be saved?"

Cloud shook her head. "No. I don't think it can be. But it's nothing Gift has done."

"Dee," Rab said, selecting one of the other seats. Button sat down beside him.

"What?" Cloud asked, glancing his way.

"The Feathers call her Dee, her Top-sider name."

"I know that," Lilly said, waving a hand at him.

So, Rab concluded, it *was* one of Lilly's good days. Lucky for them.

"The brightworms inside the dome have flourished," Cloud continued. "They're everywhere now and the Feathers have opened up a new tunnel to the surface. It's just too light and warm inside the dome. The mushrooms can't survive."

"I see," Lilly said. "Then that's what I must tell the Kun."

"What will he do?" Cloud pressed her. "About our people in the tunnels, I mean."

Lilly shook her head. "I don't know, but I suspect he won't allow them to stay there. Without the mushroom crop, there's no point. I'm sure you've worked that out for yourself or you wouldn't be looking so worried."

"Do you have any idea where he might move them?" Rab asked, garnering Lilly's attention.

"No, I don't. He could send them to any of the settlements."

From the opposite seat, Cloud was looking at him knowingly. He was thinking about Gift, of course, and what might become of her now.

"Are there many of us left?" Lilly asked.

She sounded a trifle distant now, although perhaps it wasn't that familiar old flash of uncertainty he was hearing but concern for her people instead. She hadn't forgotten them. Even Lilly, at her worst, wouldn't forget the place where she'd been born and the people with whom she'd shared most of her life.

"In the tunnels, you mean?" Cloud replied.

Lilly nodded and Button, who had been sitting silently beside Rab as the others talked, got up and left the room.

"Maybe half who were left behind. I can't say for sure. We weren't there very long and didn't get to speak to anyone but Gift. But you have to remember it's been a long time. Some of our people were old already."

"Like me?" Lilly prompted. "Oh, it's all right," she went on, waving a dismissing hand at Cloud. "I know I'm old, although I can't exactly remember how old. But I don't suppose that matters. The Kun has looked after me very well here."

"Yes, he has," Cloud agreed, sounding a little subdued.

Rab knew his wife; she'd be thinking that the Kun had done a far better job of seeing to Lilly's welfare than she ever had. She'd be wrong. In the ways that really counted anyway. If it hadn't been for Cloud, Lilly would have died while still a relatively young woman.

Button slipped back into the room. She was carrying a small metal cup and, as she passed by Lilly to reclaim her seat, handed it to the old woman.

Lilly accepted the cup automatically, almost as though she'd been expecting it to appear. As she tilted the cup to her lips, Rab caught a whiff of a strong and unfamiliar odour. Whatever Button had brought Lilly, it wasn't plain water. He glanced at Cloud but she didn't appear to have noticed.

"The Kun will also want to know what you discovered in the library," Lilly said after taking another sip from the cup.

It took a moment for Rab to realise that Lilly was talking to him.

"If you're asking me about a possible cure for the disease, then I'm afraid the answer is nothing. I couldn't find anything useful in any of the books."

Rab didn't like to lie. He hadn't even bothered to look at any of the books. There'd be nothing in any of those old books that touched on the vegetation on *this* planet. But he couldn't tell Lilly that. Explain that the only reason he'd asked to go along was to protect Cloud. That he'd known all along the books would be of no help whatsoever. But if Lilly had the Kun's ear, then the Kun also had hers. And what about the woman sitting beside him? Where did Button's allegiance lie? With her own people or with the Feathers who had provided her with such a comfortable lifestyle?

Some things were best kept secret.

"Did you bring any back with you?"

"Books?" At first, Rab thought she was talking about the diseased mushrooms.

Lilly nodded and, again, brought the cup to her lips.

"Well, no."

What sort of question was that?

"And what about the condition of the library? The Kun might be interested in that, too."

Well, since she'd brought it up …

Rab did his best to lean forward in his seat but his legs were stretched out far in front of him.

"Why are the Feathers so interested in the library?" he asked. "Gift told us that the tunnel-dwellers aren't allowed to take the books to burn anymore."

"I'm afraid I wouldn't know, Rab. The Kun only tells me so much."

Rab would like to believe that. Maybe it *was* so, but …

"I'd think the Kun's own scouts could tell him more about the library than I can."

"*About* it, yes. They can tell the Kun how many books are left, but they can't assess its condition. Its worth, if you will."

"It's worth? As what?" He'd raised his voice. He hadn't meant to.

Button lightly touched his arm. "I think they've been trying to read them, Rab."

He glanced at Lilly. If Button was betraying some sort of confidence that existed between the two of them and the Kun, it hadn't registered with Lilly.

"Gift more or less implied that, too," he said. "She said that sometimes the Feathers go into the library and look at the books."

"Then I guess that explains their interest," Button replied.

"But if they are trying to read the books, why haven't they asked me for help? I think I'm the only one left who can read."

"Perhaps they've found someone else," Cloud suggested. "A few of the tunnel-dwellers could read," she said, glancing at Lilly for confirmation.

The old woman shrugged. "Not me," she said. "I never saw the point. John Braham could read. Sunny, too. Ruby. Benjamin Caine …"

Cloud didn't even flinch at the mention of her birth father's name. Hadn't for a very long time.

"… some others," Lilly continued. "But I don't know of anyone who is teaching the Kun to read. Then …" she said with another shrug, "… I don't really see him that often."

"Well, whether he eventually learns to read or not, it won't help him save the mushrooms," Cloud said definitely. "They're finished. And that's what you're going to have to tell him, Lilly. I don't see what else we can do. Our people will starve there in the tunnels if something isn't done."

"I'll tell him."

Lilly rose, seemingly a signal for Button to rise, too, and take the small metal cup from the old woman.

"And you'll come back and see me again?" Lilly asked, grasping Cloud's hand.

"I would have come before now, Lilly. You must know that. But I'm not allowed. Until today, I didn't even know where you lived. I'd always assumed it was in the palace."

"In the palace?" Lilly's face crinkled with amusement. "Heavens, no. Whatever gave you that idea," she said, releasing Cloud.

They hadn't yet asked Lilly to intercede for Neila; Rab had never found an appropriate moment. Now it seemed they'd been dismissed.

"Lilly," Rab said hurriedly before Button could shepherd them away, "could you use your influence with the Kun to have Fin's wife assigned to personal service? She's injured and it's unlikely she'll ever be able to work the mines again."

The old woman simply stared at him. She didn't appear to have any idea what or who Rab was talking about.

"If something can be done, it will," Button offered readily and, with arm extended, invited them to accompany her to the door, leaving Lilly standing alone by the long low seat.

As Button opened the door, Cloud snatched the chance to glance briefly back into the room where Lilly stood watching. Button accompanied them in silence across the enclosure to the high wall where she retrieved the key from her skirt and unlocked the little wooden door.

As Rab was about to step through into the lane, Button grasped his arm.

"Did you see Twist while you were in the tunnels?" she asked in a small voice. She seemed oblivious that Lilly's cup was still in her hand.

Rab had rarely ever seen Twist, even when he had lived on and off among the tunnel-dwellers. She had been the smallest and probably the youngest of the girls who had been brought back into the tunnels with Cloud and Button all those years ago. Neither of the two younger girls had been able to adjust to tunnel life as well as Cloud and had moved, for the large part, unseen and unheard on the fringe of tunnel society.

"I didn't," Rab replied, then glanced at Cloud.

"No. I'm sorry I didn't, either. But we saw so few people, Button. She could have been there and we just didn't see her."

"Perhaps," Button agreed although it was clear to Rab that she wasn't convinced. "But she might have left the tunnels and evaded the Feathers. Some of us are living free on the surface. At least, that's what I've heard."

"I've heard that rumour, too, Button."

So had Rab. But tunnel-dwellers weren't fit for the surface.

"She might have tried to find Galen," Button said almost in afterthought.

Cloud reached out and placed her hand on the younger woman's shoulder. "If we're sent back to the tunnels again, we'll ask about her. I promise."

Button nodded and closed the small wooden door.

"We won't be going back there," Rab said once they were some distance down the lane, heading for home.

"I know," Cloud replied.

They were almost home before Rab felt comfortable enough to ask. "Who's Galen?"

Cloud took a moment to answer. "He was the elder of the band Twist, Button and I lived with."

Rab could understand why Button thought Twist might have sought out Galen now. Someone leaving the tunnels would have to join up with Top-siders to survive.

"He must be dead by now though," Cloud continued, "and I'm not so sure Twist would have gone seeking him out anyway. Life for a captive with them wasn't any better than life among the Feathers."

Rab had learned very little about Cloud's experiences while she'd been a captive of the Top-siders. She didn't like to talk about it and Rab wasn't inclined to press her. There were things he preferred not to remember, too.

"Galen was a hard man and those girls were far too young for the work he made them do. I managed. I was bigger. But it was particularly difficult for Twist. If she tried to escape to the surface, I doubt it was to join up with Galen."

"But if he's dead …"

Cloud grunted. "Noon was no better."

"Noon?" Rab prompted.

"His daughter. Well, she was supposed to be his daughter, but I always suspected she was an earlier captive. She knew how to play Galen though. It was more or less understood that she'd take over once Galen died."

"That's unusual, isn't it? To have a woman elder?"

"If you'd ever met Noon, you wouldn't think it strange at all," Cloud replied.

Rab hadn't met Noon, but, from Cloud's brief description, he thought he might have met someone with some of the same qualities. No one would have questioned Sunny's rise to leadership – even a Top-sider.

"Do you think it's true?" Rab asked after a moment. "Do you think some of your people could have left the tunnels?"

"It's possible, I suppose," Cloud answered, stopping. "But they can't have survived. I mean there are so few Top-siders now, aren't there? Any that are left will have moved far to the west. I've been in the west and there's nothing but desert there."

"But things may be better in the west now, too."

"Maybe," she replied. "But I doubt it. Didn't you read there were un-inhabitable regions on Earth, even when it was at its best?"

"Yes, but this isn't Earth, Cloud."

"Doesn't matter," she said with a shake of her head. "Some places, like some people, never change."

She started off again towards home with Rab hurrying after her. If she was right, then Gift was probably right, too. More than likely Glint, Poppy and the rest of the band were all dead – including Gift's young daughter.

Chapter 5

"SEEMS our uninvited guests left us a gift."

Rab had left Cloud to sort through the jumble of her precious medicines and food, thinking his time would be better spent tidying their rifled possessions. Tomorrow they expected to be sent back to work in the fields. They'd done what they'd been sent to do in the tunnels and the rest was up to Lilly. Neither of them had any delusions about being informed of the outcome of her report to the Kun.

"What?" Cloud asked, spinning round. She had an uncapped canister in her hand.

Rab held up a crudely knapped knife.

"That's Top-sider work," Cloud said, approaching. She passed him the open canister and took the knife from his hand. "Where did you find it?"

Rab pointed. "On the floor over there."

Cloud hefted the knife a couple of times. "It's badly made. Are you sure it isn't yours?" she asked, handing it back.

Rab was taken aback. "Are you saying I can't knap a stone better than that?"

Cloud smiled. "No, I mean are you sure you just didn't find it somewhere once and forget about it?"

"Positive," Rab replied. "I wouldn't keep something that crude. Whoever made it didn't have much of an idea about what they were doing." He handed the canister back to Cloud and placed the knife in plain sight on the little narrow shelf hacked into the blockwork beside their bed.

Cloud's eyes drifted to the shelf. "But they did have *some* idea," she said. "Well, at least that settles who stole from us." Her focus shifted towards the lane outside. "Where do you think they came from?"

"Don't know, but maybe you're wrong about how few Top-siders are left in the west."

Cloud's focus jerked back to him. "What do you mean?"

"If there are any Top-siders around here, they'd be using Feather weapons. Ones they've stolen during the raids. That knife is old-style."

"Oh." Cloud dropped down onto the bed. "That can't be good," she said, glancing up. "That means whoever it was is desperate."

Rab almost laughed. "Aren't all Top-siders desperate?" he asked, slipping down beside her.

"You know what I mean. If it was a Top-sider who came from further away, and I'm not saying that it was, but if it was —" she left the rest unsaid.

***

Instead of being pressed back into harvesting again with Cloud, Rab found himself rostered to work on a curious project. The Kun had ordered that a fourth protective wall be erected around the settlement, leading Rab to wonder if there had been reports of a possible Top-sider raid.

Rab had been assigned to the construction party, as was Fin who had been time-bartered from the forge master. Neila had been given Rab's former duties, working with Cloud. It was easier work for her, although still taxing. Her limp had not improved and on the evening of the first day, when he'd seen Neila return, walking side by side with Cloud, Rab began to question just how much longer Fin's wife could go on. The Feathers had little use for exhausted humans. Those few they favoured were sometimes turned over to Feather families where their responsibilities were limited to cooking, maintaining their master's ts'un and assisting with child rearing. As far as Rab had observed, Neila didn't number among the Feather's favourites. When the time came, her only chance might be Lilly – or, perhaps it was Button their hopes should really be pinned upon.

Work on the fourth perimeter wall was gruelling. Even when he was younger, Rab would have struggled to cart and set the heavy stones. And so far they were only working on the foundations. The higher the wall grew, the more punishing the work would become. Each morning they arrived on site, they'd find a new delivery of blocks from the quarry waiting for them and each time Rab felt he could not lift or place another stone, he remembered the humans who were working in the quarry, those who hacked and chipped at the wretched stone and especially those four young ones who'd recently been taken and were now drawing the blocks to the settlement on coarsely wheeled carts, night after night after night.

On their fourth day working on the wall, one of the ropes they had been using to drag the blocks into place snapped, sending those on the rope sprawling forward into the hard and unforgiving ground outside the settlement. The workers dragging on the second rope were lurched sideways when the tension on the block collapsed. Rab had come away with minor bruises and cuts to his face as a result of his lurch forward into the stones and dirt while Fin had been among those with an injured shoulder. Until a new rope was secured, and a good and sturdy one, work on the site was stalled.

Rab owned a rope – a good and sturdy one – one he was convinced would be more dependable than anything the Feathers might care to produce. They tended to reserve their best tools for themselves. After a frustrating attempt to explain to one of their Feather overseers that he intended to return to his ts'un and retrieve the rope, Rab gave up. The Feather didn't appear to have understood a word he'd said or grasp any of the gestures he'd made to explain that he was about to walk off the site. Doq'iri did not walk off on-the-job … unless they were begging for consequences, like a long stint out in the quarry. And so Rab was surprised when he was able to pass through the gate unchecked. He didn't look back to find out why the Feathers were allowing him to go, just hurried on through the middle and inner gates. Once through the last gate he stopped rushing. The longer he took to retrieve the rope, the longer his injured comrades had to rest. He was just entering the little lane that would take him directly to his ts'un when he spotted someone he didn't recognise emerging from the ts'un.

The intruder noticed him at the same time. Rab rushed forward. The intruder rushed sideways, rounding the neighbouring ts'uns and leaving Rab some distance behind. He'd thought he'd only suffered those few injuries to his face in his recent fall but as soon as he started running, Rab felt a stabbing pain in his left knee and upper back. He must have banged his knee and wrenched something in his back when he'd pitched forward. But he kept running and was actually starting to make some headway. The person he was pursuing was only small. And judging by the tattered and filthy clothes, a Top-sider, just as he and Cloud had suspected.

Rab had thought there was only one of them. He'd only seen one emerge from his ts'un, but on reaching the inner wall behind the row of ts'uns, he saw a second Top-sider. This one was a girl. A long and tangled mass of black hair gave her away. She was gesturing frantically but silently for the running thief, who Rab now decided was a boy. Kids. They were only kids, which explained the crudely knapped knife. The boy threw something to the girl, who caught it deftly, launched it over the wall, then proceeded to clamber up the wall herself.

The boy had almost reached the wall when Rab pulled up in disbelief. He wasn't going to catch them and there was no way he would even attempt the same manoeuvre he'd just seen the girl perform. The boy quickly followed suit and, like the girl who had just disappeared from sight, began to scale the wall with astonishing agility. He was up and over, leaving Rab little to no opportunity to study how he had done it. Slowly, Rab approached the wall – all urgency now gone. His knee was threatening to give way under him and his back, below the shoulder blades, felt like it was on fire.

It wasn't possible for those kids to do what they had done. And yet they had. Rab ran a hand across the wall. It wasn't exactly smooth but smooth enough and yet somehow those two kids had managed to find the tiniest of imperfections in the surface and use them as footholds. More impressive still, they'd obviously done it six times on three different walls: three times to enter and three times to leave the settlement. Chasing them down was simply out of the question. They'd be long gone before he could wind his way around the defences.

Turning, he walked back to his ts'un. The first place he checked was the little shelf above the bed. He wasn't surprised to find the knife gone. When he inspected their food and healing supplies, he discovered a few of the canisters out of place again. None seemed to be missing but he was betting that the contents of a few of them would be depleted. Retrieving the rope he'd come for, Rab began making his way back to Fin and the waiting workers. They were just kids – desperate as he and Cloud had decided – but kids just the same and now they'd been spotted, they'd likely never return to this same settlement again.

He found Fin and the rest of the workers digging in the trench. The stone they had been hauling had been left in place, waiting on Rab's return. The Feathers were some distance away with backs turned, gazing towards the southern horizon.

"What's going on?" Rab asked, dumping the rope. It sent up a puff of loose soil by his feet.

Fin looked up from his labours, set the pick he'd been wielding to one side and climbed out of the trench.

"There's something out there," he said, wiping the sweat from his brow with an upraised shoulder. "The Feathers spotted it just after you left."

Rab tried to follow the Feathers' line of sight. With a little imagination, he might just see something. Kind of a haze way off to the south, low on the horizon.

"What do you think it is?"

Fin shrugged. "Too big to be Top-siders on the move. Dust storm maybe." He reached down to retrieve the rope. "Whatever it is, we'll find out soon enough. It's probably nothing though." He motioned for his co-workers in the trench. "If we get this stone into place, they might let us rest for a while."

Rab tore his gaze from the unusual haze just as Fin pointed towards an old man lying in a small patch of shade by the wall. The old man had his right elbow cupped in the palm of his left hand.

"Nat's wrenched his arm pretty badly. I think his shoulder's out of place. Can you do anything for him?"

Procedures like that were usually Cloud's job. First she'd administer a small amount of purple mushroom extract and then, relying on Rab's brute force, instruct him where to push. Today he'd have the benefit of neither Cloud's expertise nor her medicines. Rab doubted he could get away with a second excursion back to his house to retrieve any of the extract from Cloud's supply.

"I'll do my best," he told Fin. "You and the others see to the stone. But be careful with that rope. It's a good one but I've only ever used it to haul Cloud out of the ravine."

Looking down, Fin grasped the rope with both hands and gave it a snap. "Seems fine. Better than they'd have come up with." He jerked his head, indicating the Feathers over his shoulder, then with a party of workers in tow, headed towards the abandoned stone.

Rab made his way to Nat, squatted and then gently lifted the clothing away from the old man's right shoulder. It had popped all right; Rab could see the bone sticking up unnaturally under skin that was beginning to bruise.

"Well?" Nat said, grimacing in obvious pain.

"I'm going to have to manoeuvre it back into place, Nat. Best thing for you to do is relax."

Rab felt like a fool for saying it. Somehow Cloud always managed to say exactly the same thing with more conviction and confidence.

Rab seated himself more securely and gently grasped Nat's right elbow, positioning it tight into his body. Slowly he began to draw the old man's arm out until it was lined up with his splayed out right leg and, slower still, he moved the arm outward from Nat's body. When he felt resistance, he stopped, switched to easing Nat's upper arm forward then switched again, turning his lower arm back towards his chest. When he heard a pop, he stopped and looked at Nat's face. The old guy didn't look particularly relieved but then nor did Rab expect he would.

"Any better?" he asked nonetheless.

Nat nodded slightly.

As Rab slowly assisted Nat to his feet, he glanced again towards the Feathers. They'd turned around and noticed him and Nat 'dawdling' by the outer wall. One of them, a female, was hurrying towards them, gesturing with her hands and clicking angrily.

Rab pointed towards Nat's shoulder.

"He's hurt," he shouted, loud enough for the Feathers and his fellow workers to hear. "He can't do any more work today."

The Feather didn't appear to understand. Where once this inability to communicate had been a frustrating affair, now it was simply expected. Sometimes the right gesture from either party would solve the problem; sometimes nothing would and Rab was beginning to have a suspicion that this would be one of those times when he was destined to utterly fail to get his meaning across.

He pointed to Nat's shoulder again and then grabbed his own shoulder. "He's hurt," he said again as the featherwoman bore down on them. "Injured. Understand?"

Of course, she didn't. Reaching them, she made a lunge for Nat and if it hadn't been for Rab leaping between them, would likely have undone Rab's repair work.

Feathers were strong. Deceptively strong. That was no secret but when the featherwoman turned on him instead, Rab was taken by surprise. She wrenched him forward and sent him sprawling in the dirt behind her. When she was about to make the same move on Nat, all Rab could think of to do was reach out, grab her legs and pull. She crashed to the ground beside him. Rab got to his feet first in time to see the second Feather running towards them. Rab didn't notice Fin — not at first — but suddenly he was right there.

The featherwoman had just pulled herself up from the ground when, calmly and deliberately, Fin began to talk — *in Feather*.

Rab listened, dumbfounded, glancing first towards the featherwoman and then towards the featherman who had finally reached them. They seemed to understand everything Fin was saying. Like Rab, he pointed towards Nat, who had backed up against the rough stone of the outer wall. He was clutching his shoulder protectively and his face, justifiably, had turned ashen.

Fin fell silent and the featherwoman started talking. She sounded angry and Rab guessed she had something of a right to be. After all, he had just dumped her into the dirt in plain sight of another Feather. The featherman had nothing to say and it was only then Rab realised that the woman must have been his superior. He was following the conversation though – intently. His beak of a mouth was pursed and the rind that took the place of a head of hair was drawn forward, forming a kind of ridge over his yellow eyes in one of those rare easily interpretable Feather-type expressions.

The little featherwoman blinked as rapidly as she spoke. Rab hoped that Fin could follow what she was saying. Evidently he followed enough to at least make a reply that seemed to placate the featherwoman, who harshly clicked something at her companion and then, with a parting fling of her multi-jointed left hand towards Rab, stomped off, gesturing for her companion to follow.

Rab's attention swung to Fin.

"How long have you been able to speak Feather?"

"A while," Fin replied guardedly.

"Didn't you think it might have been a good idea to tell us?"

"Not really." Fin placed a hand to Rab's arm. "I don't think this is the time or place to explain, do you?"

Most of their fellow workers were bending now, taking up the ropes that had been dropped while they'd been watching the altercation between Rab and the Feathers. Perhaps Fin was right.

"So what did you say?" he asked instead.

"I explained what had happened to Nat and that you'd just set his shoulder back in place. She said that he didn't have to work anymore today."

"Seemed to be a lot of talking for just that."

"Yeah, well, she did have a few other things to say, so I'd stay out of her way for a while if I were you."

A needless warning as far as Rab was concerned.

Fin turned to Nat who was still cowering by the wall. "You go home now, Nat, and take care of that arm."

"I'll have Cloud stop by to see you tonight," Rab added.

"Are you sure?" Nat asked uneasily and, supporting his right arm by the elbow, pushed off from the wall.

"It's all right," Fin told him. "She said you could go."

Rab tracked Nat's glance towards the Feathers. They didn't seem the least bit interested in him or Nat any longer. They'd returned to their post on the perimeter of the work site as though nothing at all had happened and, once again, were just standing there, backs turned, surveying the horizon.

"Go."

At Rab's prompt, Nat took off as quickly as old legs could carry him towards the gate of the outer wall.

Once Nat was safely gone, Rab started walking with Fin towards their fellow workers who were hauling once again on the wall stone.

"I had a brief run-in with those thieves again when I went back for the rope," Rab told Fin quietly as they walked.

Fin looked over at him in surprise.

"They're just a couple of kids. Top-siders most probably. I doubt they'll be bothering us again."

"Any idea where they came from?"

Rab shook his head. "As much as I have about how you learned to speak Feather."

"Later," Fin said dismissively and took up his former place on the rope.

As Rab moved into position behind him, he glanced over towards and then past the Feathers. That same haze was still there just visible on the horizon.

***

Once again, Cloud was obliged to make an inventory of their supplies. She'd been relieved although more angered than he'd expected when Rab had explained that the thieves had only been children. At the moment though his real interest was in Fin, rather than any further loss that might or might not have befallen their food and medicines.

Fin was sitting across from Rab at their small table while Cloud was making occasional banging noises on the bench behind them.

"I'm not as good as Lilly," Fin was saying, sounding almost apologetic. "But I get by."

Get by? That was an understatement.

"I presume there was a good reason you kept this from us?" Rab pressed the younger man.

He should have been angry. Had been, at first. Now he was beginning to feel cautiously pleased.

"I figured the fewer people who knew the better it would be," Fin replied. "Even Neila doesn't know. I've learned things, Rab," he continued, leaning forward conspiratorially. "Things I'd never have learned if the Feathers had known that I could understand them."

"You could have told us," Rab insisted.

Fin shook his head.

"Yes, why didn't you?" Cloud asked. Her inventory completed, she came to stand behind Rab. "What harm could that have done?" she asked, casually placing her hands on Rab's shoulders.

"A lot," Fin replied. "What if the Feathers found out I was listening to everything they said? And what if they found out that you knew it? I intended to tell you when it was time."

"I'm not sure spying on them was such a good idea, Fin," Rab said. "Anyway, what use has it been? You say you've learned things? But what things, Fin? And just *what* time were you waiting for?"

Fin leaned back in his chair. "There's a lot the Kun doesn't tell us."

Rab repressed a sigh. Fin's revelation wasn't exactly startling. There were many Assemblies Lilly did not attend and even when she was in attendance she might not speak. And if Lilly didn't convey something to them, then it simply went unknown.

"And I think there's a lot he's not even telling his own people."

Rab thought about that a moment and concluded he wasn't 'particularly startled by that, either. Most leaders hid things, he supposed. Even when he'd been young, he'd suspected there had been many things the elders of his own small village had kept from them 'for their own good'.

"Fin, you're not telling us anything we don't already know," he said at last.

"Rab's right," Cloud said. "All they *ever* tell us is where to go and what to do for them next. I think you've taken an awful risk. Now they *do* know you speak and understand Feather and they're going to be very suspicion why you hid that from them."

"Yes, I know," Fin agreed. "But that featherwoman was about to strike Nat. Bad enough his shoulder got hurt. But if she broke any of his bones?" Fin shook his head. "I think it would have finished him."

Rab understood that at least. What else could Fin have done? If he had stayed silent, the featherwoman likely would have snapped old Nat's arm like a piece of dry tinder.

"What's done is done," Rab said.

"Maybe we should keep Fin out of their way for a few days," Cloud suggested.

"How?" Rab asked with a glance over his shoulder.

"I think you're both missing the point," Fin said with no trace of apology now. "I'm trying to tell you something important. I was about to tell you before you left for the tunnels, but, well," he said, running a hand through his hair as he got up from the table and began to pace, "you had those two Feather scouts with you and they knew what is out there – at least what is *supposed* to be out there. They would have known what to do. But when you came back and said you hadn't seen anything, then I knew I had to tell you." Fin ceased pacing and fixed Rab with his gaze. "I don't know what's going on … not really … but something is." His attention shifted to Cloud. "And it's got to do with Qworkas."

Rab felt one of Cloud's hands squeezing his shoulder.

"White Qworkas?" Rab prompted.

Fin opened his mouth to speak but before he got a word out, Neila came bursting through the entrance. In her arms, she had Tickie, holding him the way someone might hold a useless bundle of old cloth. It looked like she'd snatched him up in a hurry.

"Top-siders!" she screamed. "They've set fire to the settlement." Her balance gave way and if it hadn't been for the doorway, she might have slumped to the ground before Fin reached her.

Neila had to be wrong. If there was fire nearby, Cloud would have smelled it first.

"I can't smell anything, Neila. Are you sure?"

"Yes, I'm sure," Neila replied, leaning into Fin's chest.

And then the horn sounded. Two blasts in quick succession and then a pause. Two blasts and a pause. The call for alarm.

"See?" Neila said, head cocked to the sound of the horn. "They're firing lighted arrows or spears or something into the western ward. You can't smell it from here yet. But you can see it. Come look for yourself."

Rab rushed outside with Cloud close on his heels.

On the opposite side of the settlement, the black of the night sky was beginning to glow as jagged teeth of red-hot flame and fire snapped at it from below. It looked beautiful and deadly at the same time. There were billows of blackish smoke, too, slaves of a steady wind that was gusting towards the centre of the settlement, and every now and then, a blazing strip of something, Qworka-skin or fat-soaked cloth from the roofs of some of the ts'uns most likely, went twirling up into the air, showering bright sparks and greyish ash.

"It's just begun," Fin said, drawing Neila closer.

"We have to get over there and help," Cloud insisted, pulling on Rab's arm. "Maybe it can be put out."

Maybe.

But Cloud was right. Every able-bodied doq'iri and Feather in the settlement would be needed. And that meant Neila had to stay behind. Rab was about to suggest as much, when Fin pushed Neila to one side and grasped her by the arms.

"You have to stay here with Tickie, Neila. With that injured leg of yours, you can't help."

Perhaps that wasn't the best way for Fin to have said it, although he was correct. Neila knew that, too, but the expression on her face betrayed something other than understanding and acceptance. She looked beaten — sad and beaten. Rab had always admired Neila. She was one of those people who, come what may, struggled without complaint to do the best, more than the best, they could each day. He couldn't look at her disconsolate face any longer and let Cloud drag him away.

Fin caught up with them quickly. Rab didn't ask about Neila. She'd stayed behind as Fin had asked and that demanded more courage than running with them to fight the fire. Fin's woman was good, if not strong. He had chosen well.

By the time they reached the western ward, the fire was well underway. Humans and Feathers were running in all directions, humans shouting, Feathers frantically clicking and snapping instructions that only their fellow Feathers could understand. And every now and then, another flaming spear came arcing over the high inner wall into the settlement. Some landed harmlessly on open ground where the burning head spluttered for a while before petering out. Too many found their mark, spearing the flammable roof of another ts'un.

Breathless, Rab pulled up and grasped Fin by the shoulder.

"What are the Feathers calling for?" he rasped.

The smoke was acrid … stinking … Qworka fat had a foul stench when it burned. It got into the eyes of the renderers who prepared it, into their skin and clothes. By the end of tonight, they'd all be reeking of the stuff much worse than any fat renderer.

Fin wiped a hand across streaming eyes. "They're asking for dirt. Buckets and buckets of dirt."

Dirt?

Of course! If it came to it, the damage to the ts'uns could be repaired, but water couldn't be coaxed, on demand, from dry skies. Even now, every drop of water was too precious. The fat-soaked roofs were the real problem. Whenever a spark hit them, they caught like dry tinder and then the next roof would catch alight from the drifting embers.

"Dirt won't solve anything," Rab barked. "We have to strip the skins and cloths from the roofs."

Someone, human or Feather Rab didn't notice, rushed past him, painfully bumping one of his shoulder blades and almost knocking him off his feet.

"*All of them*?" Cloud asked, incredulous, as she caught Rab's arm and stopped him from falling.

"Enough to make some sort of break." He was glancing around, assessing the wind direction and attempting to locate the fire front. "We should start there," he said, pointing. "Fin, you go and tell the Feathers that. Try to make them understand."

The expression on Fin's face said it all. How did Rab expect him to do that? He was just a doq'iri.

"I know. I know," Rab said. "But you have to try. With ten times as many Feathers and humans, we couldn't get enough dirt up onto the roofs to stop this. The Feathers are too small to launch it high enough anyway and even if we could collect enough, we're too few in number to make any difference. Besides, we run the risk of being speared if we try to put out the fires that've already started. But the spears aren't reaching over there."

After a moment of hesitation, Fin rushed off. Rab grabbed Cloud's hand and began to run with her towards one of the as yet untouched ts'uns.

"How can we possibly get enough roofs off in time?" Cloud said, gasping for air as she ran beside Rab. "We can't just rip them off. Each one has to be unstrapped."

"If the Feathers see we're making even some headway, they'll help."

At least, that was the strategy he was counting on.

They'd reached the ts'un Rab decided was the best to start on. He released Cloud's hand and together they began frantically untying the straps that held the cloth roof in place. The knots the Feathers used to tie down their roofs were a kind of a slip-knot affair, easiest of all of their knots to untie. Each time Rab began drawing another strap through the hole that had been bored into the wall to secure it, he glanced towards the front of the settlement, seeking Fin. At first he couldn't see him and an ugly thought crossed his mind that Fin might have been impaled by a flaming spear as he'd rushed ahead into the frantically scurrying mob of Feathers. Then, amid the glowing and wafting smoke, he finally spotted Fin running towards him. There were perhaps twenty or more Feathers running with him. Either he'd got them to understand or, Rab's biggest concern at that moment, they intended to prevent him from stripping more of the ts'uns. But as the Feathers drew closer, they began to splinter off. Some ran to Rab's right, others to his left. Fin ran with the group rushing left.

Rab didn't have time to triumph in Fin's victory. At least twenty to thirty more ts'uns had to be stripped of their roofs. It was slow and often blind work. Although the wind wasn't especially strong, it was constant and enough to drive the thick and stinking smoke their way. The glow from the fire lent them some light but the holes through which the straps were threaded were still difficult to see and had to be located by guess and feel.

No sooner had he and Cloud unstrapped the first ts'un of its roof than a group of humans who had gathered on one side of it began dragging the roof off the walls. Rab had no idea where they had come from and he didn't question their timely arrival, just rushed off towards the next ts'un, where he found more of the Feathers already at work unstrapping its roof.

They worked through the remaining ts'uns as quickly as they could – Rab with different teams of Feathers unstrapping the Qworka skins and fat-treated cloths, gangs of humans dragging them away to safety beyond the reach of the flaming spears. He had lost sight of both Cloud and Fin, but as long as they stayed clear of the incoming spears, they should be safe for now. Whenever the rare opportunity arose, Rab chanced a look towards the fire. They seemed to be winning the battle; the fire appeared to be contained to one section of the ward now. The ts'uns there couldn't be saved. Their roofs and whoever and whatever had been inside them was lost. Rab hadn't been able to make out much about the raid itself. A contingent of Feathers and maybe some humans were probably on the outside of the inner wall, defending the settlement, pushing back the raiders who he had little doubt were Top-siders. It had been a long time since the last Top-sider raid and this was the first time they had ever pre-empted an attack using lighted spears.

It was almost dawn by the time the fire in the western ward showed signs of burning itself out. Rab's gamble had paid off. The thirty or so unroofed ts'uns had created an effective break and ultimately only a small portion of the settlement had been completely lost. In the morning they'd count up the dead, Feather and doq'iri. Very likely on the opposite side of the defensive walls, there'd be Top-siders lying dead as well and Rab wondered, with some sadness, if the two children who had stolen from him would be among them.

In the wan dawn light, he found Cloud, soot-covered and reeking of Qworka fat, crouching with some others against the wall of one of the ts'uns they had managed to save. He dropped down beside her and, lacking words or breath enough to speak had he had them, took her dirty face into torn and bleeding hands. Noticing the state of his hands, she eased them away from her face and began to dab at the open wounds with the ragged tail of her shirt. It stung, but Rab didn't attempt to stop her.

A few of the older humans and Feathers were doing the rounds with flasks of water and when an old featherwoman passed within range, Rab reached up and greedily snatched two, handing one of the flasks to Cloud.

"It worked," Cloud said after a long draw from the flask. "But I wouldn't expect any thanks from them." She jerked her head, indicating a group of milling Feathers who were picking about among the remains on the ground.

Rab shrugged. He wasn't looking for thanks. Not even recognition that he'd been the one who had come up with the idea. Best to stay invisible.

"Seen Fin?" he asked instead.

Cloud pointed.

Rab followed her pointing finger and spotted Fin, crumpled against the wall of another ts'un. He raised his flask in acknowledgement when Rab caught his eye.

"You know in all the confusion last night, there's something we didn't even stop to question," Cloud said, tapping Rab's shoulder with her flask.

Rab was betting there was a lot they hadn't stopped yet to question. Like where the Top-siders had come from. They weren't responsible for that dust haze far to the south. No Top-sider could have reached the settlement so quickly from so far away.

"What?" Rab asked distractedly, turning to Cloud.

"Neila," she answered simply.

Rab wasn't getting it. "What about Neila?"

"She said that Top-siders were launching lighted spears over the walls and setting the ts'uns on fire."

"So?"

"I could see the fire from outside our ts'un," Cloud explained, shifting in the dirt and angling herself towards him, "but I couldn't see the spears coming over the walls. I'm guessing you couldn't, either. So how did she know that's what had started the fire? She was inside her ts'un with Tickie when it began."

It was a good question. How *had* Neila known about the lighted spears? Rab glanced towards Fin, whose eyes were closed as he leaned his head back against the soot-stained wall of the ts'un. On quick reflection, Rab realised that Fin wouldn't have the answer. He had been with them at the time and everything happened so quickly after Neila had raised the alarm that he probably hadn't stopped to think about it, either.

Rab scrambled onto his feet, dragging Cloud up with him.

"Then let's ask her."

Cloud glanced around, clearly undecided. "What about all this? We can't just leave."

Rab shrugged. "Why?"

"What about the injured?"

"The Feathers will tend to their own."

"And ours?"

Rab pulled on her arm. "Your medicines are back in our ts'un. We have to go there anyway."

Finally Cloud saw the logic and allowed Rab to hurry her away.

They didn't get far before Fin called to them.

"Wait up. Where are you going?"

Rab turned as Fin caught up with them. The empty flask of water was still in the young man's hands.

"To get my medicines," Cloud explained.

Fin flung the flask away. "I'm coming with you. I want to see if Neila and Tickie are all right."

"Then let's hurry," Cloud urged them. "If the Feathers see us leaving, they might try to stop us."

Rab took in the devastation around them. Somehow, he doubted that any of the Feathers would even notice three doq'iri rushing back to their ts'uns. They had bigger problems. The western ward lay in ruins. Even the walls of some of the burned-out ts'uns had cracked from the fierce heat and ragged chunks of stone and brick were lying scattered on the ground all around. The injured were being led on a meandering path between the broken walls to a place of safety away from the haze of smoke and the suffocating stench. So far Rab hadn't spotted any humans among the injured. He wasn't all that surprised. This was a Feather ward and the damage had been done to Feather ts'uns. But it was a miracle that no human had been injured during the attack or the subsequent efforts to put out the fire. There may be human along with Feather dead and injured outside the settlement walls, but they hadn't been brought in yet and there'd be no attempts made to bring them in until the Kun was satisfied that the raiding Top-siders had retreated. All in all, it hadn't been a terribly successful raid. The Top-siders must have been extraordinarily desperate to have risked it.

They pushed their way home through a constant stream of uninjured Feathers and humans moving quickly towards the western ward. Neila wasn't among them. She wasn't standing outside her ts'un waiting on their return, either. Their ward was largely deserted and very likely Neila was inside with a sleeping Tickie, who'd probably spent a good part of the night awake, excited by all the commotion.

Rab left Fin to see to his wife and child and, with Cloud, continued on to their own ts'un. Time enough later to ask Neila how she had known about the raid. It was hardly important now when there were medicines to be collected and brought back to the injured. It had been a long night. It was going to be an even longer day.

Cloud had barely made it to the bench where she stored her medicines when Fin came bursting into their ts'un.

"She's not there! And nor is Tickie!"

Behind the soot and ash, Fin's face had turned white.

"Maybe she's in another ts'un," Rab suggested hopefully.

Fin began shaking his head. "She wouldn't do that."

"Then she's gone to help the injured," Cloud said, abandoning the canisters of medicine on the bench. "The Feathers may have ordered her to go. There's hardly anyone around here. They must have all been sent."

"*Then where is Tickie?*" Fin looked near to collapse.

Rab went to him, took his shaking arm, and led him to a seat.

"We'll look for them, Fin," he said. "They can't be *missing.*"

"Of course they can't," Cloud agreed, seating herself in the chair opposite Fin. She reached out and took his hand.

"I'd like to know where they are, too," someone screamed at them from the laneway.

Rab's head snapped around to find Willa, a woman roughly the same age as Neila, hanging limply from one hand off the doorway.

"Petie's gone, too," she said through trembling lips. "I left him with Neila when I went to help with the fire."

Cloud jumped up from the table and carried as much as walked Willa to her abandoned seat.

"Do you think that's what the raid was about?" Fin asked, looking despairingly at Rab. "A diversion so they could steal the children?"

Cloud was on her knees beside Willa, trying her best to calm her. "A lot of effort to go to just to steal two children," she said.

Fin leaped to his feet, setting his chair tumbling to the floor. "*Just* to steal two children!"

"I'm sorry, Fin," Cloud rushed to say, rising. "I didn't mean it that way. If —"

"If their plan was to steal children," Rab interrupted before Cloud could anger Fin further, "then they'd have come up with a better way to steal more." Rab shook his head. "I think someone just grabbed at an opportunity."

"What do you mean?" Cloud asked. Her brow was crinkled the way it always crinkled whenever she was puzzled.

Rab turned to Fin. "I'm wondering if those two kids didn't take them, Fin. Maybe I was wrong about them not coming back again."

"The Top-sider kids?" Cloud asked, the furrow in her brow deepening.

"Will someone please tell me what's going on?" Willa shouted. "You're talking like someone has stolen some loaves of mushroom bread. These are children." Her troubled eyes darted to Fin. "*Our children!*"

"Rab could be right, Willa," Fin said, calming a little as he reseated himself. "A couple of Top-sider kids broke into Rab's ts'un while they were away," he explained. "Stole food and a bit of medicine. It might have been them who took the boys."

"Why?" Willa snapped at him.

"Same reason they took children in the past," Cloud suggested.

Willa swung on Cloud. "Girls! They took girls then, didn't they?"

Willa was too young to have had any experience with Top-sider raids down in the tunnels, but it was common knowledge that things like that had happened in the past.

"Yes," Cloud replied, sounding uncharacteristically contrite.

"Girls. Boys. I don't think it matters but it can only be a good thing," Rab said.

"Good! How!" Willa was almost hysterical.

"Look, Willa, I know you're worried." Rab came down onto one knee beside the distraught woman. "But if it was Top-siders who took Tickie and Peter, then they have no intention of hurting them."

"What then? Why would they take them?"

Chapter 6

"SAVE them? Save them from what? Us?" Willa was rocking backward and forward, arms wrapped around herself as Rab voiced the only conclusion he could draw.

"No, Willa. Of course not. But let's face it," he said. "We're essentially slaves here, aren't we? And they are free."

"Free to starve."

"Maybe those kids don't see it that way. I saw them again this morning running from my ts'un. They were very young, Willa. Maybe not even ten years old."

Fin rose again from the table.

"Then that's it then," he said with determination. "We have to go after them. They've got Neila, Tickie and Peter. And we're going to get them back." He started towards the entrance."

"We can't, Fin," Rab said, stopping him. "Not yet. If the Feathers didn't see the Top-siders coming, how do you think you're going to see them going?"

Fin wrenched himself loose. "You can't expect me to just sit here. We can still follow them. That many Top-siders will have to have left tracks behind."

"The tracks will still be there later. It doesn't look like there's going to be rain any time soon. And they couldn't have taken Neila. How could she have got over the wall?"

Fin's face turned blank. Clearly he hadn't stopped to consider that.

"Then where is she?" he whispered at length.

Cloud came up behind him to wrap an arm around his shoulder. "That's something we can do now, Fin. Find Neila. And when we do, she'll be able to tell us what really happened."

Before Rab was aware she'd even moved, Willa was already in the laneway. Fin slipped away from Cloud and hurried after her.

"Which way did the kids go before?" Cloud asked, trailing Rab as he hastened after the pair.

"Behind the ts'uns. They scrambled over the wall."

Cloud looked at him with disbelief.

"I didn't think it was possible, either," he said before she could argue with him. "But they did it. Up and over."

"But if you're right, this time they had to get two children over with them. How could they have done that?"

"On their backs maybe," Rab said after a moment of thought. "In slings perhaps."

"Clever kids," Cloud observed.

"They're Top-siders," Rab replied. It didn't need further explanation. "Fin," he called. "This way."

With Rab in the lead, they followed the path the two Top-sider children had taken to the wall. Rab expected to find nothing there. Willa looked disappointed; Fin frustrated.

"Well," Fin said, spreading his hands. "Now what? If they went over this wall, then they took Neila with them."

"I can't see how," Rab said.

Examining the wall more closely, he discovered the tell-tale scuff marks he *had* expected to find. Of course, the scuff marks could have been left from the previous times the kids had scaled the wall – but there were an awful lot of them. Cloud came up and began to trace the marks with her fingers.

"Someone's been climbing here," she said, sounding surprised.

Did she think he'd made it up?

"Well, they're not here now," Fin barked. "I'm going to search outside the walls. You three can do what you want."

Willa dashed after Fin and, resigned, Rab followed. He soon pulled up when he realised Cloud wasn't with him. Turning, he found her starting up the wall.

"Cloud," he shouted, drawing the others' attention. "You can't climb that!"

"If they can, I can," she called back.

"And so can I," Fin declared as he rushed past Rab, heading back to the wall.

"No, Fin," Rab shouted. "If you fall and get hurt, who'll look after Neila?"

Fin appeared to see the reason in Rab's warning and paused just short of the wall.

"Cloud," Rab called again. "Get down."

Although how he couldn't imagine, she found a second foothold in the wall.

"I'll be fine," she shouted back. "If you just stop distracting me."

Cloud was a good climber – the best they had – but, on this nearly sheer wall, she was pushing her luck. All Rab could do was hope that, when she fell, and he had no doubt she would, she'd only bust a few bones that would eventually mend.

"She'll make it."

Rab turned around to find Willa standing behind him. Her eyes were trained on Cloud.

His heart was pounding. The easiest thing to have done was to make their way out of the settlement through the gates. But Cloud didn't always choose the easiest thing. All she'd find on the other side of the wall was another two walls she'd have to scale. They could have wound their way out of the settlement in the time it would take her to scale them. And once she did, then what? She'd be on the outside and the rest of them would still be there on the inside. Did she intend to pursue the Top-siders by herself?

Halfway up Cloud stopped to rest and Rab took the opportunity to call to her again, beg her to jump so that he and Fin could break her fall.

"It's easier the further up you go," she shouted down to them, face pressed into the wall. "You can't see it from down there but there are better footholds nearer the top. Should be simple from here on. Just have to catch my breath."

"I knew she could do it," Willa muttered, clutching hold of Rab's arm.

Well, maybe she could after all. But that didn't mean Neila had. Rab glanced at Fin. He had his head tilted back and was intently following Cloud's every move. He had to be thinking the same thing.

Rab held his breath. Almost there. Cloud got one hand to the top of the wall and pulled. There! She executed a quick scoot and turn and all Rab could see then was the back of her. Her legs were dangling off the far side of the wall.

"They're here!" she shouted from atop the wall, swinging her head around.

It was the last thing Rab expected to hear.

"Neila and the boys?" Fin called up to her.

Understandably his voice was choked with fear, because clearly something was wrong. If Neila and the boys had landed safely on the ground on the opposite side of the wall, then why hadn't they gone with the Top-sider children or, if they'd got away from them, made their way back through the gates?

Rab didn't want to ask it, but someone had to. He could feel Willa's hold on his arm tighten as he spoke.

"Are they all right?"

"Can't tell," Cloud called down. "But it's not Neila and the boys. It's Neila and Pi'a'weh."

With that she disappeared completely. Rab listened but when he failed to hear an ominous thump decided that she was making her way down the other side. He waited a little longer – long enough to convince himself that she was probably halfway down the wall, where should she fall, her injuries were likely to be minor.

"We'll go around," he said, reaching out to grasp Fin's shoulder. "Through the gate. Meet them on the other side."

Fin turned away from the wall and, for a moment, Rab wasn't certain that the younger man had understood a word he'd said. Then suddenly, something changed in his face and Fin took off. Willa seemed to be fixed to the spot.

"Come on, Willa, we have to go with Fin," Rab said, shaking off her tenacious hold.

Still she didn't move and Rab was obliged to grasp her about the waist, at first almost dragging her along beside him. The lanes were mainly deserted and quiet until they reached the burned-out section of the settlement where the air was still thick with the stink of singed cloth and Qworka-skin and the ground littered with smouldering debris. There were no bodies; the dead and injured must have already been carried away.

They threaded their way through the carnage, spawning delicate eddies of smoke and stench in their wakes, and no one attempted to stop them. After all they were only doing what everyone else was doing – moving around the site, cleaning up the mess and salvaging what there was to be salvaged. As they passed through the inner gate, they encountered a small party of Feathers and humans. Whatever was slung between them swung side to side as they tramped along. Rab didn't look too closely, unwilling to find out what it was. An injured Feather or human perhaps or, more likely, a dead Top-sider. No raid ever ended in victory for the Top-siders.

They turned east, rounding the inner wall without coming upon any-one else, human or Feather. Cloud's impulsive decision to climb the wall had been a lucky one. Had she not taken it in her head to do such a dangerous thing, they'd have made for the middle gate instead and never found Neila and Pi'a'weh lying at the base of the wall on the eastern side of the settlement. Rab had never walked this far between the walls before. He didn't like the oppressive feeling it gave him. There was adequate space – the three of them hurried along abreast – but, unless they attempted to scale the walls, there was only one way out. Did Fin and Willa feel imprisoned the same way he did? Or were they simply too concerned about their children to even notice how the walls pressed in from either side?

Rab tried to think about something else. Like how both Pi'a'weh and Neila had ended up on the other side of the wall together. Every time the thought that they might not find Neila alive began to surface, he pushed it away. That kind of thinking just made the walls feel closer.

As soon as he spotted Neila, Fin started running. Willa was close on his heels. Rab took his time. Cloud had the matter in hand and, besides, it didn't look to him as though Neila would be going anywhere anytime soon. She was lying worryingly still at the base of the wall, legs bent at an alarmingly unnatural angle. Cloud was crouching over her. Pi'a'weh appeared to be conscious although he was sitting very silently, back propped against the rough stone of the opposite wall. One of his long hands was clutching the back of his head.

Fin skidded to a halt and dropped to the ground beside Cloud. Willa remained standing although, on getting a better look at Neila, her hands flew immediately up to her mouth. By the time Rab reached them he almost knew what to expect. If Neila wasn't dead, she was in a very poor state at least. He came up quietly behind Willa and looked down at Fin's wife. He didn't look at her legs, knowing already that at least one, if not both, were broken.

Fin was on his knees now, brushing long strands of wispy hair from his wife's pale face. There was a streak of blood staining one cheek but, apart from her legs, Neila didn't show any other obvious signs of injury.

"How is she?" Rab asked tentatively.

Both Fin and Willa seemed to have been struck mute.

Cloud glanced up from her ministrations. "Can't say for sure. She's alive though," she said, turning her gaze on Fin. "That's a really good thing, considering we don't know how long they've been lying out here."

"Ask him," Willa said, finding her voice. She was pointing at Pi'a'weh.

"I did," Cloud replied, "but I couldn't understand a thing he said."

"Let me try," Rab said and walked the short distance to where the little featherman was sitting.

"What happened, Pi'a'weh?" he asked, coming down on one knee beside the featherman. "Can you tell us?"

Pi'a'weh blinked – once – twice – in that disconcerting Feather way.

Rab didn't seem to be getting through to him. "Pi'a'weh!" he said sharply. "Can you talk? Speak Feather. Fin will understand you."

The little featherman's focus drifted towards Fin, who didn't appear to be listening. He was holding Neila's limp hand as Cloud continued feeling all along her body, looking for breaks and injuries.

"Fin," Rab called. "You have to come here and translate for Pi'a'weh."

Fin raised his free hand in impatient dismissal.

"Leave Cloud to tend to Neila. Pi'a'weh may be able to tell us what happened to Tickie."

That got Fin's attention. He called for Willa.

"You kneel down here and hold her hand. If she says anything – anything at all – call me."

Willa's hand wandered down from her mouth. She was slow about it but finally did as Fin asked. Dropping to her haunches, she reached out and took Neila's hand, but her eyes were fixed on Cloud.

Fin scrambled up from the ground and hurried over to Rab and Pi'a'weh.

"Ask him –" Rab began before Fin cut him off.

"I know what to ask him," Fin snapped, then launched into a flurry of feathertalk, clicks and all.

Rab failed to understand any of it. Fin was talking very fast. Pi'a'weh seemed to grasp what Fin was saying, at least most of it, judging by the changed look of his face. The heavy cap crowning his head eased back from his forehead, leaving Rab with the impression that the little featherman was growing less anxious.

Fin stopped talking and Pi'a'weh began to click and speak in his distinctive wheezing manner. Rab had an easier time picking up some of the words but he failed to pick up enough of them to string them all together into some comprehensible account of what had happened.

When Pi'a'weh finished talking, Fin began to explain.

"Pi'a'weh said he was inside our ts'un with Neila when someone came in and stole the boys."

Already Pi'a'weh's account sounded suspicious. What was he doing inside Fin's ts'un with Neila? And how could someone just *take* the boys?

"Fin, that doesn't –"

"Yes, I know. I can't get him to tell me what he was doing there. Or maybe he did and I just didn't understand. But he says that they were knocked out. Both of them. Someone hit them on their heads from behind."

Pi'a'weh *had* been holding his head.

"Go on," Rab prompted.

"Pi'a'weh came to first and saw two children running out of the ts'un with the boys. He chased them and by the time he got to the wall heard Neila running after him."

"Then they weren't hit very hard," Rab observed.

That was good.

"No," Fin agreed. "But somehow they both got to the top of the wall. He explained how, I think, but I didn't really understand. Anyway neither of them made it down the other side without falling. At least I think that's what he said and …" his attention flicked briefly towards Neila, "… it makes sense that's what happened. And if both of Neila's legs are broken … Rab, I don't know what we're going to do." His voice was beginning to break.

Rab put a hand to Fin's shoulder.

"First we get Neila back inside. Get her cleaned up and warm. Cloud will know what to do."

Rab wasn't just trying to placate him. Cloud would know what to do – in the short term at least. After that? Well, if Neila didn't ever wake up, then there wasn't much even Cloud could do. Then there was also Pi'a'weh to think about. How badly was *he* injured?

"Does Pi'a'weh think he's hurt badly?" Rab asked, glancing at the little featherman. "Did you ask him?"

"No," Fin admitted. "I didn't think to."

"Ask him now," Rab said, squeezing Fin's shoulder.

Together they could probably carry both Neila and Pi'a'weh back inside the settlement but it would be better if they didn't have to try.

"He says he'll be all right," Fin said after a brief few words with the featherman. "He said the fall swallowed his spirit for a while and hurt his back some, that's all."

Swallowed his spirit? It took a moment for Rab to understand. The fall had knocked the wind out of him.

"He says he can walk but didn't think he could have carried Neila and that's why he waited here with her."

If Cloud hadn't climbed that wall, it would have been a very long wait.

Rab was bigger and although it took some coaxing, eventually convinced Fin that he was the one who could more safely carry Neila. Willa never let go of her hand. Between them, Cloud and Fin got Pi'a'weh to his feet and helped him make it back to the gate. Either Fin had misinterpreted what Pi'a'weh had said or the featherman was understating his injuries but in Rab's opinion, without aid, Pi'a'weh would have stood little chance of making it back, even without Neila.

Again they passed through the gate unchallenged. They were just another party returning with the injured. Rab, with Neila lying limp in his arms, wove a tenuous path through the smoking debris littering the lanes. At one point he thought a Feather might have recognised Pi'a'weh, but nothing came of it. Doq'iri. Feather. It really didn't matter much at that point – each was helping the other.

By the time they arrived back in their own ward, Neila was beginning to stir, offering Rab a bit of hope. Her legs were broken but Cloud could set them. Perhaps she'd never walk well again, but that had been the path she'd been heading down already. Even a lame human might be of some use to the Feathers. She could weave for them; Cloud could teach her how. Taking care of Tickie was another matter. But they had to get Tickie back first before they could even think about that. Top-siders had him and Top-siders were nomadic. Rab knew only too well how difficult it would be to track down a nomadic band of Top-siders.

"I want Neila taken back to our ts'un," Fin called ahead to Rab. "I can care for her better there."

Rab didn't argue, but if the Feathers had anything to say about it, it might be Cloud who'd be charged with the care of Neila. But even there, Rab had his doubts. He couldn't see the Feathers agreeing to waste Cloud's talents on caring for an ailing human woman. But right then, he really had to put Neila down and if that meant inside her own ts'un, then so be it.

Their ward was still deserted. Anyone who had stayed behind would be inside their ts'uns, caring for the children who were too young to be of use in the burned-out ward. Rab placed Neila in her own bed and turned around to assist Pi'a'weh to the nearest chair. He'd made it back on his own legs, for the most part, but couldn't have gone much further. His breathing, which was commonly ragged and wheezy, was coming now in worrisome fits and starts. If he died right there inside Fin's ts'un, how could they possibly explain it?

Rab left Neila to Cloud's and Fin's care and set about making Pi'a'weh comfortable, which mainly amounted to requisitioning a blanket from the end of the bed and wrapping it around the featherman's drooping shoulders.

Poor Pi'a'weh. He'd never had a truly healthy moment since Gift had speared him. Rab couldn't see it end this way. Not from a simple fall. It just wasn't right.

"Pi'a'weh," he said, coming down on his knee in front of the featherman. "What can I do to help you?"

"This – *click!* – good," Pi'a'weh wheezed.

Good?

Well, he wasn't, but Rab had a notion that the little Feather might benefit from something Cloud kept inside their ts'un.

"Cloud," Rab said, rising. "I'm going to our ts'un for green-weed."

"Bring it all," Cloud replied. She was leaning over Neila but glanced up to look at Rab. "All the medicines we've got."

Rab made to pass Willa who was hovering in the entrance but she caught his arm.

"What about the boys?" she asked irritably. "We have to find the boys."

Rab slipped his arm free. "Just let me get the medicines first, Willa. Pi'a'weh can barely breathe at the moment. He's not able to tell us anything more."

Willa wouldn't be satisfied with that and Rab knew it, but he didn't have the time or the patience to appease her. Tickie was missing, too, and the sooner they tended to Pi'a'weh, the sooner they could decide how to go about finding the two missing boys. Rab didn't bother to sift among the cans and canisters on their bench top, instead he just gathered an armload, tossed it into a blanket, and returned to Fin's ts'un, somehow without dropping any along the way. He tipped the lot on the bed by Neila's feet.

"Here," Cloud said and, reaching over to sort among the jumble, passed him a canister he knew now contained green-weed, "give Pi'a'weh some of that. Just a little," she cautioned as Rab made his way over to the featherman.

Like purple mushroom extract was to humans, green-weed was to Feathers. Too much could kill. Cloud had been lucky when she'd risked treating Pi'a'weh with the stuff after Gift had wounded him. At the time, she hadn't known how much of a risk she had taken. Rab intended to give the featherman *just a little* indeed.

Pi'a'weh took a small piece off the string Rab offered him and swallowed without showing even the slightest hint of hesitation. The little featherman trusted them – always had. For some reason that made Rab feel sad.

"Better?" he asked.

The little featherman nodded clumsily and Rab began to relax. Pi'a'weh actually even looked slightly better – for a featherperson anyway, whose hard, dark rind of skin never revealed much to the human eye.

"Well?" Rab heard Fin ask. He was seated on the bed by Neila's side. The last time Rab had looked he'd been clutching Neila's hand. Probably still was. Rab didn't turn around to find out.

"Can you help her?"

He was talking to Cloud.

"I'm doing what I can, Fin. Be patient. You can help by heating some of this in water."

"I'll do it," Rab said, leaving Pi'a'weh's side. "You stay with Neila."

It occurred to him then that Cloud might have given Fin a job to do for a reason. Too late now. He took the canister from her outstretched hand and, popping the lid, smelled the distinctive aroma of purple mushroom extract. He took the canister to the hearth and, laying it to one side, began to stoke a small fire. As it began to build, he glanced back to check on Pi'a'weh. The little featherman seemed to be regaining more of his strength. Rab could barely hear that tell-tale wheeze anymore and, when Pi'a'weh looked his way and his face crimpled into what passed as a Feather smile, Rab breathed a silent sigh of relief. The green-weed was working its usual magic.

"Can you describe the two children who took the boys, Pi'a'weh?" Rab asked.

"Doq'iri," Pi'a'weh replied.

Thin-skins. Well, they already knew that.

"Tizwi stand," Pi'a'weh continued.

Rab glanced back again just in time to see Pi'a'weh's hand raised, palm flat.

So – a girl about as tall as Pi'a'weh's head was when he was seated.

"Tet stand." Pi'a'weh dropped his hand a fraction.

A boy a little shorter.

Had to be the same two children he'd seen.

"And it was them who hit you and Neila?"

"Of course it was them," Fin snapped from Neila's bed. "Who else could it have been?"

Rab turned to Fin. "If they did it alone, Fin, that's good. If they had help …" he left the rest unfinished.

"Tizwi and tet," Pi'a'weh said emphatically. "This eye tizwi and tet go." He slapped his hands together then quickly brushed the left past the right.

The way he said it, with a pre-emptive click, made the last word sound more like 'ko' than 'go', but Rab took the Feather's meaning.

"You saw them running from Neila's ts'un?" Rab asked just to confirm it.

Pi'a'weh nodded.

"So it was you I heard!"

Rab's gaze shot towards the entrance. He'd forgotten about Willa.

"When I left Petie with Neila, I thought I heard someone else in the ts'un." She looked towards the trio at the bed. "I thought it was Fin, but it was him!" Her hand was raised, pointing now at Pi'a'weh.

Again Pi'a'weh nodded. Rising, he walked to Rab's building fire, withdrew a thin stick of lighted kindling and began gesturing with it like a spear over his shoulder. Returning the stick, he pointed towards the western ward, then towards Neila. "Say Neeya," he said.

So that's how she knew about the fire and how it was started. Pi'a'weh had told her.

Rab caught Cloud's eye. They were probably wondering the same thing: why had Pi'a'weh come to warn Neila?

A little hiss sounded at the hearth. The pot Rab had set to boil was overflowing. He nudged it sideways out of the flame. Retrieving the canister, he took a very small pinch of purple mushroom extract and dropped it into the pot. Finding a small cup, he poured some of the concoction into it and then carried the cup to Cloud.

"Just a sip, Neila. Do you think you can do that?" Cloud asked.

When she received no response, Cloud glanced at Fin, who raised Neila's head a fraction. Cloud brought the cup to Neila's lips and gently began to tip. Most of it dribbled down Neila's chin but, judging by the little cough Neila emitted, some of it must have gone down.

"That's all I want to do for the moment," Cloud said as Fin lowered Neila's head back to the bed. "She didn't take much but I hope it's enough to calm her before I try to set her legs. We're going to need some splints and bindings. Any ideas?" she asked, looking at Rab.

He had none at all. Things like that were in short supply.

"This," Pi'a'weh exclaimed and hurried to the entrance.

Rab watched the little featherman squeeze past Willa, then disappear lop-sidedly into the lane outside.

"I think he's gone to get something," Fin said. As far as Rab could tell, Neila wasn't even aware of Fin holding her hand.

"Let Neila rest until he gets back, Fin," Cloud suggested. "Sit at the table and I'll get you something to eat."

When Fin just shook his head, Cloud motioned for Rab to follow her to the table.

"That's it?" Willa barked from the entrance. "My boy is missing and all you can do is sit around waiting for that featherman to come back."

"Willa, there isn't a thing we can do about Tickie and Peter now. The Top-siders are long gone," Rab told her. "First we have to see to Neila, then we can plan what to do."

"You call this *planning?*"

Willa was virtually screaming now and all that had done was attract a glare from Fin. Neila didn't stir at all.

"I know all about how you lost Gift, Rab," Willa said, taking a backward step into the lane. "And I know it took you ten years to find her. I never really understood how that could have happened – *until now.*"

Willa's last words were uttered with such bitterness, the sting of them lingered in the entrance like a physical presence after she had left.

Rab stood, about to follow her, but Cloud grasped his hand, drawing him back into his chair. "Let her go, Rab. She's angry and upset. You've got to expect that."

"What if she decides to go looking for Peter herself?"

Cloud smiled thinly. "She won't. Oh, I don't say she won't start out but she won't get very far before she turns back. Willa was hardly more than a girl when she was marched here, Rab, and she's never been outside since. One good look at the terrain out there and she'll turn back."

Rab wasn't so sure. He'd never particularly liked Willa, but then he'd never actively disliked her, either. She was just kind of there. He shook his head at Cloud, but sat down again just the same.

"Maybe she's right to go," Fin said from Neila's bedside. "The longer we wait, the further away they get." He made to rise but changed his mind. "If only Neila wasn't hurt," he added in a whisper.

Fin couldn't go. Rab could. But the Feathers would soon discover him missing. What would the consequences be for Cloud then? All those years ago when he'd roamed the surface in search of Gift with Fin and Stitch safe in the tunnels, his only responsibility had been to himself. Now he had someone else to consider. Would the Feathers regard Cloud as too valuable to punish or would they punish her anyway? Cloud and he were getting older. At some point in the future the Feathers would have to find someone else with the skills Cloud possessed – someone younger. If he left the settlement, would the Feathers simply take the opportunity to replace her now? That's what life on this planet had always amounted to: one moment of waiting after another. Waiting in dread for snow time to come. Waiting in desperation for it to leave. Waiting for the day when your usefulness would run out.

And still they were waiting. Willa had called it wasting time and maybe she was right.

Pi'a'weh soon returned, appearing in the entrance to the ts'un with some short strips of wood and a large piece of Qworka-skin in his hands. He held up one of the strips of wood, looking quite pleased with himself – assuming Rab had read the subtle change in his usual expression correctly.

He had a right to look pleased. What the little featherman had brought them would serve admirably as splints.

"Thank you, Pi'a'weh," Cloud said as, rising, she took the wood from Pi'a'weh with obvious gratitude.

Pi'a'weh handed the piece of Qworka-skin to Rab and, then retrieving something from the folds of his clothes, handed that to Rab as well.

Rab looked down and, after unwrapping its cloth covering, discovered that what Pi'a'weh had handed him was a knife – probably the finest, sharpest knife Rab had ever seen. It was clear that the featherman intended for him to cut the Qworka-skin into lengths, so Rab laid the skin on the table and began to work. When Pi'a'weh seated himself and took to holding the opposite end of the skin, the job became much easier. Every so often, Rab glanced up, wondering if, during one of those glances, he'd catch a hint of uneasiness in the featherman's strange eyes. All it would take was one slip and he could easily cut the little featherman's hands. But Rab saw no fear at all. Once again, that same odd thought struck him: Pi'a'weh trusted them.

"How are you doing?" Cloud called.

"Almost finished," Rab replied.

Once he had what he thought were enough strips for the bindings, Rab carried them over to Cloud. He could hear Pi'a'weh's distinctive little wheeze as he followed otherwise silently behind.

"Fin, I want you to go to my ts'un now and make yourself something to eat," Cloud said.

Fin looked up, clearly disturbed by Cloud's suggestion.

"What about Neila? No," he said, shaking his head. "I'm staying here to help."

"I don't think that's a good idea," Cloud insisted. "Rab can help. He's helped me in the past and he knows what to do." Cloud glanced at Rab as she spoke.

Good luck, Rab thought to himself. There was no way Fin was going to leave Neila now. At least, Rab didn't think so until Pi'a'weh stepped around the end of the bed to place one of his multi-jointed hands on Fin's shoulder and spoke a few brief words in Feather.

Fin made some sort of reply, also in Feather.

Whatever Pi'a'weh's response was, he seemed to be winning Fin over. His hand slowly slipped from Neila's.

"Just for a little while," Fin said at last to Cloud. "Then I'll be back."

"That's fine, Fin," Cloud agreed. "It won't take us very long at all."

Rab doubted that was true. Both of Neila's legs were broken and she was languishing in a weakened condition. Cloud wouldn't be rushing anything.

Rab waited until Pi'a'weh and Fin were well out in the lane before speaking.

"Can you do it?" he asked.

Cloud shrugged. "I think so. But I'm not sure she'll ever walk properly again."

As far as Rab was concerned, that was the best prediction Cloud could have made. For a moment there, he was convinced she was going to say that she wasn't sure Neila would even fully regain consciousness.

"Lucky you took it in your head to climb that wall, Cloud," Rab said, moving to the foot of the bed in anticipation of his wife's instruction.

"Wasn't luck," Cloud said as, with delicate hands, she began to feel her way along Neila's left leg. "When I was looking at the wall, I saw blood. High up. I just didn't want Fin to know about it."

News Rab wasn't heartened to hear. Maybe the blood was Neila's or Pi'a'weh's.

Maybe it wasn't.

Chapter 7

RAB kept his eye on Fin as he worked. With chisel and hammer, Fin and his team were honing the top of one of the foundation stones of the new defensive wall. After the fire in the western ward, the Kun had ordered work on the fourth outer wall doubled. Unless Pi'a'weh had informed him about Tickie and Peter, which Rab doubted, the Kun wasn't aware that two doq'iri children had been stolen during the raid. Likely he wouldn't have cared much about the loss of the children but he'd certainly have been alarmed to know how easily a couple of young Top-siders had gained entry to his 'fortress'.

That was Feather business. But Tickie and Peter were *Rab's* business. And Fin was too. But the younger man wasn't coping well. How could he be expected to cope with his allegiances torn between that of his ailing wife and his lost son? He couldn't leave the settlement on account of Neila's injuries and he couldn't stay because his son was out there somewhere, waiting for his father to come and rescue him. Unlike Willa, Fin couldn't have left the settlement with the Feathers none the wiser that he had gone. Fin was well known to the Feathers – a good and valued worker. Willa went generally unnoticed, skirting around the edges of life in the settlement. She had stolen out of the settlement in search of Peter, but Cloud's prediction that she would soon turn back had been wrong. Willa had been gone for most of the day and there hadn't been any indications that the Feathers were conscious of her absence or, if they were, that they were concerned. Maybe he should just go after her and the boys, the very thing he'd pleaded with Fin not to do. Indecision was making him almost physically sick. Fin had to be wrestling with the same uncertainty, only for him it would be ten, a hundred, times worse; still he pressed on shaping and then hauling the wall stones, slinging that pick and dragging that load with determination. It was probably what kept him going.

If not for Pi'a'weh, things would have played-out differently. Fin would have refused to return to work on the wall and God knew what consequences that would bring down on him. But Pi'a'weh had stepped forward of his own accord to care for Neila. That, too, had Rab wondering. First about his motives. Second about why Pi'a'weh appeared to have the freedom to do as he chose in the settlement. Even Feathers had jobs to do; Rab never saw any idle. Had they made a mistake in trusting Pi'a'weh? The little Feather had no reason to show them kindness. If it hadn't been for Gift, he would never have been injured. But if it hadn't been for Cloud, he would never have survived. Who knew how Feathers balanced good and bad? Certainly not Rab. He couldn't even weigh such things for himself. From the day he'd met Sunny, he'd struggled over every decision he ever made. Although, if he were honest with himself, the struggle had probably always been with him.

Rab raised his hammer, about to strike another blow on the head of his chisel, when Eli, who'd been occupied on the other side of the stone, stopped working.

"Look!" he said, pointing over Rab's shoulder.

Rab looked. Since the fire yesterday, he hadn't given another thought to the strange cloud of dust they'd seen on the horizon the day before. But it was still there and growing larger. When he squinted his eyes, he could almost make out discrete movement within it. Something large was coming their way. Not a dust storm. Dust storms didn't behave that way. Not the band of Top-siders who had attacked their settlement, either. They'd be moving away from the settlement not towards it. Besides, the cloud was far too large to have been raised by a scattering band of Top-siders.

Dropping his hammer and chisel, Rab hurried over to Fin. The Feathers didn't even notice. They, too, were scanning the horizon, reflecting on the meaning of the cloud.

Crack! Fin's pick came down hard on the stone he'd been shaping, sending a large sliver spiralling. It barely missed Rab's eye.

"Fin, hold up," Rab barked, anxious to avert another near miss or worse. "Take a look to the south. It's the tunnel-dwellers. I'm sure of it. They're coming this way – every last one of them."

***

It was clear now that the Kun had made his decision before Rab and Cloud had even started out for the tunnel city; that should Cloud declare the mushroom crops doomed, then the abandonment of the tunnels was to commence without delay. Understandably, it was not something the Kun had imparted to Lilly and if he had given any consideration as to how this one settlement was going to accommodate so many refugees, he hadn't been prepared to share those details with his own people, either. There had been no call to Assembly before or even after the dirty and spent horde of tunnel-dwellers and their attendant Feathers began flooding through the gates. Rab had kept his eyes peeled for Gift and found her among the first of those to arrive. He'd immediately shepherded her along with her scant belongings to his and Cloud's ts'un. She'd been resting there for the good part of a day and still the tunnel-dwellers were coming, but the flood had diminished to a trickle. The last were mostly children, who couldn't keep up the pace the Feathers had set, and they were accompanied by their parents, at least those who had parents. The orphans had more or less attached themselves to anyone who would take them. Rab failed to spot Charlie and Patrick among the scatter of children but had little doubt that sooner or later he'd come upon the crafty pair.

The Kun had ordered not only the removal of every living being from the tunnels, but every piece of furniture and merchandise that could be carried. The ground outside the settlement walls was now littered with overflowing carts and as the number of carts increased so did the difficulty of channelling the living through the narrow outer gate.

It never occurred to Rab that Fin would take advantage of that confusion, but that's exactly what he did, something he, Cloud and Gift only learned when Pi'a'weh came hurrying to their ts'un late that evening.

"I can't believe he left Neila behind," Cloud said, dropping heavily onto the edge of the bed.

Gift was seated by the fire, where she'd spent the good part of the day, recovering from her long and difficult journey; she'd hauled one of the heavy carts a good part of the way.

When Gift and Pi'a'weh locked eyes, Rab wasn't sure what to expect. It had been many years since they had seen each other and, in all that time, in his rare and brief bouts of conversation, Pi'a'weh had never spoken Gift's name.

Gift rose from her chair and, with a confidence Rab suspected hard-won, walked briskly across the room towards the little featherman.

"Pi'a'weh," she said, offering one of those smiles that had become so few over the years, "it's good to see you again."

For a moment, Pi'a'weh seemed at a loss. He'd come to advise them of Fin's disappearance, not anticipating an encounter with the human who had nearly killed him.

His head tipped awkwardly a fraction to one side. "Dee?" he said tentatively, terminating his obvious uncertainty with a little click.

"Yes, it's Dee."

"Come in, Pi'a'weh," Cloud called, waving impatiently. "And tell us everything you know about Fin."

The little featherman eased past Gift into their ts'un.

"Neeya say Fin – click! – go that p'ace," Pi'a'weh replied, pointing towards the laneway.

That place. Pi'a'weh had used that expression once before – when he had warned them about the white Qworkas.

"Where the white Qworkas are?" Rab asked. "The met'ah Qworkas?"

Pi'a'weh spun around to look at Rab. His eyes blinked in rapid succession and his beak of a mouth dropped open in a rare Feather expression of surprise.

"Met*ah*," he said in an agitated fashion.

"We have to bring him back," Cloud declared, leaping from the bed.

"And Willa," Rab reminded her.

Peter's mother never had returned to the settlement. Either she was made of tougher stuff than they realised or she'd met her end sooner than expected.

"Yes, Willa, too," Cloud agreed.

"That's the woman you told me about?" Gift asked. "The one who left to search for her son?"

Rab nodded.

"And Neila is all alone now," Cloud added.

Rab glanced again towards Pi'a'weh. No! Neila wasn't quite all alone now. Was he prepared to risk talking in front of the little featherman? There didn't seem much to lose.

"We have to go after them," he said, settling the matter. "We should have gone after Willa straight away. Maybe it's too late for her – but not for Fin. He knows how to survive out there. For a while at least."

"But what if he finds those Top-siders first?" Cloud asked. "It's not like he'd negotiate to get Tickie back."

"Maybe he would," Rab replied hopefully. Fin wasn't the same brash young man he once had been. Perhaps he had finally learned to think first before he acted.

Cloud was shaking her head. Clearly she didn't believe Fin had changed that much.

"Then that's just more reason to leave now, isn't it?" Gift said. "Fin got out in the confusion."

Maybe they *could* slip out in the confusion. But what of Pi'a'weh? Would he stand idly by and just allow it? And there was Neila to consider, too. Could they trust Pi'a'weh to continue caring for her? Not just in the immediate future but forever. There were no guarantees that they would come back. There were no guarantees about anything.

"You're right," Cloud said to Rab. "And so is Gift. There's no time to waste." She strode towards Gift and the large metal crates where their few possessions were stowed.

Rab opened his mouth to speak but Pi'a'weh beat him to it.

"This eye Neeya," he said.

"And the moment we are gone, you'll tell the Kun," Rab suggested, stepping up to stand directly in front of the little featherman.

It seemed to take a moment for Pi'a'weh to absorb what he had said.

"No," Pi'a'weh replied at last with what passed as a vehement shake of his rigid head. He worked his mouth, clearly in some frustration before he spoke again. "Friend."

It was the clearest human word he'd ever spoken.

***

Maybe it was stupid to have allowed Gift to come with them – not that he could have stopped her. But she was tired already, having walked all the way from the tunnel city, hauling a heavy cart. At least she and Cloud seemed to have temporarily put their differences aside. Perhaps what he really should have been concerned about was Pi'a'weh.

Friend!

Was he? He had no cause to be. Sure, Cloud had saved him once – but only because Gift had wounded him in the first place. To Rab's mind, their actions hadn't done much to earn his friendship. Yet it seemed that's what they had: the friendship of a featherman.

Still Rab couldn't stop worrying. It might have been smarter to insist that Cloud stay behind, too, but there was little likelihood she'd agree to him leaving the settlement without her. Of the three of them, she was the first one the Feathers would be sure to notice missing. The confusion caused by the damage in the western ward and the arrival of tunnel-dwellers immediately afterwards could only last so long. Long enough to find Fin? Maybe. Long enough to then go after Willa? Doubtful. Long enough to track down those Top-siders and get Tickie and Peter back? Even more doubtful. The Top-siders were long gone, melting back in their practiced and proficient way into the dust and obscurity of the surface. Even if they found Fin, he'd never be coaxed back to the settlement. Not without Tickie. He'd left Neila behind and that, itself, spoke of a single-minded determination to find and bring back his son. It would come down to a battle of wills. Three against one. Fin would lose. The question was would Rab be prepared to take it that far? Neila was Fin's wife and Tickie was his son. Did Rab have the right to decide which of his priorities Fin should put first? The answer to that, at least, was clear.

As they neared the gate to the inner wall, Rab glanced down the congested lane towards the western ward. In the night, he shouldn't have been able to see very far at all. But tonight the lane glowed. Every surviving ts'un had its hearth burning to lend light to the darkness and illuminate the chaos. They'd either be coming back here with Tickie and Peter or they wouldn't be coming back here at all. Neila's fate lay entirely within the hands of Pi'a'weh now and there wasn't a single thing they could do about it.

They were bumped and jostled as they walked, lightly laden with the scant supplies they had been able to quickly assemble. The lanes were choked with Feathers, tunnel-people, dust, and the stink of burned Qworka-skin. Shadows waxed and waned in a constant procession along the walls of undamaged ts'uns. Children cried and whimpered while the Feathers who had been assigned to put order to the chaos barked and clicked instructions to the shambling tunnel-dwellers. Here and there overladen carts, small enough to have been manoeuvred through the narrow gates, were being dragged along. Just ahead of them, one cart had overturned and they were obliged to weave around the six or so shouting tunnel-dwellers who were attempting to right it and gather its scattered contents. The noise and smell of it all muddled Rab's already tangled thinking. The air still reeked from the charred contents of the burned-out ts'uns and the stench was only magnified by the fires the Feathers had set to light the dark night. And underneath it all, like a pervasive current, coursed something else that was at once both familiar and strange. It seemed that along with their children and their wares, the tunnel-dwellers had brought with them the lingering musky scent of the tunnels. It took Rab some moments to identify exactly what it was – shimmerers! The new arrivals smelled like shimmerers. It was a strange realisation because, until that moment, Rab had never noticed that shimmerers had any scent at all. Perhaps, in the tunnels, they hadn't, but now that he was aware of it, the smell was beginning to verge on nauseating.

Rab tried to put his mind on something else. He looked around for Charlie and Patrick and, again, failed to spot them. What were the chances of coming upon them in this shifting mass of humanity and Feather? Still, this anonymity was a good thing. It meant they could squeeze through the first of the gates unchallenged. Just the way Fin had done – how long before them? Half a day? Less? It couldn't have been too long. Pi'a'weh rarely left Neila's side and he must have come back to be told by Neila that Fin was gone.

As hard as he tried, Rab couldn't shake his doubts about the little featherman. By rights he should bear a lingering resentment to humans, especially Gift. But during their brief encounter this evening, Rab would have said that the Feather had actually been pleased to see her. Maybe that was the 'Feather way', but Rab really didn't think so. There was something odd about that Feather – always had been – and, at the back of his mind, Rab had always been aware of it.

Most of the tunnel-dwellers had already made their way inside the settlement but the ground outside the outer gate was littered with carts too large to be drawn through the narrow entrances and the smouldering remains of the fires that had been made while the tunnel-dwellers had waited for admittance. Here and there a tunnel-dweller could still be seen walking among the disorder, looking for something or someone, rummaging among the contents of a heavily-laden cart.

"Was nothing left behind?" Rab asked of Gift as they passed by one of the carts.

"We brought all we could," Gift replied. "Even the remaining books from the library. They're here somewhere. Two full carts of them."

No sooner had she said it than Rab spied one of the carts that had once been used to transport the 'shroom crop in from the field. Like many of the old transport carts, it had been cut down to a manageable size and in the light from the dying fires, he could see just well enough to realise it was loaded with books. Hauling 'shrooms across the surface was understandable. But hauling heavy books? What was the Kun going to do with those? Burn them the way Sunny had once done? But the Kun had *stopped* the tunnel-dwellers from burning books according to Gift. It was just another puzzle. Seemed they'd had more than their fair share of those in the last few days.

"Where should we start?" Cloud asked, drawing Rab's attention away from the cart and its remarkable cargo. "We have no idea which direction Fin took."

"West," Rab replied mechanically.

He wished he'd managed to find his old binoculars. They weren't where he'd expected them to be and there was no time to waste in searching. He felt even more naked without his spear; but it was a certainty they wouldn't have been able to walk quite so nonchalantly out through the gates of the settlement if he'd been carrying a weapon.

"It's where the Top-siders come from, isn't it?" he explained, anticipating Cloud's next question.

"Normally," Cloud said, her tone betraying some doubt. "But these Top-siders must have come *in* from the west. Do you really think they'll go back that way since they've made all this effort to come so far east?"

Rab sidestepped the brightly glowing coals of an abandoned fire directly in his path. "They wouldn't have brought the children all the way. They'll have left them behind somewhere. We just have to hope it wasn't *too* far behind."

"I don't know. Those two kids were with them. And if they aren't far away, then Willa would have found them, wouldn't she?"

"We don't know Willa went west. In the state she was in, it wouldn't surprise me if she went off in completely the wrong direction. She wasn't thinking straight."

"She should have waited," Cloud said, her frustration with Willa's rash behaviour plain to hear. "She didn't give us any time at all to plan. Now Fin's gone and done the same thing."

"I can understand why they did it," Gift said bluntly. "When your child is gone, all you want is to get them back and anyone who stands in the way of that is your enemy."

Her bald statement put an end to any further words from Cloud. More than that, it finally opened Rab's eyes. Why hadn't he seen it before? When Fin and Cloud had left Glint's band of Top-siders, they had left Gift's baby girl behind. He knew why Cloud had done it. She and Fin were journeying into the unknown. They had started out from the Top-sider camp not certain if he and Gift were even still alive. It would have been madness to carry a child under those conditions. Rab wouldn't have brought her, either. But evidently Gift had a different opinion and, in all these years, nothing had changed her mind. While Cloud's animosity towards Gift had been seated in resentment for obliging him to risk his life returning the injured featherman; for Gift, it was all about Cloud's abandonment of Sunny. And there wasn't one damn thing he could do about it beyond steer clear of the subject at every opportunity.

"Come on," he said, putting a hand to Cloud's back. "We're leaving the light from these fires behind. We can't waste time but we still have to be very careful from now on. No one noticed us leaving but in the morning they're sure to realise we're gone. Especially you, Cloud."

"Perhaps she shouldn't have come then," Gift suggested.

Beneath his hand, Rab could feel Cloud stiffen and was grateful when she made no reply.

***

Their trek through the night had been slower than Rab had hoped but uneventful. In the morning, among the scattered stands and clumps of thorny urse that were gradually beginning to invade the land beyond the settlement, they saw the tracks the Top-siders had left behind. Had he come this same way, Fin would have seen them, too. Maybe they *should* have started out after the Top-siders straight away. Another mistake? It wasn't the first Rab had made in his life. Wouldn't be the last. When they came upon a fresh grave hurriedly concealed beneath branches of cut urse, Rab changed his mind. In their retreat, the Top-siders had been carrying their dead and injured. Anyone coming up on them unexpectedly in the darkness would have ended up the same way. If any physical harm was to come to Tickie and Peter, it would have happened then. They *had* been right to wait. Rab had dealt with a lot of Top-siders in his day and the most useful and reliable strategy he'd ever learned was patience.

Top-siders were motivated by need. The need for food, shelter, and safety. Once they had also had the need for young girls – ones they could rear and integrate into their society as child-bearers. But with the return of the Feathers and the Top-siders' progressive isolation, that practice had ceased entirely. Now it had begun again – only this time they had stolen two boys. And it hadn't been a raiding party who had done the stealing, but two small children. Rab just couldn't reconcile that their abduction had been planned. The two children had simply taken advantage of the raid and, for whatever reason, stolen the boys of their own accord. The Top-siders wouldn't reject the boys, leave them behind somewhere to die. These days, a strong boy was just as valuable as a strong girl, perhaps even more valuable as far as a Top-sider was concerned.

And so they continued on, following the Top-siders' tracks that snaked among the barbed thickets of urse, only stopping briefly to eat and rest. The threat that the Feathers would come after them drove them just as hard as their desire to find Fin, Willa and the boys. So far they had seen no sign of anyone trailing them, although without his binoculars, Rab was constantly troubled by the possibility that they were back there, just out of sight.

For a long time Rab had been fighting a niggling little impulse to just take off into the wasteland with Cloud. Now that it was done, the impulse to never return to the settlement was even stronger. Could they do it? Survive out here all alone or, if need be, join up with the very Top-siders who had stolen Tickie and Peter. He kept the thought to himself. Time had a way of settling questions and, in Rab's experience, the answer was rarely anything he anticipated.

On the fourth night out from the settlement, Cloud woke Rab from a fitful sleep.

"What's that?" she asked gruffly, shaking his arm.

Rab was reluctant to rise. Cloud's hearing was sharp – too sharp some-times. Often she was the first to hear things that, in the morning, proved to have been of little concern at all. A fallen pot. The flapping of the cloth on their roof in a gust of wind.

He rose on an elbow and listened. He could hear something – kind of a low-pitched persistent drone, but it was what was happening to the ground beneath him that worried him more.

"Earthquake?" Gift said sleepily, putting words to Rab's concerns.

"I don't think so," Cloud replied. "I think the noise is coming from the sky."

She'd said that very same thing a long time ago when they'd been shel-tering in the abandoned village just outside the tunnel city. And she'd been right then. Rab was loath to dismiss her now although he couldn't imagine what could be making such a strange sound this time. It certainly wasn't Qworkas like before.

"Landslide," he suggested at last.

"Maybe," Cloud replied and, taking advantage of the coming dawn, looked towards the distant hills. "If it is, it's a big one."

Rab struggled onto his feet. It was too late now to worry about snatching any more sleep.

"Whatever it is, it's too far away to concern us," he said. "We're awake now, so we might as well get an early start."

As they ate their first small meal of the day, Cloud kept glancing towards the hills. Soon she had Gift doing it too. Rab was relieved to start out again. The way ahead was strewn with sharp-edged rocks and stones. They'd have to keep their wits about them to avert a fall. But it was good to have something else to think about other than that noise and the strange shaking of the ground that had accompanied it.

Towards evening, they came upon more evidence that something had been there before them. At first, Rab thought that the Top-siders must have been dragging a cart of some kind and that the cart had become damaged. But there had been no sign of a cart being dragged before and no remains left behind now. The thickets of urse were crushed over an extensive area, many flattened completely, and there was widespread disturbance to the ground all around. No single cart could have churned up so much dirt or left such long, wide and deep gouges. The tunnel-dwellers hadn't come this way on their trek from the tunnel city, so they weren't responsible. And it certainly wasn't connected with the noise they'd heard in the early hours of the morning; there was nothing Rab knew of that could produce *this* sort of damage.

"Fighting Qworkas?" Cloud suggested, bending down to inspect one of the deep furrows.

Qworkas fought. There was no question about that, but generally their contests were conducted in the air and typically short-lived. Besides …

"No blood and no feathers," Rab pointed out.

"And no Qworkas," Gift added, glancing overhead. "I haven't seen a single one since we left the settlement."

"Then what caused this?" Cloud asked, rising. "It can't have had anything to do with Fin." She spread her hands. "I mean the ground is just too messed up here. Even the urse looks like it's been torn up. If Fin had got into a fight with the Top-siders, I wouldn't expect to see anything like this." She began to wander away, head down inspecting the ground as she walked. "Something really big went on here."

"Perhaps there was a skirmish between two Top-sider bands," Gift said.

"Using what?" Rab asked. "Hands and feet couldn't have done that." He pointed towards the furrow where Cloud had been kneeling. "Even if they had spears, they couldn't have left gouges like that. Something large and heavy was here."

"Very large," Cloud called back to them, waving for them to approach. "See," she said once they joined her. "There are gouges here, too." She pointed back towards the first furrow they had come upon. "That's a fair distance apart."

Rab shook his head, confounded. "Maybe it's got something to do with the Feathers. Something they dragged or something they started to build here and then tore down."

"Really?" Cloud snapped.

Gift's head whipped around and she caught Rab's eye.

He just smiled. He'd only ever known Cloud to lose her temper when she was worrying on something, specifically something for which she felt responsible. In this instance, Rab guessed her concerns were about leaving Neila entirely in Pi'a'weh's hands. Rab had his own concerns about that but sharing those concerns with Cloud would only make matters worse.

"Then just why was the urse all torn up and left? And just where did they drag something from?" Cloud asked. "And if they weren't dragging anything but building something, where did they get the stones and where did the stones go? All I see is small rocks and urse. There's no quarry out here."

"She's right," Gift said. "The Feathers haven't been out here for a long time. There's nothing here for them. And the Top-siders can't be responsible."

"Well, I don't know what it is," Rab said, "but I do know it isn't helping us find Fin. We should keep moving. He can't be too far ahead of us now."

"But we've lost their tracks in this," Cloud reminded him.

"Then we'll just have to look around until we find them."

It was Gift who finally spotted the trail of the westward-moving Top-siders. In fact, the trail veered slightly north of due west and hadn't been all that easy to locate. They had it now though and it quickly became as plain a trail as it had been before. With luck the Top-siders had lingered, arguing about what they had stumbled upon, and lost some time. But if they didn't come upon the Top-siders or at least Fin soon, they'd either have to turn back or find a source of food and water. Their supplies were starting to run low. Urse wasn't edible and they hadn't come upon any water. But to turn back? Now? Until that moment, Rab hadn't realised just how truly averse he'd become to ever going back again.

If only it hadn't been for Neila …

Chapter 8

RAB had taken to counting stars again as he lay, dozing on and off, on the hard ground, Gift and Cloud sleeping soundlessly beside him. They wouldn't have forgotten about the recent find but it seemed he was the only one whose sleep was disturbed by it. Whatever had caused the destruction of the urse and left those deep gouges in the surface couldn't have anything to do with Fin, the Top-siders or the abduction of Tickie and Peter. But something had happened – and not too long ago. The wind and rare rains hadn't gotten to any of it yet.

What had caused it? Rab just couldn't shake the feeling that it was something they should be concerned about. In hindsight, he realised that he should have been paying more attention to what was going on around him than to something they had left a day's trek behind. If he had been paying attention, listening to the dark night, smelling the gentle breeze, he wouldn't have dozed off once again, unaware that someone was creeping up on them until he felt the spear tip press into the top of his shoulder.

Lurched out of his light slumber, Rab's impulse was to jump up from the ground. Instead he remained motionless, anxiously waiting until whoever was holding that spear to his shoulder circled around in front of him. He could feel the tip of the spear twisting in the padding of his jacket as the person or Feather who was holding it moved towards his feet.

"Human," the intruder said, looking down at Rab lying prone on the ground in front of him.

Their intruder had spoken loud enough to wake Gift and Cloud.

Cloud sprang up from the ground and might have made it to her feet if someone Rab didn't notice before hadn't pushed her back down onto her haunches beside Gift, who had more cautiously eased herself onto her knees.

"Three of them," the second intruder observed.

Their visitors were human, too. Rab could tell from their stature and voices, although their faces remained obscured beneath heavy hoods.

Top-siders. With luck, the very Top-siders they'd come to find.

"Get up," the first of the Top-siders ordered Rab.

"I would," Rab said, easing his hand from his side to point towards the spear tip that was still pressing into his chest. "But your spear is making that a little difficult. I don't suppose you'd care to move it?"

After a brief hesitation, the Top-sider did as Rab asked.

"Thanks," Rab said, coming to his feet.

"You're from the Feather settlement," the Top-sider said in a tone that left Rab in no doubt that he wasn't seeking confirmation. "What are you doing out here?"

"Looking for someone," Rab told him readily.

The Top-sider raised his spear, pointing the tip towards Rab.

"That doesn't tell me a lot."

"Not a lot to tell," Rab replied. "At least nothing I'm sure you don't already know … assuming you're who I think you are."

"And that would be?" the Top-sider prompted.

"Part of the band who recently raided the Kun's settlement."

Behind him, Cloud's eyes would be boring holes into the back of his head. She never did hold with his methods of dealing with Top-siders. True, Cloud had spent many years of her early life living with them but Rab had spent a good many years of his adult life tapping their knowledge and plying them for information. He'd learned long ago that when he wanted something, and wanted it quickly – the direct approach worked best. Half-truths and even the most innocuous attempts at deception had a way of morphing very quickly into outright lies and duplicity. They lacked the time and Rab lacked the patience for either.

"And if we are?" the Top-sider pressed him.

"Then you're who we're looking for. You seem to have something that belongs to us. Two things actually, and, to put it simply, we'd like them back."

The Top-sider snorted. "Just like that!"

"That, I think, would be unlikely," Rab agreed, "but as you can see, we have nothing to offer in return."

"You have them," the Top-sider said, motioning with the spear towards Cloud and Gift.

"Actually, *I* don't have them," Rab replied. "They speak for themselves. And I don't think either one of them is going to offer themselves in trade."

"I might," Gift said, surprising Rab, as she rose from her knees and stepped forward, "if you really do have what we're looking for. Otherwise, the deal is off. You go your way and we'll go ours."

"That's pretty big talk from a very small woman. We say who goes where and when here, not you. We can do what we want with you."

Gift shrugged. "You can try. But I can assure you that if you do try, one of you will end up dead."

"Really? I can't see how that's possible since we're the ones with the spears."

"But I'm the one with the cropping knife."

No sooner were the words out than the second Top-sider, spear raised, stepped up to join his companion.

Did Gift have a knife? Or was she bluffing? Rab supposed it didn't matter. The knife or at least the threat that Gift would use it was all the bargaining power they had. It wasn't the way Rab usually operated, but Gift had committed them to doing things her way.

"Hand it over," the smaller of the two Top-siders commanded, menacing Gift with the tip of his spear.

"I don't think so."

"Then we kill the man or the woman." The taller Top-sider again.

"Go ahead," Gift told him. "I'll still kill one of you."

Rab had almost forgotten how much of a force Gift could be. As much as any Feather on this planet, her nature had been chiselled sharp-edged and sometimes lethal by this harsh and unforgiving land.

"I'd listen to her if I were you," Rab suggested calmly. "It wouldn't be the first time she'd stabbed someone. She's very good at it."

"A tiny thing like that?" the taller Top-sider scoffed. "The only knife she knows how to use is a cooking knife."

"You think so?" Rab goaded. "Fine, take the chance then. But it doesn't take size to use a cropping knife efficiently. Only speed and accuracy," Rab reminded him. "And she has that, I promise you."

"Just what is it you think we've got?"

The taller and more talkative of the Top-siders was obviously the leader. Maybe these were two of the Top-siders who had raided the Kun's settlement and maybe they weren't. But if they had the children, then they were already aware that the settlement walls could be breached. If they were of a different band, then it would be an enormous mistake for Rab to reveal anything about the flaw in the settlement's defences.

"Like I said before, if you're who I think you are, you already know. If you're not, then I don't see any advantage for me if I tell you."

"Except your life."

"And yours. You're scouts. Our business is with your elders. We only talk to them."

"And you expect us to just take you to them?"

"I don't expect it. But she has the knife and you are outnumbered. It might be the smart thing to do — unless one of you isn't all that interested in making it back to your band. I really don't care which of you that is. I'll leave that up to her."

"The little one, I think," Gift mused. "Or on second thought — maybe the bigger one. He seems to think size makes such a difference."

"Just let me know which," Rab said casually. "I'll hold the other one for you."

"No need," Gift replied. "Shouldn't take a moment."

"We're wasting time," Cloud snapped, snaring the Top-siders' attention as she got to her feet. "Just do it and get it over with. I'm tired of waiting around."

Before Rab had time to register Gift move, her knife was pressed to the neck of the taller Top-sider, just below his left ear. She wasn't bluffing after all, but her action had prompted the shorter Top-sider to press his spear into Rab's chest.

"Make a decision, Top-sider," Gift said. "But make it fast. Cloud is running out of patience."

"Well?" Rab prompted. "What's it to be? We fight here and now or we come to an understanding? As I see it, there is only one reasonable choice." Beneath the hood of his coat, the Top-sider's eyes were darting this way and that. Rab kept his gaze trained on those anxious eyes. "Your friend there can be dead in less than a second. Maybe you'll have the time to kill me, but in the time it takes you to do that, she'll have the time to kill you. Three dead. And for what? Just doesn't seem like a good deal to me, considering all we're asking is to be taken to your elders."

The shorter Top-sider turned uneasily towards his companion. "What do I do?"

"Put down your spear," his companion replied. "We'll take them to the elders like they ask. Then *they'll* be the ones outnumbered. We'll see how cocky they are then."

"Finally," Cloud barked and bent to gather her pack. Her hand shaking.

Casually Gift lowered her knife and, bringing out a small Qworka-skin pouch from inside her coat, resheathed it. She cast a glance towards Rab as she passed him and seemed more amused than relieved. He couldn't say the same of himself.

***

Their uneasy truce with the two young scouts ensured that the bulk of their journey to the Top-sider camp was made in silence. There were a few brief moments when they could not be overheard and Cloud took advantage of those moment to express, in no uncertain terms, her unhappiness with Gift's rash decision to challenge the two young men. Rab didn't try to placate her; he hadn't been all that happy with Gift, either. Her threats had worked – this time. But it was a strategy Rab wouldn't recommend they use again in the future.

The Top-sider scouts led them further westward into territory peppered with hillocks and shallow depressions, where the urse was no longer as plentiful. Ahead Rab spotted a low chain of hills that appeared to be the scouts' destination.

They reached the base of those hills before evening and scrambled after the scouts up loose scree towards the wide, open mouth of a cave. Looking through the opening, Rab saw a familiar light shining down from its roof not far from the entrance – brightworms. The cave provided shelter from the elements, but it was too large to offer much in the way of concealment. Out here, Rab supposed, they didn't need it. So far, the Feathers had made no attempt to settle the land to the west and, as yet, showed no indications that they had any intention of doing so.

"You wait here," the taller scout instructed Rab when he made to follow them inside the cave. "The elders will decide if you can come in."

"And what if they say we can't?" Cloud called after the pair making their way into the cave.

The scouts simply ignored her, so Rab returned to his companions.

"Well," Gift said, glancing at him as she shrugged off her pack. "I'm not just going to stand around here waiting. We haven't eaten anything since yesterday." Dropping to her knees, she began to rummage inside her pack. When she found what she was looking for, she raised her hand, offering Cloud some of her food.

Cloud pushed her hand away.

Gift shrugged and began to eat. "Why don't we just follow them inside?" she suggested between mouthfuls.

"We wait," Rab said. Looking at Gift eating was beginning to make his mouth water. "We're from the settlement. They'll want to know everything they can about it. They'll let us in, if only to ask us questions."

"No need for them to do that," someone called from the entrance of the cave, causing Rab to spin around. "They've already asked me."

Fin! So he *had* made it here before them. Rab didn't know whether to feel relieved or angry.

"Tickie and Peter?" Cloud shouted. "Have you got them?"

"They're here," Fin said, smiling as he approached. "And they're both fine."

"What about Willa?" Rab asked, rushing towards Fin.

The smile on Fin's face quickly faded. "I never saw her. I thought she must have gone back."

Rab shook his head.

"She must have turned herself around out here," Cloud said, a trace of sadness in her voice. "We should have tried to stop her, but I thought she'd be all right."

"Maybe she is," Rab replied, although he knew how unlikely that would be. Willa was dead or, at best, lost and that meant she soon would be dead. There'd be no looking for her. If she hadn't followed the tracks the way Fin had done, then she could be anywhere. Maybe they would stumble upon her, but the chances of that were remote. Peter was on his own.

"Gift!" Fin said uncertainly, snapping Rab out of his pointless thoughts. "It is you!" he said, rushing past Rab and Cloud to hug Gift who had just risen from the ground. "I didn't expect to see you out here. You, either," he said, glancing at Cloud. "That's why they were confused." He gestured towards the empty entrance of the cave.

"Who was confused?" Rab asked.

"The scouts," Fin explained. "I said that a man might come following me. No one else."

"I'd like to know how they even saw us," Rab said. "You were almost a day ahead of us."

From the pocket of his coat, Fin produced Rab's binoculars.

So that's what had happened to them!

"I'll have those back if you don't mind," Rab said, snatching the binoculars from Fin's hand.

The expression on Fin's face suddenly darkened as his focus darted back to Cloud.

"Neila." The way he said his wife's name, so faintly and with such distance, it sounded like a goodbye.

"She's the same, Fin," Cloud said, hurrying forward to grasp Fin's arm.

"You left her all alone?" he accused.

"She's not alone," Cloud told him. "We left her with Pi'a'weh."

"Pi'a'weh! I never wanted to leave her with him even for a second. Now you've left her for days."

"I trust him," Cloud replied.

"And he trusts us. At least he seems to," Gift said, stooping to gather her pack. "I wouldn't."

Rab had barely heard Gift's last words. Fin wouldn't have heard her for, at that very moment, a dirty but otherwise unharmed Tickie came pounding out of the cave.

"I told you to wait with the others," Fin said, spinning around with the intenton of intercepting his son.

He didn't stand a chance. The second Tickie spotted Cloud, he bolted right for her.

Cloud dropped to the ground to embrace the hurtling child, who was all smiles and unintelligible chatter until his eyes settled on the woman standing behind her.

"I'm Gift," she said, bending down on one knee, the pack slipping off her shoulder. "Some people call me Dee. You must be Tickie. Your father and I came from the same village," she said, prompting Tickie to look towards his father for confirmation.

When Fin smiled, it seemed to settle his son's remaining misgivings. He reached out and taking one of Cloud's hands and one of Gift's, began leading them towards the entrance of the cave.

"I have new friends," he said as he toddled along, clearly still a little exhausted from his long journey. "Nicer than Feathers."

"I can't wait to meet them," Gift replied.

As he followed behind with Fin under the glow of the brightworms, Rab noticed his fragile smile.

"What?" he prompted.

Fin stopped walking, leaving Tickie, leading Cloud and Gift, to draw further ahead of them. "Gift is in for a bit of a surprise," Fin told him, waving a hand when Rab opened his mouth to speak. "Best you see for yourself. I intended to leave at first light with Tickie and Peter, but now I'm not sure what to do about Peter. If Willa is dead —"

"They were just going to let you take the boys?" Rab asked, interrupting.

"Of course. They never wanted them. Those two kids were punished when the elders found out what they'd done."

"I'm afraid you're going to have to explain things a lot better than that."

Fin started off again and Rab fell into step beside him. The bright-worms glowed brighter in this part of the cave, so Rab could clearly see Tickie leading his two charges towards a sharp bend. In a moment, they'd be out of his sight. He wished Fin would walk faster.

"The kids were only supposed to scout the settlement," Fin was saying. "Locate the warehouse and such. Get in and get out unobserved. They weren't ever supposed to steal anything from anyone and bring attention to themselves. And they certainly weren't supposed to take the boys. The attack was a diversion. To draw us all to the western ward while another party undertook a raid on the warehouse."

"No one got through the gates, Fin," Rab said as the three ahead of them disappeared from view. "If that's what they told you, then they were lying."

"They didn't come through the gates." Fin made a motion with his hands. "They went up and over the walls the way the kids had done."

Rab began to walk a little faster. "We couldn't get over those walls."

"Not true. Abby did," Fin reminded him. "These Top-siders have spent their entire life out here, scaling cliffs, walking day in day out on rock with shoes so thin they provide hardly any protection at all. The Feathers are fooling themselves. Those walls aren't any deterrent. Not to these Top-siders. The younger ones are the best but soon there'll be none left, then I don't know what they're going to do."

They'd reached the bend and, down the broader adjoining tunnel, Rab caught sight of Tickie, Cloud and Gift again. He began to relax. "What do you mean 'soon there'll be none left'?"

"Them," he said, pointing ahead. "They're all that's left of Glint's band."

"Glint! He's here?"

"No," Fin replied soberly. "Glint is dead. Poppy, too. Most of the older ones. And there are no more children. Those that were born since

Abby and I left all died. Those two kids who stole from you are the youngest they have left. And God knows how they've survived out here."

"Wait," Rab interrupted. He'd just thought of something. "If this is Glint's band, then Sunny must be here."

"That's what I meant when I said Gift was in for a surprise."

Rab could hardly believe it. Sunny! Here!

"But I'm afraid she's going to have to wait to see her. Sunny and the boy, Patch, are out gathering tinder."

A smile creased his mouth. So, it had been Gift's own daughter who had stolen from his ts'un. What were the chances?

"If Glint's not in charge, then who is?" he asked.

"His name is Skylar."

They'd come to the end of the tunnel and, gathered under the light of the brightworms stippling the ceiling of a largish inner cave, the remnants of Glint's band. The cave wasn't anywhere near as grand as the tunnel city's Market Square. There were no stalls, no wares being sold or traded, in fact little in the way of possessions of any kind. But it was an adequate enough resting place for a rag-tag band of Top-siders who were constantly on the move. Though a few of the Top-siders remained seated on the floor, most had begun to cluster about Cloud and Gift. At a rough guess, Rab put their number at around thirty. That was all that was left of the sixty or so Top-siders Cloud had told him made up Glint's band? And, just like Fin had said, there wasn't a single child among them. Few women, either.

"That's him over there." Fin nodded, singling out a man whose back was turned to Rab. "I'll take you to him. There's something you don't know yet, but I think I'd better let Skylar tell you. It makes sense of what the Kun told his people."

"The Kun? What's the Kun got to do with this?"

"Ask Skylar."

Rab hurried after Fin into the thick of the milling Top-siders. He thought he recognised a few of them. Cloud and Gift obviously had and judging by the anxious look he'd noticed on Gift's face as he squeezed past her, it hadn't taken long at all for her to realise that, since this was the remnant of Glint's old band, then had her daughter survived, she must be here among them. Tickie had disappeared somewhere in the huddle, but, so far, Rab had failed to see any sign of Peter.

The Top-siders were all chattering at once and Cloud seemed to be almost as welcome among them as Gift – Dee, as they knew her. In the confusion, Rab thought he might have spotted Sandy, but Fin was leading him directly to Skylar and Rab didn't get much of a chance to confirm whether it was the same woman he'd met travelling south with Glint's small scouting party almost a decade ago.

"This is Skylar," Fin said, tapping the shoulder of the man standing in front of Gift.

When the man turned around, Rab was surprised to discover that he was relatively young.

"I don't think I remember you," Rab said.

"No," the elder replied, "we've never met. But I've heard about you. Why don't we let Dee and Abby catch up with the others? It's quieter and more comfortable over there," he said, pointing towards a spot near the back of the cave where someone had piled a stash of ragged cloth on the ground.

So this wasn't the first time they had used this cave. There weren't many comforts but enough for this group of travellers. Rab followed the elder and Fin trailed on behind.

"I'm sorry the children caused you so much trouble," Skylar said, slipping to the ground ahead of Rab and Fin.

He didn't apologise for the trouble he'd caused the Kun's settlement.

"They should never have taken those two boys. And they certainly shouldn't have stolen from you personally."

"Fin said you punished them."

"That's right," Skylar agreed. "They're to gather tinder and do all the cooking for us until I'm convinced they've learned their lesson."

"But two young children out there all alone. Isn't that dangerous?"

"If it wasn't dangerous, it would hardly be much of a punishment, would it? Besides, would it be any more or less dangerous for me to be out there alone? Or any one of them?"

He gestured towards the group of Top-siders gathered about Cloud and Gift. They were seated on the floor of the cave now, looking like they had settled in for a long visit. Rab could hear their talk but make little of what was being said.

What Skylar said was true. All Top-siders, whether adult or child, did their equal part.

"But I'm sure you'll understand that I won't be asking them to give back what they stole from you," Skylar was saying.

Rab understood.

"If they'd come to us and asked," he said, turning back to the elder, "Cloud would have been happy to give them food. More than they ended up stealing from us."

"Cloud?" Skylar's brow furrowed.

"Abby," Rab explained. "Cloud is her Top-sider name."

"I see," Skylar replied. "Fin always called her Abby. But I'm afraid Sunny and Patch weren't likely to approach anyone inside the Kun's settlement. Even humans. They think all the humans there are friends of the Kun."

"Friends?" Rab said with a smile. "I wouldn't go that far."

"But that's what we've always thought and so, when the scouts saw three of you and not the one Fin had warned us to expect, they panicked and assumed you had been sent by the Feathers."

Rab shook his head. "We snuck out and I suspect there'll be a price to be paid for that when we go back. And it won't be gathering tinder and cooking."

"What will they do?" Skylar asked.

"Cloud is special to them. She knows how to make things grow. I don't think they'll punish her too severely. As for Gift, if she decides to come back – I don't know. Fin and I are just common workers." He shrugged and didn't bother to add anything more.

"Even so," the elder said, glancing briefly towards Cloud, "perhaps you and your people did the right thing by going over to the Feathers. At least you have good food and shelter."

"Yes, we have that," Rab agreed half-heartedly.

"We don't," Skylar replied. "We're starving and this cave is the best shelter we have ever found but it's too close to the Feathers' settlements to risk staying here too long. The wild 'shrooms we used to find on the surface are disappearing. Ground grubs, too. We have to dig deeper and deeper to find them. Lately we've been finding some sort of animal though – and, despite the bitter taste of its meat, it's good enough to eat whenever we can get it."

"Probably a Punn'tu," Rab said reflexively.

Fin turned to him with a questioning look on his face.

"I saw one in the tunnels. They've been eating the 'shrooms there."

"Perhaps," Skylar agreed. "It does seem to favour mushrooms. But there aren't very many and when we do find them, it usually means the mushrooms nearby have been eaten. A lot of the surface seems to have been taken over by that thorny bush. It's good for tinder and weapons. Nothing more."

"The Feathers call it urse," Rab explained, "and they don't eat it, either. I think it's the warmer temperatures. Even the Feathers don't seem to be able to grow their crops too far from the rivers and creeks. I suppose that's why they've never gone too far west and why you've been able to evade them. But Fin says you're the last."

"The last of the Top-siders?" Skylar said, emphasising the somewhat derisive name for his people. "I doubt that. But we're certainly *among* the last and the people you see here," he said, encompassing his fellows with a spread of his hands, "*are* the last of our band."

"Then there are others still on the surface?"

Inside the Kun's settlement, there was little word about the people who still roamed free on the surface. Most of what they heard were unsubstantiated rumours and conjecture.

"Some. We come upon a few others now and then. Not many."

It seemed to Rab that there was more Skylar wanted to say but was unsure how to go about it. His gaze drifted to the rock floor beneath his feet and stayed there for such a long time Rab was beginning to wonder if his audience with the elder was finished.

"You're unexpected company," Skylar took up at last, raising his eyes. "Unexpected but welcome. Glint spoke a lot about you and I've always wanted to meet up with you. I never suspected it would be this way though. Perhaps I shouldn't have punished Sunny and Patch so severely. They've brought me what I've been hoping for."

"Me?" Rab said, astounded. "Why would you be hoping to meet me?"

Rab glanced towards Fin, seated beside him, but the elder's strange confession appeared to be news to him.

"Glint said you know things."

Rab shifted uneasily on the bundle of loose rags. A long time ago, he'd told Glint all he knew and Glint would have told his people. As far as Rab was aware, there was nothing more he *could* tell. Unless …

"Oh, we know this isn't Earth," Skylar said, reading Rab's discomfort. "Glint told us everything about that."

Rab breathed a sigh of relief. After all these years, he just wasn't up to repeating the same old story, battling the same old scepticism.

"I knew things, Skylar – once. But what I knew isn't much use now. I can't help anyone. Not even the people back in the settlement." He looked briefly towards Fin. "Ask him. He'll tell you how useful I am there. I do the Feathers' work when I'm told to do it. I go where and when they order me to go. Just like everyone else."

"Glint said you'd seen things no one else had ever seen. He said you could even read."

Yes, thanks to Sunny, he had seen things no one else alive today had ever seen and, thanks to Ruby, he could read. But …

"Neither of those are of any use now, either," he told the elder.

"It's just one question, Rab," Skylar went on. "If you can't answer it, then you can't. Even if you can, I'm not expecting it to help us. Any of us. I simply want to know. If you were going to die, wouldn't you want to know why?"

Rab was beginning to feel uncomfortable again.

"Ask your question then?" he said, resigned.

"I want to know what is happening to our people."

"I don't follow –"

"Not why our babies die, Rab," Skylar said, cutting him off, "or why our young women rarely survive childbirth or why many of us never reach old age. We understand all that. What we don't understand is why so many of our people seem to disappear."

"Into the settlements, you mean?"

Skylar shook his head. "No. I mean off the surface of the planet."

Chapter 9

RAB snapped a look at Fin whose mouth was hanging open.

"Is this what you wanted me to ask Skylar?"

"This? No!" Fin said, finding his voice. "I thought he was going to talk about Qworkas."

"You've seen them, too?" Skylar interrupted. "These *other* Qworkas?"

"No. Pi'a'weh tried to warn us about them," Rab explained, turning back to the elder.

"Pi'a'weh?"

"The Feather Gift – Dee – wounded."

"He survived?" Skylar asked almost indifferently.

"Yes, he survived," Rab agreed, growing exasperated.

"Well, he is right about the Qworkas," Skylar continued. "We've seen them. From a distance. They're not like any Qworka I've ever seen before. But that isn't what I wanted to talk to you about."

"Look, Skylar, people can't simply be disappearing."

"But they are, Rab. We've seen the signs over and over again."

"*What* signs?"

"Abandoned campsites."

"That's easy to explain. They moved on somewhere else."

"Leaving everything they owned behind? Sometimes we find their cold fires. Sometimes their possessions – not scattered about but left where they might have been stowed for the night. Once we even came on a cart that was still in good enough condition to be useful. But it was just left there, too."

"Then they died."

"Who buried them?" Skylar asked.

Rab shrugged. "Other Top-siders," he suggested, glancing away.

He was growing concerned about Cloud's whereabouts. She was still there, seated in the midst of a circle of Top-siders. Tickie looked to be asleep in her lap and, beside her, a woman Rab didn't recognise was cradling another sleeping child – Peter hopefully. Gift wasn't among them, but seated off to the side with another woman, the one Rab had at first suspected might be Sandy. He felt sure now that he'd been right. It was Sandy – an older Sandy but definitely the same woman who had brought them food when they had stayed briefly with Glint's scouting party all those years ago. She and Gift were roughly the same age, he recalled, and she'd had a small baby with her then – a boy baby. What were the odds, Rab wondered, that the boy who had stolen from his ts'un wasn't Sandy's son?

"We found no graves," Skylar was saying, grabbing Rab's reluctant attention away from Gift and his wife. "We should have found graves. And even if we simply missed seeing the graves, then their possessions wouldn't have just been left there."

"Did you take their things when you found them?"

Skylar smiled. "Of course, we did."

Rab offered up an inward sigh. "Well, if people are disappearing, and I doubt it, then I'm afraid I can't explain it any better than you. There has to be another explanation for what you've seen. Maybe Feathers took them and, unlike us, they wouldn't be interested in taking anything that belonged to a Top-sider. Did you consider that?"

The elder shook his head. "The first camps we found were far to the west where the Feathers have never been."

"What do you mean 'the first'?" Fin asked, leaning forward.

"Just some days ago, we came on another abandoned camp. Only this one wasn't very far from here. Whatever is happening to our people – it's spreading."

"Spreading east?" Fin asked. "Towards us?"

"It looks that way," Skylar replied. "So you see, my concerns aren't simply for my own people. Perhaps we're next. But then after that – you."

"No, this can't be," Rab protested. "It's impossible. People just don't *disappear*. They have to go somewhere. Even if they were killed and – eaten, say – there'd be some evidence left behind."

"Eaten by the Qworkas, you mean," Fin suggested.

"Qworkas don't kill us for food, Fin. They just don't."

"And I used to say there was no such thing as a launch pad," Fin reminded him.

"All right, Fin, you've made your point. Maybe there are Qworkas who are happy to make a meal out of humans but, even so, there'd still be something left behind to show it. Blood. Feathers. *Something*."

"There is something," Skylar said, breaking into their argument, "but we've never been able to understand it. It's like the ground around the camp site has been ripped up and trampled over. Sometimes even that thorny bush in the area — urse, you said? Well, it looks as though it's been scorched."

Rab could have described the site he, Cloud and Gift had recently come upon exactly the same way. And they hadn't been able to explain it, either.

"And there are gouges?" Fin prompted, expectantly. "Long, deep gouges in the ground?"

"Yes," Skylar agreed. "You've seen one of those sites?"

"On my way here, tracking you," Fin replied, then looked directly at Rab. "And since *he* was following right behind *me*, so did he."

"I saw it," Rab agreed. "But that's all I saw. There was no evidence of any camp fires. No possessions left behind. Nothing. Just that disturbance on the ground."

"As I said, Rab, sometimes that's all there is."

"Skylar," Rab said after a long and thoughtful pause. "I can't help you. I wish I could but I can't. If Top-siders are disappearing, then there has to be some simple explanation for it and my guess is that Feathers have taken them. They haven't been brought into our settlement. I can tell you that at least. But they could easily have been taken to some other settlement. Or even to work in the roosts or the mines. I'm sorry," he said, a shadow at the mouth of the cave drawing his attention.

"Perhaps you're right," Skylar said. He didn't sound very convinced.

Two children were entering the cave. The girl's arms were laden with urse branches while the boy was wheeling a small cart overflowing with more tinder. Rab glanced towards Gift, but she made no attempt to rise. In fact, she appeared not to have noticed the pair.

"In the morning, you'll have to leave just as Fin intended, but you're welcome to stay with us tonight."

Rab looked away from the children in time to see Skylar point towards the shadows further back in the cave. For the first time, he noticed a large and haphazardly arranged pile of Qworka-skin bags containing, he guessed, food the Top-siders had stolen from the Kun's settlement.

"We have food for the moment," Rab told the elder. "Enough to get us back."

"It will only keep so long," Skylar reminded him.

"What about Peter?" Fin asked. "If his mother is dead, then what use is it to take him back to the settlement? Can't he stay?"

"With us?" The elder sounded surprised.

"Why not? He's healthy enough. He might live."

"And he might die," Skylar replied.

"What do you say?" Fin asked, turning to Rab.

"I don't know, Fin. It's not our decision."

"Peter can't exactly decide for himself," Fin reminded him. "And if Skylar's willing to take him, then I think that's what we should do. He'd be better off taking his chances out here."

"I'm not sure I agree," Skylar said. "But I won't turn the boy away. He'll be cared for, but that's all I can promise."

"We'll think on it, Fin," Rab said. "Make a decision in the morning."

As Fin was offering his half-hearted agreement, the two children wandered past with their burden. The boy gave Rab a thorough inspection, nearly toppling his small cart in his distraction. The girl barely looked his way. She was Gift's daughter all right, although beyond that mane of black hair, there was hardly a trace of physical likeness between them. She must have inherited her father's looks. Rab wouldn't know. The only time he'd seen Sunny's father, his face had been contorted in pain. Sunny wasn't a pretty child. Her light-coloured eyes were set too far apart, and her nose had a slight kink to it midway down; a visible clue, perhaps, to the severe and sober spirit residing within? Finally seeing her up close, Rab could now understand how a little girl like that could have got it into her head to scale the settlement's defences. The boy's finer features didn't suggest the same self-assuredness. If it hadn't been for Sunny, Rab had a suspicion the boy would never have attempted to scale the walls at all.

Over by the seated Top-siders, Tickie was beginning to stir, while Peter remained fast asleep locked in the arms of the woman seated beside Cloud. She made no attempt to rise when Cloud struggled onto her feet.

"The children should have our meal prepared soon," Skylar said.

As if to confirm it, Rab began to smell the bitter aroma of burning urse. Looking over his shoulder, he saw a waft of smoke billow out through a narrow tunnel at the back of the cave. Somewhere behind him, there had to be an exit to the outside where the children had built a large fire.

"What about Gift?" Rab asked as Cloud, leading Tickie, came up to join them. The boy rolled more than toddled into his father's lap while Cloud seated herself between Rab and Fin.

"She's over there with Sandy," Cloud replied, nodding towards the pair on the opposite side of the cave.

"Does she know about Sunny?" Rab asked, garnering Skylar's attention.

"She must," Cloud replied, "but when the two children walked in, she didn't even look their way."

So Cloud had noticed that, too.

"You know, don't you?" Cloud asked, glancing at Skylar.

"About Dee and Sunny? Yes," Skylar agreed. "We all *know*."

Rab was left with the distinct impression that Skylar had no intention of continuing that line of discussion. And Cloud didn't pursue the matter either, so nor did he. Fin was distracted with Tickie, who having smelled the smoke, was obviously well aware of what was coming. The little one had to be hungry.

Twice the boy, Patch, emerged through the small tunnel to retrieve another Qworka-skin bag, which he then dragged unceremoniously behind him back through the tunnel. Rab was beginning to smell more than just smoke now. He was hungry, too – reminded of it when the air inside the cave became saturated with the aroma of the Top-siders' stolen food.

As Skylar had promised, they didn't have long to wait. Sunny and Patch seemed to be practiced hands at cooking, leading Rab to wonder just how many times they'd been dealt the same form of punishment. It was left to Patch to distribute the food. He served Skylar first with an old battered metal plate that must have travelled with the Top-siders for a long time. Rab and his companions were served next. Only when the water was to be distributed did Sunny make an appearance. Again, she served Skylar first, passing him a new and shiny cup. A 'gift' from one of the Feather settlements, Rab guessed. When it came Cloud's turn, Sunny shoved a cup into her hands so forcefully, the contents sloshed around inside. She'd been careful enough not to spill a drop though.

"Hey," Cloud snapped, whipping up her free hand up to steady the cup. "Someone needs to teach you some manners," she said, gazing after Sunny as she made her way back towards the narrow tunnel.

Rab nudged Cloud in the ribs.

"Look at the cup she gave you."

Cloud tore her eyes away from the retreating child. "Why that little …" she began, then broke out laughing.

"Is something funny?" Skylar asked, glancing up from his plate.

Cloud help up the cup.

"This is my cup and that there," she said pointing to an etching on its side, "is my name. Rab scratched it there a long time ago. It was among the things Sunny stole from our ts'un."

Skylar's face darkened and he glanced over his shoulder. "I'll punish her again," he said. "We don't steal from our own kind."

Technically, that wasn't true. By stealing from the Feathers, the Top-siders were stealing food from the mouths of every human in the settlements. Rab let it go.

"Don't," Cloud said with a shake of her head. "I've got it back now."

Sunny appeared again and began the slow process of distributing water to every member of the Top-sider band. Rab made sure he was watching when Gift's turn came around. She took the cup from Sunny's hand without saying a single word – at least as far as Rab could see.

Why was she behaving that way? When he glanced at Cloud, she shrugged and went back to the last of her meal.

Sunny and Patch must have eaten outside by the fire because Rab didn't see them again until the Top-siders began to settle in for the night. Gift remained with Sandy on the opposite side of the cave and the children found a place together close to the entrance of the narrow tunnel. Perhaps their separation from the rest of the Top-siders was also part of their punishment. Perhaps not. They were a pair. Likely had always been a pair who had every intention of remaining so.

"Don't ask me," Cloud said, anticipating the question Rab was about to ask the moment they were left alone. "I have no idea why Gift is behaving that way." Getting up, she headed straight for the mound of piled-up cloth, selected a few choice pieces and returned with them to Rab.

"I don't know if this is allowed," she said, handing him a wad of cloth, "but no one stopped me and I don't intend to sleep on the hard ground again when something better is available."

***

Despite Rab's suspicions that he'd never be able to sleep under the glowing light of the brightworms, Cloud had to shake him awake.

"Fin is up and moving." She was bundling up the bedding she'd slept on the night before, preparing to return it to the mound of cloth. "He'll be anxious to get back to Neila. You'd better get up now. Tickie has already come by twice to check on you."

Rab struggled up from his makeshift bed, running a hand through his matted hair.

"Have you spoken to Gift yet?" he asked without thinking.

"No," Cloud snapped and, reaching down, wrenched Rab's bedding from the ground and began to bundle it angrily with her own.

As she started to hurry away, Rab reached out and grabbed her arm.

"I'm sorry," he said. "It's just –"

"I know what it is, Rab," Cloud shot back at him. "I've always known what it is. Blaze made you feel like you had to be a father to those children. But Gift already *had* a father then – and she let him go. She spent years with Glint's people and she *chose* to let them go. I wouldn't have expected it but it appears to me that she's also chosen to let her own daughter go after all these years apart. Just how long was she with you, Rab? Hardly any time at all. And still you won't let *her* go. She's moved on but you're stuck in the past. Always have been. You're always thinking backward. About where we came from. How we got here. But you know, it doesn't matter anymore. Hasn't mattered for a long time. We aren't *from* Earth. Not really. And knowing more about how we got here won't change a thing. We're here. Now. And we've been here for a very long time. Sooner or later you're going to have to let it go. *All of it.*"

Out of the corner of his eye, Rab noticed one of the Top-sider women approaching. In her arms, the woman was cradling a dozing Peter. Reluctantly, he let Cloud break free of his hold and move away.

"Is it true you want to leave this boy behind," she said, stopping in front of Rab.

Rab hadn't actually decided anything yet. That had been Fin's decision, but he was more concerned about Cloud right at that moment.

"Maybe," he said hurriedly, looking after Cloud. "I'd need to talk to the others first."

"I've spoken to Fin," the woman told him. "He still thinks it's the best thing to do. And I think Abby will agree if you do."

Rab wasn't so sure about that.

His hand made its way to his sleep-matted hair again. "I don't know," he said, unwittingly betraying his frustration.

"Fin says the boy's father is dead."

"Yes, he is," Rab agreed, struggling to focus. "He died before Peter was born."

"Then what will happen to the boy if you take him back?"

"I guess someone will take care of him."

"You?" the woman pressed him.

Oh, no. Not again. Cloud simply wouldn't have it. Rab shook his head. "Someone else."

"And then? I mean what will happen to him after he's grown?"

"He'll become a miner, I suppose. Like his father was."

"That's what Fin said, too," the woman replied soberly.

If she knew that, then why … oh, Rab understood. She was trying to pressure him into agreeing with Fin's decision. Well, why not? Peter would be sent to the mines. That's the way it was for humans in the Feather settlements. Peter's father had belonged to the Kun – personally – and whenever the Kun lost one of his workers, their son or daughter, if they had any, were slated to step up and replace them. Peter wasn't old enough yet, but in ten or so years, it would be a different matter.

Rab took a really good look at the little boy. He wasn't a particularly robust child, taking more after Willa than his father. And then his thoughts turned to delicate Neila – and Patch who, although slight, seemed to be holding his own among the Top-siders. Without Sunny, maybe he couldn't do it. But here, among the Top-siders, Peter would have Sunny – and this woman. With the Feathers, there'd be little he or anyone else could do to protect Peter.

He made his decision. And maybe Cloud would just agree with it, too. In the long run, it didn't matter, he supposed. Fin wanted the child to stay. He wanted the child to stay.

"If you want the child, he's yours," Rab said.

The woman's face brightened just enough for Rab to feel more comfortable with his decision. Her hand drifted towards the boy's fair head. "If you ever meet up with my band again – and I'm gone – and you want to see the boy, ask for Skylar's son. We're going to call him Gaige," she said, her voice betraying a little of the joy she was obviously feeling. "Is that all right?"

"You call him whatever you want," Rab said, offering up a hard-won smile as he reached out and touched one of the boy's dangling legs.

"Thank you," the woman said barely above a whisper and then, turning, hurried away.

Rab shook his head. She could have told him right from the start that she was Skylar's wife but she hadn't. If she'd thought it would have influenced his decision, she'd have been wrong.

"You're letting Peter stay?"

Rab spun around. How long had Fin been standing there behind him?

"It seemed the best thing to do." He glanced towards Cloud who, having returned their heap of bedding to the untidy pile, was attempting to get Tickie prepared for the journey ahead of them. "What do you think Cloud will say?"

"She'll agree," Fin said with confidence. "These are good people – basically. You forget we got to know a lot of them."

"Skylar's wife?" Rab asked.

"Yes," Fin replied. "A good forager then. I suppose she still is."

Rab hoped so. For Peter's sake, he hoped so.

"Seems Gift is coming with us," Fin said.

Rab turned around and looked towards the opposite side of the cave where Gift had spent the night. She was slinging the old pack she'd carried from the tunnels across her back.

"Did she say so?" Rab asked, turning back to Fin.

"Never said a word. In fact she hasn't spoken to me since we walked in here." He shook his head. "That girl is her daughter, isn't she? I mean we haven't got it wrong somehow, have we?"

"I don't think so. Besides, even Skylar implied it." He spotted Cloud approaching with Tickie and decided to forego any further talk of Gift and her decision.

"Tickie's ready," Cloud said on arriving. "But he wants to say goodbye to Skylar." Bending, she retrieved her pack.

"I'd like to, as well. Where is he?" Fin asked, scanning the cave. "I haven't seen him since last night."

Rab spotted him by the entrance to the cave and pointed. "There," he said, then glanced around, hoping to see Sunny and Patch again, but there hadn't been any sign of them this morning. "I guess there's nothing keeping us here then."

"No," Cloud agreed in that same curt manner she'd used with him before. "The sooner we leave, the sooner we can get back to Neila."

"Mamma?" Tickie said, brightening as he grasped Cloud's hand.

"That's right," she said, tightening her hold, and began to make her way to Skylar.

Rab, with Fin beside him, started after them.

"Your mother will be anxious to see you," Cloud was saying. "She and Pi'a'weh ran after you, you know, but they couldn't catch you."

"I went over the wall," Tickie said with a giggle as he hurried along beside Cloud.

"Yes, you did."

Skylar was waiting for them by the entrance. Rab thought about telling him of their decision to leave Peter behind, but doubtless the elder already knew.

"There are extra supplies here," Skylar said, gesturing towards a small pack at his feet.

"You keep it," Rab told him. "We'll make it back to the settlement with what we have."

"It's really yours anyway," Skylar reminded him.

"Next time you raid a settlement," Rab said, stooping to collect Skylar's parting gift, "just make sure you keep Sunny and Patch back at camp."

Skylar smiled and fell into step with them as they made their way through the tunnel that connected the cave to the outside.

Glancing back, Rab saw Gift bidding a solemn goodbye to Sandy. He turned away quickly before Gift could see that he was watching her. They were about halfway through the tunnel before Rab became aware that she'd tacked herself on to the rear of their little party.

Skylar left them at the entrance.

"You keep a lookout for those Qworkas," he called after them.

Instinctively Rab's eyes turned skyward, uncertain if the elder was joking. What was it about living top-side lately that had humans and Feathers seeing things that simply weren't there?

He was surprised when he looked down and saw Sunny and Patch standing ahead of them in the middle of a nearby thicket of urse. Perhaps they'd been sent out foraging again or maybe they'd come outside of their own accord. Then Patch waved at Tickie, betraying his motivation at least. Sunny, on the other hand, gave nothing away as she stood motionless among the urse, eyes locked on their departure.

As they passed, Rab refrained from looking back to find out how Gift had reacted to this perhaps final encounter with her daughter. Instead he turned his thoughts to Neila and that made him pick up the pace.

Soon Rab and Fin fell into an old pattern, each of them offloading their packs and alternating who carried Tickie. The boy was a bigger handful than Stitch had ever been. Perhaps Rab was just getting older. By the time they came to the patch of disturbed ground again, Rab was almost at his wit's end with Tickie's constant chatter and squirming. Fin wasted a little of their time searching around the site again, hoping to discover something they had missed before. But there was nothing more to find and so Rab pressed them on a bit harder, further into the darkness than he normally might have. It was Cloud who finally called a halt to the second day of their journey back to the settlement. She set about preparing their meal and the way she did it, with such distraction, left Rab with no doubt that something was stewing in her mind.

"I guess it's up to me," she said bluntly as Gift dumped an armful of gathered urse onto the ground beside the fire Fin had made.

Rab glanced at Fin hopefully, but the younger man simply shook his head.

"I thought you'd stay with the Top-siders," Cloud said, looking briefly at Rab and Fin. "I think it's safe to say we all did. So?" she prompted, turning to Gift. "Are you going to tell us or not?"

Gift lowered herself to the ground and began to work on the fire. "I can't see that's anyone's business but mine," she replied.

Rab couldn't fault her there but, like Cloud, he was also curious.

"I think it's mine, too," Cloud countered. "I'm the one who left Sunny behind and that's always been the trouble between you and me, hasn't it?"

While he had only figured that out recently, it appeared that Cloud had known it all along. Of the two of them, Cloud was undeniably the smarter, but Rab had always known that.

"And you think that gives you the right to question me about *my* decisions?" Gift asked, fixing her eyes on Cloud.

"Yes, I think it does. All these years you've blamed me for leaving Sunny with the Top-siders instead of bringing her to you. But now, when you have the chance to get her back, not only don't you try, you don't even speak to her."

"What would have been the point?"

"The point!" Cloud shot a look towards Rab. "Fine," she snapped after a moment and turned away. "Keep your secrets." She thrust some food towards Gift. "I really don't care anymore."

Casually, Gift took the food from Cloud's hand.

"I have no secrets," Gift said, studying the food in her hand. "The explanation is simple," she said, looking up. "Sandy raised Sunny as her daughter. She thinks Patch is her twin. What have I got to offer her?"

So, Sunny and Patch were more of a pair than Rab had even realised. Their stubborn attachment made even more sense now. And so, too, did Gift's response.

"Oh," Cloud muttered contritely. "And I suppose you're going to consider me responsible for that, too, now," she said, confidence building. "It was you who speared Pi'a'weh, not me. And if you hadn't done that, then you wouldn't have had to leave Sunny."

"And if Fin hadn't made the spear," Rab interjected, "Gift wouldn't have been able to spear him." Fin made to interject when Rab added "And I encouraged him. In the end, maybe we're all responsible for Gift's decision." Snapping a nearby branch of urse, he tossed it into the fire. It sputtered and then flamed, spending embers into the darkness. "So maybe we should all just leave it at that."

Through the drifting embers, he was aware of Cloud and Gift just sitting there, mutely looking at him. Perhaps he shouldn't have weighed in to their argument. Or perhaps he should have weighed in a long time ago.

Fin stood up, capturing Rab's attention. "Or maybe no one is responsible," he said soberly, stooping to collect a sleeping Tickie. "We don't always have the luxury of making a good decision. Sometimes all we get is the chance to make *a* decision and hope it's the right one."

He could have been talking about his own decision, Rab realised, the one he made to leave Neila behind and go chasing after Tickie.

"For what it's worth," Fin continued as he carried Tickie a safe distance from the fire. "I think Abby made the right decision when she left Sunny behind with Glint." Laying Tickie on the ground, Fin stripped off his coat and placed it over the slumbering child. "You forget, Gift, that we didn't even know if you and Rab were still alive." He started back to the fire. "I was there, too. It was also my decision, so if you want to blame someone, it should be both of us. But I think you are right, too," he added, folding himself back down onto the ground in front of the glowing fire. "It is best for Sunny to go on believing she's Sandy's daughter. Yes, it's a lie but the way things are," he shrugged, "it's a lie she's better off living right now."

Inwardly Rab flinched. They could have been Sunny Braham's words. 'Let the believers go on believing.'

She'd said that to him once and said it with such passion, it was almost as if she'd been warning him of the challenges ahead. And there had been challenges. She'd been right about that. Challenges to his courage, his resolve, his very spirit even – but those challenges had been faced and lost so very long ago.

Just what new challenge was Fin alluding to? Likely even he didn't know. They never did.

Chapter 10

TICKIE had worn out long before they came within sight of the settlement. Years ago, when he'd carried Stitch the same way, the muscles of Rab's neck and back had burned. Now, almost twenty years on, his muscles screamed just from the anticipation of having to take his turn carrying Tickie.

Cloud and Gift had fallen back into their practice of communicating with each other only when necessary. It seemed neither one of them had forgiven him for his interference. Perhaps they were just stewing on the things Fin had said. Either way suited Rab for the moment. Fin had little to say now, either, his thoughts clearly fixed on Neila. Rab was just as anxious to get back to the settlement – if only to get Tickie off his back. He tried not to think about what would happen to them on their return. Slaves weren't meant to wander off whenever they chose. There'd be a retribution. For all of them. Except Tickie, of course. But if Neila didn't recover, she'd be in no position to look after the boy. What would happen to him then? Rab was mulling over the possibilities when Cloud, who had moved up to take the lead, suddenly stopped walking.

Rab hurried up to her. They were almost home. Surely nothing could go wrong now.

"What's the matter?" he asked. His sudden dash had disturbed Tickie who began to squirm around on his back.

"There's something over there," she said, pointing south. "See it?"

Rab looked, spotted what appeared to be another enormous dust cloud and called for Fin to look south.

"Dust?" Fin shouted back.

It couldn't be another throng of human refugees. Even if a few stragglers had been left in the south, they wouldn't cause a cloud that large.

"What's going on?" Gift asked.

She'd been walking the slowest of them all, not surprisingly, since she had little incentive to hurry back to the settlement.

Rab pointed towards the latest ugly brown stain low on the southern horizon.

"If it's a dust storm, it's a big one. Can we make it to the settlement in time?" She glanced back the way they had come. "It's a long way back to any shelter."

"It's a fair way off yet," Fin said.

"Should we risk walking through the night?" Cloud was still looking south. "I mean," she said, swinging around to take in her three companions, "if we're close enough to the settlement, we should be able to see their fires when it turns dark."

The light from the few scattered stars in the sky couldn't pilot them. If they had paid more attention to the coming and going of the stars through the night sky, perhaps they might have been able to use them as a guide. It was an ancient technique the people of Earth had used; or at least that's what Rab had read. But maybe, on this new Earth where there were so few stars, it simply wasn't possible.

But Cloud was right; although they'd had to rely on Gift's younger eyes to spot the glow in the distance, the lights from the settlement fires were there. At first they showed as just tiny specks on the eastern horizon; but the specks grew progressively larger as they pressed on.

It was dawn, an insipid dust-choked dawn, by the time they came within sight of the settlement. The carts that had been clustered outside the walls had all been moved away, leaving the jagged workings of the new outer wall and the gathering of humans and Feathers outside it clearly visible. But there were more Feathers milling around outside the settlement than usual. Perhaps fifteen or so. Work on the new outer wall had progressed in the time they had been gone. The foundations had been completed and the first blocks that would form the base of the towering wall had already been laid. The humans were working on the rounded section on the southernmost side of the settlement but that wasn't where the Feathers' attention was directed. All were looking towards the approaching dust storm.

But why so many Feathers? The settlement had weathered dust storms before, and preparations generally amounted to a precautionary effort to get all foodstuffs, weapons, and tools under cover. It hardly took fifteen Feathers to coordinate that. Top-ranking Feathers at that; most of them had their fine feather cloaks draped about their shoulders.

"I don't think they're all waiting for us," Fin said dryly as he slipped Tickie from Rab's back and set him upon the ground.

No – but someone would be waiting for them.

Raising a shoulder, Cloud wiped some of the dust from her cheek. "What do you think they'll do to us?"

"Maybe they'll be too distracted by the dust storm to bother," Gift suggested.

Fin began to laugh. It was a hollow sound devoid of humour. "I wouldn't count on it. And before they do punish us, I want to say I'm sorry. I never intended for all of you to get involved. I had to find Tickie and bring him back. None of you had to come after me."

"We've stuck together so far, Fin," Rab said evenly. "Hardly the time to change that now."

Cloud touched Rab's arm. "They've seen us," she said, drawing his attention to the cluster of Feathers.

Actually four of them had seen them.

***

Cloud glanced constantly towards Rab as she walked, anxious but reluctant to speak in the presence of their cloaked escorts. Fin was taking it all in, too, head swinging first one way and then the other. Even Gift appeared mildly concerned, exhibiting a certain curiosity that had been absent since they'd left Skylar's encampment. Tickie was the only one who seemed calm, his sole interest by then, Rab supposed, returning to his mother and the familiarity of his own ts'un.

At first, as they'd made their way through the lanes towards the Kun's palace, Rab started to wonder if Gift might have been right after all. Apart from the four Feathers escorting them, no one, Feather or human, showed any interest in their return. The lanes of the settlement were buzzing. Feathers and humans were rushing about with a purpose Rab had only ever witnessed ahead of a rumoured Top-sider raid. Although dust storms frequently blew themselves out before reaching the settlement, resources were too precious to take the chance on the vagaries of the weather, so some advance preparations were to be expected. But no preparations had ever reached this kind of fever pitch before. Just what were the Feathers anticipating?

So Rab was both surprised and concerned when, at the base of the platform leading to the Kun's palace, it looked like they were about to be separated. Fin, Gift, Cloud and Tickie were led off to the left by three of the cloaked Feathers and when Cloud reached out, making a grab for Rab, he was roughly torn from her and hauled by a single Feather in the opposite direction. As he was drawn away from his companions, Rab glanced over his shoulder. Only Cloud looked back at him and she kept looking back at him until all seven of them had disappeared out of sight around the corner of the platform. Even if he could have made himself understood, Rab's escort wouldn't have explained why they'd been separated.

From the moment they had left the settlement, they'd known this time was coming. The only way to have avoided it was to have never returned at all. He and Cloud could have stayed with the Top-siders. Even Gift. Sure, it would have been awkward for her, living side by side with her daughter and, for the rest of her life, never revealing who she was. But what of Fin and Tickie? And Neila? In the end, it was just like Fin had said. Sometimes you don't get to make a good decision, only the *right* one. And coming back, *sticking together*, had been the right decision. Only now they weren't together, were they? And that was something Rab hadn't foreseen.

His Feather escort led Rab down the same lane they had used to reach Lilly's quarters, but his escort bypassed that entrance and kept walking, pulling Rab along beside him. As near as Rab could figure it, they were rounding the side of the palace, heading towards the rear. Finally the Feather stopped by a narrow door that, at any other time, would easily be overlooked. Button had used keys to unlock the door to Lilly's quarters but it appeared this Feather wasn't so privileged to have keys to unlock the door leading to the Kun's palace – even if it was only the back door. Instead he reached up, grasped the knotted end of a heavily-wound rope and pulled. A bell rang inside the compound and soon Rab could hear footsteps on the opposite side of the wall. The little door opened and Rab was obliged to stoop to pass through it. He turned, expecting his escort to follow, but the little Feather who had opened the door shut and bolted it immediately, leaving Rab's escort outside the palace walls.

"Now what?" Rab asked, turning to the Feather who had opened the door.

The Feather simply motioned for Rab to follow.

Lilly's quarters were elegant in comparison to the rear of the Kun's complex. Then, Rab supposed, he wasn't seeing the best section. The ground was nothing but dirt and the many ts'uns they passed were all crammed tightly together. This was probably the servants' quarters – and the most menial of the servants at that. As they neared the palace proper, the number of ts'uns became fewer and farther between until there were none at all – only a wide space that was, in some respects, reminiscent of Lilly's courtyard. Here was the stateliness Rab had been expecting; granted a simpler kind of stateliness when compared with the pictures he had seen of the gardens and courtyards that graced the palaces and temples and churches on Earth. But this wasn't Earth and what the Kun's gardeners had accomplished on a planet that, just a decade ago, had supported only the most humble forms of plant life, was nothing short of miraculous. Where Lilly had one tree, the focal point of her modest courtyard, the Kun had ten. And this was only the back side of the palace. Unfortunately Rab was in no frame of mind to appreciate it.

He didn't understand why they had been separated. And he didn't understand why he, in particular, had been brought to the palace to be informed of his punishment. It didn't bode well for him at all. The Feather who'd escorted him wasn't forthcoming with any explanation and the Feather who was now leading him through the dim labyrinthine corridors of the palace itself wasn't any more obliging.

He was brought to a room lit by a series of windows high in the walls, much like Lilly's quarters, only this room was very much larger. The floor was covered in brilliant white tiles that allowed the walls to ring with the echo of Rab's footsteps. The Feather beside him passed quietly. The soles of his Qworka-hide shoes must have been finely worked indeed, beaten and softened to such an extent they'd have been absolutely useless on the rocky ground outside the settlement.

In three places, the walls were adorned with weavings so large the tops of two of them reached the base of the high windows. The third weaving was as yet incomplete. Beneath it was an odd contraption that reminded Rab of the little loom Cloud used to use down in the tunnels, the one she'd work her fingers raw on as she rewove cloth for the tunnel-dwellers. The strange devise beneath the unfinished weaving was very likely a loom as well, crafted from large urse branches, its many arms probably hinged together with bolts forged in the settlement's furnaces – perhaps even by Fin. Loose threads were hanging from the underside of the loom, dangling in a tangled mess on the floor. Evidently as the completed weaving emerged on the other side, it was inched higher and higher up the wall. Whoever was weaving it was almost finished. Perhaps it wasn't so strange that the Kun adorned the walls of his palace but it did strike Rab as strange that two cultures, so widely separated as those on Earth and the Feathers who inhabited this planet, would choose similar ways to enhance their day-to-day life. Tapestries! That was the word he was trying to think of. Stranger still that the subjects they chose for their tapestries were so similar because, as impossible as it seemed, Rab thought he could remember the same quasi floral-like patterns on any number of the ragged and time-worn carpets he used to see in the tunnels.

Towards the end of the room was a haphazard array of large and thickly padded red cushions and, seated cross-legged upon one of those cushions, a Feather. There was a book lying open on the cushion in front of the Feather and between the opened book and the Feather's head another strange contraption the like of which Rab had never seen before — an oversized piece of glass suspended on arms and legs that, like the loom, looked to have been fashioned from the branches of a large urse. The Feather was peering through the glass, his focus on the book. At first Rab didn't recognise him. Without his fine cloak, the Kun looked just like any ordinary Feather. It was only when he drew closer that Rab could pick out the subtle differences in facial features that distinguished one Feather from another.

Unless he was deaf, the Kun must have heard Rab's approach but he gave no sign of it … not immediately. But after a long and silent pause, during which Rab's escort quietly backed away, the Kun finally raised his head. He waved his hand, but the wave hadn't been directed at Rab, so he stayed where his escort had left him, just beyond arm's reach of the cushion supporting the open book.

From a doorway to the left of the Kun, Lilly Benson emerged. Button came trailing after her and Rab wasn't at all surprised to see the familiar little stool in her hands. Until Lilly's entrance had distracted him from the tapestries and the little figure seated on the cushion, he hadn't noticed that five of the Kun's personal guards were standing in the dark, some distance behind the Kun, at the very head of the room.

So he had been ordered to a private audience with the Kun himself. Over the matter of his brief desertion of the settlement? That didn't seem likely.

Rab watched while, as was her custom, Button positioned Lilly's stool just to the left of the Kun, then stepped to the rear once Lilly was seated.

Rab almost jumped when the old woman, unbidden, began to speak.

"The Kun has been informed that you and a number of others left the settlement without permission. He wants to know why?"

Rab doubted that the Kun didn't already know.

"To retrieve two human children who were stolen during the raid."

As Lilly made a brief clicking sound, the Kun listened then uttered a few featherwords of his own.

Lilly nodded and turned again to Rab. "And that was the only reason?"

"Yes," Rab replied, puzzled.

"The Kun wants to know what you saw out there."

"Saw? Nothing other than what we always see. A lot of urse."

Again, Lilly translated for the Kun and then waited a moment for his reply.

"Then if urse is all you saw, the Kun is curious how you got that boy back."

"Does he mean did we see Top-siders? Well, yes, we saw a few, but we managed to steal Tickie away from them in the middle of the night. I can't tell him what's happened to them."

Technically the last at least was true.

"And you saw nothing else? No one else?"

"What else and who else is there to see?"

Lilly turned once again to the Kun, exchanging featherwords at some length, before she looked back at Rab.

"The Kun also wants to know what you've done with Itzeh's property."

Itzeh's property. By that, Rab assumed he meant Willa and her son.

"They're dead," Rab said without hesitation.

"Then you'll compensate Itzeh," Lilly said after a brief consultation with the Kun.

Rab supposed he should have enquired just how he was to do that but he really didn't care. His real concern was for Cloud and Fin and Gift – where they were – what was happening to them. He could sense the Kun's eyes trained on him over the top of that strange glass devise and so let his focus drift away from Lilly and settle directly on the Feather leader.

"The Kun also wishes me to inform you that you'll be punished for having left the settlement."

Rab shrugged, making a deliberate show of the gesture.

There were no details forthcoming about the method of his punishment, either. Maybe that kind of tactic worked on Feathers. It wouldn't work on him. Rab had spent most of his life ignorant of what would happen from one moment to the next. The Kun would get to it sooner or later.

"And so will the others," Lilly added.

Rab had expected that, too.

The Kun looked away and, raising his hand, waved it three times in rapid succession at Lilly. If a human had done that, Rab would have taken it as a gesture of impatience. With a Feather, it was hard to know.

"However," Lilly took up, "the Kun is aware that you have a particular skill and, before you're punished, he requires you to use it."

"Does he?" Rab snapped, startling Lilly.

Behind her, Button began to frown.

Lilly hurried on. "You can see that there's a book open in front of the Kun. He demands that you read it to him."

"All of it?" Rab asked with a heartless smile.

"It might be to your benefit to cooperate, Rab," Button said, stepping forward.

This was a strange day indeed. First an audience with the Kun – and now this – Button, who never ever interfered while Lilly was translating for the Kun, suddenly had something to say.

"How?"

"Just do it," Button said gently. "If not for yourself, then for the others."

Rab wanted to press Button further but had the impression that she had gone as far as she was willing, or perhaps permitted, to go.

"What does the Kun want to know about the book?" he asked instead, directing his question at Lilly, who immediately launched into another series of clicks and feathertalk.

"First, if it's the right one," Lilly said, addressing Rab. "The one that shows how you got here."

"How I got here?" He looked from Lilly to Button. "Does she mean how *we* got here? Humans?"

Button nodded.

"But you know that as well as I do. Why didn't you tell him?"

"Lilly told him where humans came from, Rab, but I believe that isn't what he wants to know. He wants to know how it's possible to travel from one planet to another."

"Button, I can't answer that."

"Then show him in those books."

"I wouldn't know where to look. They're all mixed up now. A lot have been burned. For all I know the ones that could have shown him *something*."

"I suggest you look, Rab. It's important."

The Kun made no attempt to silence Button. He'd been wrong before. For some reason, the Feather leader was willing to allow someone other than Lilly to speak on his behalf.

"Why? Why is it so important? It's not like these Feathers can do it. It'll be hundreds of years at least before they've progressed far enough and maybe even then they'll never achieve that sort of technology. And even if I did find something in one of those books, I'd never be able to explain how it was done. Even if I could, he wouldn't be able to understand it. Is this why he ordered the books not to be burned anymore? Because he simply has to know how we got here and he thinks the answer is in one of them?"

"It's more than curiosity, Rab."

Rab shook his head. "I'd like to be told what my punishment is now."

Button lowered her eyes and fell silent. A moment later, she raised them and turned to Lilly who began to translate for the Kun.

"Four seasons at the mine in punishment for leaving the settlement in addition to another season for the loss of Itzeh's property and another still for your refusal to read from the book, during which time you'll not be permitted to return to the settlement for any reason."

Six seasons!

"And the others? What is the punishment for the others?"

"That is between the Kun and them," Lilly replied.

Button spoke up again. "Rab, you may be able to reduce your punishment if you do what the Kun asks."

"I'll do what the Kun asks if he waives punishment for the others."

It was Button's turn to shake her head. "You can't ask Lilly to say that to the Kun."

"Then have her tell the Kun this. If he waives punishment for the others, I'll do better than show him a picture in a book. I'll show him the ship, itself."

"You said it was buried!" Button's small dark eyes flashed brightly.

"And so it is. But I'll take the Kun and whoever he wants to the place. It's up to them to dig it out."

As Lilly began to translate, Rab kept a keen watch on the Kun's face. His eyes might be the eyes of an alien but they betrayed the same sort of hunger as any human's eyes might when confronted with the chance to gain what they were seeking.

"The Kun agrees," Lilly said at last. "But if there's no ship, then your term at the mines will be doubled and the others' punishment will remain as it stands." Lilly rose from her stool. "You may return to your ts'un to prepare whatever you need for the journey, which the Kun has decided will begin at first light tomorrow morning."

"What if the dust storm prevents us from leaving?"

"I asked him that," Lilly replied hesitantly. "And his answer was that will be a great pity for you."

***

Rab raced back to his ts'un, marvelling at his luck. The Kun could just as easily have turned the bargain around on him, threatening to double the punishment for the others if Rab didn't take him to the ship. But he hadn't. Button was right. There had to be more than the Kun's curiosity involved. It was something bigger. Much bigger!

Rab pushed and shoved his way through lanes choked with Feathers and humans rushing to make preparations for the approaching dust storm. When he came within sight of his ts'un, Rab grew worried. There didn't look to be a soul inside. Had they never returned?

Then he heard someone calling his name. Swinging around, he saw Cloud waving towards him from the entrance of Fin's ts'un.

"I thought I might never see you again," she said, taking his face in her hands.

So had he … and it might come to that yet.

Reaching up, he drew her hands away from his face and, clasping one of them, led her inside Fin's ts'un.

"They can't have just let you go," she pressed him. "What happened?"

"In a minute." Releasing Cloud's hand, he made his way to the empty chair beside Neila's bed. "I ran all the way from the palace."

"The palace!" Cloud said.

Rab spared a glance for Neila and the others who were gathered inside Fin's ts'un. They were all there – Fin, Neila, Gift and Tickie, who was lying fast asleep beside Neila. There was no sign of Pi'a'weh but he must have been a constant visitor to the ts'un while they were away because Neila was sitting up in bed, looking almost well. Her legs were still bound but the bindings had been changed. They were clean and as neatly wound as Cloud herself could have done. Reaching out he took a gentle hold of Neila's hand and smiled. She squeezed his hand in reply.

"You first," he said. "Where were you all taken?"

Fin and Gift were standing together at the hearth. They couldn't have been back very long; Gift was holding a woody branch of urse in readiness for making a fire.

"To a place in one of the lanes behind the palace," Cloud explained. "One of the Kun's high-ranking attendants was there. I don't know his name —"

"I think it's Irikut," Fin interjected, then shrugged. "Doesn't matter, I suppose. We were all given the same sentence. Two seasons at the roosts."

Rab's heart sank. "All of you?" he pressed Fin.

"With the exception of Tickie, of course. He stays here."

Rab hadn't expected Cloud to be given the same punishment as the others.

"I can't believe they'd waste you that way," he said to Cloud.

"I'm to work directly under the overseer. They expect me to improve the yield of the crops there."

Rab didn't like her chances.

"When do you leave?" he asked.

"Tomorrow," Gift replied, tossing the branch into the hearth. "Unless the storm keeps coming."

"But what about you, Rab?" Cloud interrupted.

Rab glanced about the room, taking in each of his companions one by one. "None of you may have to serve out your full sentence," he said, "if I can give the Kun what he wants."

Gently Cloud lowered herself onto the edge of Neila's bed. "Just what is it he wants?" she asked suspiciously.

"Answers," Rab replied. "While you'll be walking south to the roosts, I'll be going north with a party of Feathers to the ship."

"That's the punishment they gave you?" she asked, wide-eyed with astonishment. "Taking them to the ship?"

Rab shook his head. "No. The punishment they gave me was six seasons at the mine. But I made a bargain with the Kun."

"You saw the Kun?"

"I *spoke* to the Kun. He agreed that if I take him to the ship, he'd waive your punishments."

Cloud's face collapsed into a worried frown. "But that makes no sense at all."

"I agree," Fin said, stepping away from Gift and the forgotten hearth fire. "There has to be more to it than that. There's something you're not telling us."

"All I know is that he's determined to understand how we got here." Freeing his hand from Neila, Rab waved it in the air. "How our ancestors got here anyway."

"Sounds like he's *desperate* to know, if you ask me," Neila muttered from her bed. "Well, it does," she insisted when the eyes of everyone in the room turned to her. "And if that's what it takes to waive all your punishments then I think you made the right decision, Rab."

Rab had made no arrangement with the Kun to waive his own punishment but now didn't seem the time to mention that.

"It can't do any of us any harm for the Feathers to see the ship," Neila continued as she looked from face to face. "What's in it? Nothing but wreckage and a couple of ragged and smelly books. At least that's what you've always told us, Rab."

"That is all there is — apart from the bodies of Sunny and Jacob Sloane," he added in afterthought.

When he'd made that deal with the Kun, he hadn't given any thought to the prospect of coming on those bodies again. In the end it was a small price to pay.

"They're not going to be much use to him," Fin observed coolly. "Neila's right. Take him if he wants to see it so badly. Maybe Pi'a'weh knows what's so important about the ship."

Pi'a'weh. Rab had almost forgotten about the strange little Feather.

"Where is Pi'a'weh?" he asked of Cloud.

She didn't respond. Her head was down and she seemed to be lost in thought.

"He was here when we got back, then left," Gift answered instead. "He said he'd see us before we left in the morning."

Rab turned to Neila. "He did what he promised and looked after you?"

"Yes," Neila replied. "He was here every day. Sometimes all day and all night."

"There's something really odd about that Feather," Fin said, leaning down to gently stroke the head of his sleeping child. "Why would he do that?"

At last Cloud looked up. "Can you find the ship again?" she asked before Rab could answer Fin.

"I think so."

He hoped so.

***

Rab caught only brief snatches of sleep that night. Although he suspected that Cloud would not sleep at all, she had eventually succumbed to exhaustion and drifted off into a deep sleep, her head cradled against his chest. His arm quickly went numb and the unpleasant taste of dust in the air caused his throat to feel dry and scratchy. For Cloud's sake, he suppressed each cough as it threatened to erupt and tried not to think about the tingling sensation in his right arm. Sometime before dawn he must have dozed off because he woke just as the first light was seeping through the entrance to their ts'un to find himself alone in the bed. Cloud was already up and moving about.

He watched her as she set about preparing for her transfer to the roosts. If he could locate the ship again, and perhaps more importantly if the Kun was satisfied with what he saw, then Cloud, Fin and Gift would soon be able to return to the settlement. If he couldn't find the ship, well …

Rab rose, made for the battered trunks that Cloud had already opened and started his own preparations. On the way to the ship, they'd pass close to the mines. The Kun probably wouldn't allow him to return to the settlement, just to travel north again to the mines. He'd be dropped off during the return. It meant he had to pack enough clothes to last for a number of seasons – not that he had much to choose from.

"Do you want anything to eat?" Cloud asked. She was standing by the table, stashing some vials of medicine into an open pack.

Rab shook his head, dumped his own full pack by the entrance and stepped out into the lane where dust was hanging like a pall in the air.

Most of his neighbours were already about their business. Some, the majority in fact, had cloths tied over their noses and mouths. The dust storm wasn't going to blow itself out; it was going to come relentlessly on from the south. The roosts lay to the south. Surely the Feathers wouldn't force-march Cloud, Gift and Fin – and themselves – directly into it. The ship, however, was located to the north; the storm wouldn't delay *his* departure.

For as far as Rab could see down the lane, the tiny garden patches outside the ts'uns were covered over with cloth. Some of his neighbours had even hung tattered strips of cloth over the entrances to their ts'uns, little protection if the storm came in with a vengeance. But so far this storm had made slow progress. When it finally arrived, more than likely it would seep, rather than gust, into the settlement – much like the fogs that sometimes crept up from the river into Rab's old village. Without a driving wind behind it, the damage wouldn't be as severe but there'd still be losses, especially to the small stands of crops that fought to survive in the poor soil inside the settlement.

Fin was standing in the entrance of his ts'un. Like Rab, he was looking down the lane, waiting on the arrival of the guards who would lead them away in their very separate directions. Noticing him, Fin waved and started walking towards Rab.

"Where do you think they are?" he asked. "I expected them by now, didn't you?"

"Maybe it's the storm," Rab suggested.

Fin's gaze wandered towards his ts'un. "Then maybe we won't be leaving today. Neila has taken this pretty hard, but Gift seems to be able to talk to her." He shook his head. "I wish they hadn't made Gift come with us. I'd have been happier leaving Neila with her than with Pi'a'weh."

Whatever his motivation, Pi'a'weh had been diligent in his care of Neila so far and Rab didn't see any reason to doubt the little Feather's dedication now. He was about to say as much when he noticed a Feather hurrying towards them.

"Here they are now," he said instead.

But something was amiss. There was only one Feather. Maybe one was enough to escort Cloud, Gift and Fin to the outer wall where they'd be met by their guides – and maybe one Feather was enough to escort him to the Kun and his party – but surely they wouldn't have sent only one Feather to do both tasks. Besides, the Feather looked too small to be a scout or a guard and he limped as he loped along.

It was Pi'a'weh – come to look after Neila. But why was he moving so quickly?

"Are they here?" Cloud asked, placing a hand on Rab's shoulder as she stepped up behind him.

"Just Pi'a'weh. Maybe you won't be going," Rab said hopefully. "With this storm and all ..."

"They haven't come for you, either, Rab. Do you think the Kun could have changed his mind? It's not like he'd be in a hurry to tell us."

"Pi'a'weh's in a hurry to tell us *something*," Fin interjected. "But I've never known him to bring the Kun's messages."

"Come," Pi'a'weh called to them loudly as he darted this way and that out of the path of Rab's neighbours.

"What's he saying?" Fin muttered.

Pi'a'weh stumbled towards them. When the Feather grasped his arm, Rab wasn't sure if he was attempting to convey some urgency or stop himself from falling over.

"Ask him in Feather," Cloud suggested.

Pi'a'weh could jabber on forever and they'd never get to the bottom of it. Rab waited impatiently as Fin and Pi'a'weh clicked and feathertalked backward and forward. If there was some new impending disaster, no one else seemed to be aware of it.

"He says that we have to come with him. That he's going to take us some place safe," Fin explained.

From the tone of Fin's voice, Rab was guessing he hadn't made much sense of the Feather's appeal, either.

"All of us," Fin added.

"But what about the escorts?" Cloud said. "They'll expect us to be here. We can't just hide somewhere forever."

Fin asked. His speech still sounded quite strange but Rab had grown accustomed enough to feathertalk to know that Fin was rushing through the words. Pi'a'weh replied just as hurriedly.

"He said he doesn't have time to explain."

Why was Rab not surprised?

"He said that the escorts won't be coming. For any of us."

"Because of the storm?" Cloud prompted, leaning around Rab to ask the Feather herself.

Pi'a'weh nodded.

"What do we do?" Fin asked hesitantly.

"What he says," Rab and Cloud answered in unison.

When Cloud made to rush back into their ts'un, presumably to grab their supplies, Pi'a'weh sprung forward to stop her. "No," he barked and sped them off towards Fin's ts'un.

Gift's head snapped up when they burst through the entrance.

"What's the matter?" she asked, making a lunge for Tickie behind her.

Neila was seated on the edge of the bed, her bandaged legs hanging limply to the floor.

"Fin, you get Neila," Rab said. "Gift, pick up Tickie. Pi'a'weh says we have to move quickly."

"Why?" she asked, hoisting the boy into her arms.

"I don't know." He would have said more but Cloud grasped his arm.

"I have to go back and get some medicine. For Neila," she said, anticipating Rab's next question as she dropped her hand and then rushed past Pi'a'weh through the entrance.

"Tell him she won't be long," Rab charged Fin.

They met up with Cloud in the laneway. She had a pack thrown carelessly over one shoulder.

"I hope we're not going too far," Cloud said as Pi'a'weh began to hurry them away. "Fin can't carry Neila for too long and it isn't good for her legs to be bumped around like that."

Neila was a small woman and so far Fin wasn't struggling to carry her across his arms. Gift was doing fine, too, cradling Tickie as Pi'a'weh had them almost running down the lane. But they couldn't keep it up for very long. He and Cloud could spell them but even that had its limitations.

"I wish I knew what this was all about," Cloud protested. "It's just a dust storm. And there isn't even much wind."

Rab relieved Cloud of her pack. "Pi'a'weh seems to think there's an emergency. I guess we'll find out what it is when he's ready to tell us."

"Where the hell is he taking us?" Fin called ahead.

They were heading directly towards the core of the settlement. All around them Feathers and humans were making the final preparations for the impeding storm. As in their own ward, the entrances of many of the ts'uns had been covered with cloth and every lane had been emptied of the usual scattering of possessions. Rab was beginning to suspect that some Feathers knew a bit more than others about what was really going on – Pi'a'weh, in particular. That, in itself, went against everything Rab had always assumed about Pi'a'weh's position in the settlement.

Where Pi'a'weh was taking them turned out to be the lane to Lilly's quarters. At the entrance, the little Feather stopped and, drawing a set of keys from inside his Qworka-skin vest, began to unlock the door. Rab took the moment to relieve Gift of Tickie. Fin seemed to be managing well enough with Neila and Rab doubted he'd be of a mind to entrust her to anyone else.

The wooden door swung open. "In," Pi'a'weh ordered with a flourish of one multi-jointed hand. The last to enter, he stopped to secure the door again behind him.

"That p'ace," he said pointing past the central tree in the courtyard to the right – Button had told them it was the cook's quarters.

Pi'a'weh didn't appear the least concerned by the racket they were making in the courtyard. Instead he wrenched open a small door that was niched midway along the wall and proceeded to shove each of them inside.

Rab found himself in a corridor that, like the Kun's and Lilly's quarters, was lit by a row of rectangular openings near the ceiling. But the corridor was long and narrow and the internal wall so close and unadorned that Rab quickly grew claustrophobic. All he wanted was to reach the end of that corridor.

"A kitchen!" Gift complained, when they finally emerged into an open space. "Why have we been brought to a *kitchen*?"

The place Pi'a'weh had brought them was indeed a kitchen and, except perhaps for the Kun's, probably the finest one to be found within the settlement. The room was also exceptionally tidy and the way the canisters and cups and plates were all stacked so neatly spoke of the same sort of care Cloud took when she ordered her miserable supply of medicines and cooking wares. But why would Pi'a'weh bring them there so urgently?

Wordlessly Pi'a'weh crossed the floor and, bending awkwardly, began to work on a large metal ring attached to one of the rough floor tiles. Rab handed Tickie to Gift and, crouching beside Pi'a'weh, wrapped his fingers around the ring next to Pi'a'weh's long fingers and pulled. The crude tile lifted easily and a rush of colder air immediately hit Rab in the face. With it came a smell like old *ungtilis*.

Pi'a'weh pointed down into the void.

Rab looked through the dimly lighted opening into an underground room where at least one lamp must be burning.

From his crouched position over the open trap door, Rab glanced back into the kitchen – towards Gift, who was still cradling Tickie and beginning to look more like her old determined self again – towards Fin whose sole concern at that moment seemed to be keeping Neila safe in his arms – towards Cloud, who was regarding him anxiously.

It all came down to trust. Trust in Pi'a'weh and trust in his intentions. If they did what he asked, they could end up trapped in that underground room. Alone Pi'a'weh might not be able to hold them there but the glowing lamp suggested that others were down in the room already.

Out in the lane, beyond the sturdy walls of Lilly's quarters, a Feather was barking orders. The gruff command seemed to agitate Pi'a'weh even further.

"Go," he pleaded with a leading click.

"*Someone* make a decision," Gift said shortly. "I vote for going down there."

"So do I," Fin added hastily. "Neila swears Pi'a'weh is our friend."

He seemed to be.

"We go," Cloud declared.

She was the first to put a foot onto the narrow stone steps. Gift followed, but the steps simply weren't wide enough for Fin to descend carrying Neila. He passed Neila to Rab and began to descend the steps, turning part-way down to take Neila as Rab lowered her feet-first into the hole. And so Neila was passed down the steep stairway – from Rab to Fin – from Fin to Gift, who'd been obliged to set Tickie free – and finally from Gift to Cloud. There was enough light for Rab to see that Neila had been delivered safely to Cloud at the base of the steps. He motioned for Pi'a'weh. The floor tile needed to be put back into place and Pi'a'weh probably wasn't up for the job.

Rab descended after Pi'a'weh into a space that was dominated by the grotesque shadows of its occupants edging up the earthen walls, courtesy of the six or so oil lamps scattered about the room. The smell was even stronger now: a heavy blend of *ungtilis* and Qworka fat from the lamps. He found his companions gathered in a circle beneath a low ceiling of precious wood. The boards looked ancient, warped. More rare relics salvaged from a place far away and a time long ago?

His companions were blocking Rab's vision into the farthest recess of the little room but he had the immediate impression that Fin, Cloud and Gift had seen something they hadn't expected. When Rab pushed past Pi'a'weh to find out for himself, the last thing he thought he'd see was Lilly and her constant companion, Button, sitting huddled together on a pile of Qworka-skin bags in the far corner of the room.

Rab turned accusingly on Pi'a'weh. *"What have you done to them?"*

Pi'a'weh made to step backward, stumbled and might have fallen had one of the pillars that supported the floor above not been directly behind him.

"Don't hurt him," someone shouted.

Rab spun around to find Button rushing forward.

"He brought us down here for our safety. Just like he brought you. Pi'a'weh," she said, grasping the Feather's arm protectively, "Rab just doesn't understand." Then she did the most extraordinary thing, as far as Rab was concerned anyway, and launched into a short but expertly delivered dialogue with Pi'a'weh in Feather.

Button spoke Feather! First Fin and now Button. These younger ones had their secrets. What was going on? What *had* been going on?

"Care to explain," Rab said once Button had finished talking and Pi'a'weh began to relax.

"Yes, I'd certainly like an explanation," Cloud sang out, stepping forward. "You speak Feather better than Fin. Even better than Lilly by the sounds of it," she said, confirming Rab's observation, "so why is it that Lilly always interprets for the Kun? And why have we been brought down here? Was that Lilly's or your idea?"

"I'll answer your last question first," Button said. "It was Pi'a'weh's idea to bring you down into the cellar. He brought us down here, too – for our safety, like I said. As for me speaking Feather," Button shrugged. "Not even the Kun knows that. Only Lilly and Pi'a'weh know. Though sometimes I think Lilly forgets."

Cloud turned to Rab whose patience had finally been shredded.

"That's not much of an explanation," he objected angrily.

"No, I know it isn't," Button agreed. "But we're going to be here for a while and …" she glanced towards the woman in Fin's arms "… Neila, isn't it? She looks like she needs to rest. I suggest you all pull up some bags and get comfortable."

"Come and sit," Lilly called from the corner. "We have food and water and light for as long as we need it."

Cloud sighed, then reached down to take Tickie's hand. "Might as well do like she says. I get a feeling we *are* going to be down here a while."

Lilly was even smiling now as she sat there, a cup of something in one hand, motioning towards them with the other.

Rab glanced around, seeking Pi'a'weh. The little Feather was regarding him warily. Well, he had reason to be wary. But then so, too, did Rab. Nothing made any sense – least of all why Pi'a'weh seemed to think it necessary for them to shelter underground when they had weathered so many dust storms largely unprotected in the past. One thing was sure; before he left this room, Rab intended to get some answers.

Chapter 11

"YOUR cook!" Cloud said with a vehement shake of her head. "No. I can't believe that."

It was Button who had said it. Pi'a'weh was their cook. Had been their cook ever since they'd been removed to the settlement. It did explain how Pi'a'weh had been free to come and go as he pleased and why he'd been able to dedicate so much time to Neila's care.

But a cook? *To doq'iri?* Either Lilly was more highly regarded or the little Feather even less regarded than any of them had already assumed. Rab was betting on the latter. But why? Had his injuries somehow diminished his worth? If so, then Gift had a lot more to answer for than the wounds she had inflicted on his body. But Pi'a'weh didn't seem to bear Gift any malice. Rab would have. Damned certain he would have!

Seated on an overfilled Qworka-skin bag across from Rab, Button was nodding her head.

"It's the truth. And it was Pi'a'weh who taught me to speak Feather."

Now Rab was beginning to wonder if Pi'a'weh might have had a hand in Fin's education as well.

Cloud flipped a hand, dismissing Button's claim. "Then why didn't *you* ever translate for the Kun?" Her focus darted briefly towards Lilly. "Instead of my mother?"

Rab started. It had been a long time since Cloud had referred to Lilly as her mother. She wasn't. Even Button knew that now.

"It was the smart thing to do. Even Pi'a'weh thought so. The Kun knew Lilly could understand him. He didn't know I could. In fact it was Pi'a'weh's idea *not* to tell him."

Lilly, who was sharing the Qworka-skin bag with Button and nursing that same cup, looked calm and relaxed, the way she always looked whenever she was the mistress of her faculties.

"And the Kun doesn't inform the Feathers about everything," Button was saying.

"That's so," Lilly agreed, the clarity of her voice a perfect match for her current demeanour.

"Last night a runner came in from the roosts."

"That's not unusual," Rab said with a shrug.

"No. But the news he brought was and I was there to hear it."

"You just happened to be there?" Rab challenged her.

Button nodded. "Yes. As it turned out. I was finishing up one of the weavings —"

"You!" Rab interrupted. "It was you who made those weavings I saw?"

"What weavings?" Cloud asked, leaning forward.

"In the palace. In the room where I was taken. There were three large weavings on the walls."

"They're mine," Button agreed. "I don't just serve Lilly," she said, turning a kind eye to the old lady. "I serve the Kun, too. Usually as his weaver." She smiled. "See, Cloud? I did learn some of the things you tried to teach me."

"You weave for the Kun!" Clearly Cloud was having a hard time believing it.

"Yes, and last night I was weaving for him when that runner came in. And that's how I know that dust storm out there is no ordinary dust storm."

"Well?" Rab prompted.

"It's another migration."

Seated together on another of the Qworka-skin bags, Fin and Gift exchanged disbelieving glances.

"But not of the Kun's people," Button went on. "Of his enemies. Oh, they're Feathers, too," Button hurried to add, reading the expression on Rab's face, "but of a different race to the Kun. Judging from what I overheard, they must have reached the roosts during the night. So — depending on how fast they're travelling, they'll be here sometime today."

"Are you sure you understood correctly? That doesn't sound possible."

"I'm sure," Button said with an indulgent smile. "And so was Pi'a'weh when I told him what I'd overheard."

"But where have they been all this time?" Fin asked, speaking up.

"Pi'a'weh calls them the ata'iri, the *southern people*. At least that's what I understood. And I guess it explains where they've been all along."

"I don't suppose there was any mention of why these ata'iri have suddenly decided to move north?" Rab asked. He was still of a mind to doubt Button.

"Same reason the the Kun's did?" Gift suggested from her perch before Button had the opportunity to answer.

"Probably," Button agreed. "I asked Pi'a'weh but all he'd tell me was that they were the ata'iri, that they've been enemies of the Kun for a long time, and that we should go to safety because once they get here, and they *will* get here, they'll attack the settlement."

"Attack it!" Rab leaped to his feet. "Button, Pi'a'weh is telling you stories. I don't know why, but he has to be."

Button shook her head, then looked about, seeking the little Feather on the far side of the room. It seemed to Rab as though he was appraising the bags and canisters of food that were stored there.

"Pi'a'weh is no friend of the Kun," she said softly, intending for Pi'a'weh not to hear her. "I don't know why. He wouldn't tell me that, either."

That at least rang true. Why would Pi'a'weh, having been made the servant of two low caste doq'iri, not bear animosity to the Kun?

"What about white Qworkas?" Rab asked, growing increasingly suspicious. "Did the runner say anything about white Qworkas?"

Button's brow furrowed. "White Qworkas?" she said. "I've never heard anything about white Qworkas. The Kun did talk about metal Qworkas at one of the Assemblies, but he instructed Lilly not to translate that information. What's the matter?"

"*Metal* Qworkas? Are you sure?"

"Yes."

"Not white?"

"No. Why are you …"

"Metal, not met'ah," Rab muttered. "I heard him wrong."

Metal! That's what Cloud claimed Pi'a'weh had said. He could feel her staring in satisfaction at him now.

"Heard *who* wrong?" Button asked.

Rab seated himself back down and nodded towards the Feather across the room.

"That's odd," Button said, following Rab's gaze. "Why would he tell you about that?"

"There's a lot Pi'a'weh does that I don't understand," Rab said.

"I wonder if that's what Skylar's been seeing," Fin suggested.

"Who's Skylar?" Button asked.

"The elder of the Top-sider band who had Tickie. He said they'd seen strange Qworkas off in the distance."

"Well, I'd like to know why the Kun felt it necessary to keep news of these *metal* Qworkas from us," Cloud interrupted. "And what *is* a metal Qworka anyway?"

"No one knows," Button replied.

"Maybe that's the reason he didn't tell us," Fin observed. "Can't have lowly doq'iri thinking the mighty Kun isn't in complete control of everything."

"And he's not," Button agreed. "Far from it."

"I believe Pi'a'weh," Gift said, breaking her extended silence. "And I believe that he did bring us down here for our safety. These ata'iri, or whatever they're called, are coming. And when they get here, they will attack – just like Pi'a'weh says."

Just as she finished speaking, a great commotion erupted over their heads.

Rab looked up towards the ceiling, not that the dark and bare underboards of the kitchen above could tell him anything.

"We should be up there," he said, then stood up again. "If Pi'a'weh is right and the settlement is being attacked, then we have to defend it. If not for the Feathers, then for our own people." He glanced towards Fin, seeking his support, but Fin just turned away and reached out to clasp Neila's hand.

"No," Pi'a'weh shouted, rushing from the far side of the room.

He had to have been listening to every word they said.

"Rap go," he wheezed, touching Rab's shoulder with his thin hand, "Them go." Lifting his hand, he pointed at Cloud, then signalled towards Fin and Gift with the same finger.

"He's right," Gift said. "If it's one, it's all."

Rab looked long and hard at Neila. He could make the decision for himself. He couldn't make the decision for her – not for Cloud, either. Or Fin and Gift. And if he left the safety of the cellar, he'd be forcing the three of them to leave with him and possibly sealing Neila's fate forever. If the size of that dust cloud were any indication of the numbers that were about to bear down on them, then what were the chances all of them would survive?

"Wait," Pi'a'weh said more calmly now, then with a light pat of that delicate hand to his chest, began to speak in Feather.

Rab turned to Fin when the little Feather had finished.

"He said we should stay here," Fin told them, "because we're going to win."

***

Rab knew that his pacing was beginning to irritate Cloud, but even hitting his head three times on the low ceiling hadn't convinced him to sit down. He couldn't. Not when there was so much noise overhead. Just as Button had warned them, the settlement had come under attack and Rab's mind was running with images of what must be happening in the lanes and alleyways above them. He could put his hands to his ears as Tickie had done but that wouldn't block it out. The shouts and cries and the thumps and thuds caused by the tumbling of bricks and stone as the invaders poured through each ward, smashing every ts'un they came to, would still be there whether he could hear it clearly or not. And the ancient wood of the floor above him would still reverberate with the sound, showering dust onto everyone below.

Pi'a'weh had said they would win, but Rab just couldn't see it. The humans and Feathers in the settlement were surely outnumbered. And meanwhile their little band was just sitting, safe in their underground refuge, waiting for the carnage to be over. Even if Pi'a'weh was right and they did win, nothing could be the same again. The way they lived wasn't ideal but through it all there'd been one compensation: save for sporadic Top-sider raids, until now they'd benefited from a certain kind of peace.

Although Rab had pressed him about these ata'iri, Pi'a'weh had declined to say anything more. Maybe he simply didn't know anything more.

"Will you please sit down," Cloud grumbled at Rab once again. "You're upsetting Tickie."

"You're upsetting *me*," Fin interjected. "There's nothing we can do. Even if we had gone up to fight, do you think five or even six of us," he amended, glancing at Pi'a'weh, "could make any difference? He seems to think it will be all right. And he knows about these other Feathers. We don't. Maybe they're bad fighters or something," Fin added with a shrug. "Maybe their weapons are inferior. Either way, we wait it out. For however long it takes."

"If he knows so much, why is he refusing to tell us?" Rab countered. "Something isn't right here."

"Now that's an understatement if I ever heard one," Cloud said, rising to see to Neila.

They'd had Neila lie down on two Qworka-skin bags pushed together. She'd claimed she was comfortable enough but she never had settled completely. The flight down into the cellar had been too much for her. For her sake, Rab found an empty bag beside Gift and sat down.

"Finally," he heard Cloud mutter above the muffled shouts and pounding overhead.

"I agree with you," Gift said faintly, surprising him. She'd had little to say since the decision had been made to remain in the cellar. "Pi'a'weh knows more than he's telling. But I agree with Fin, too. The few of us here can't make any difference. I know you think you owe those people up there. I'm not so sure that you do. When Glint first took me from that roost, I thought I'd never stop crying but then, you know, in the end, I think I was treated far better by those Top-siders than I ever would have been down in the tunnels. I don't owe *these* people. And, as I see it, there aren't many you owe, either. Those few old ones who befriended you are dead now …" she glanced at Lilly, "except for her. When it comes down to it, it's the people down here you owe, isn't it? Cloud. Fin and Neila. Even him," she added, gesturing towards Pi'a'weh who had stationed himself at the base of the stone stairs. He'd been there since Rab had agreed to stay and showed no signs of shifting.

By and large, Gift had spoken the truth. But there were some – a precious few who had been left above. Like Nat who had worked beside him first at the mines and then, just recently, on the outer walls. And Layne – she'd always taken the time to speak to him, offer some token from her scant garden whenever he passed her ts'un. They were the ones Rab couldn't stop thinking about; they were the ones he was letting down. He could argue the point with Gift and likely she would understand. But what was the use? Just like Pi'a'weh had said, if he left the safety of the cellar, then Cloud, Fin and Gift would leave, too. Maybe even Button. That price was too high to pay.

"Perhaps you're right," Rab answered half-heartedly, conceding that he needed to put an end to a futile discussion. He'd made the decision, hopefully the right one even though he could never accept it was a good one. Now he just had to live with it.

"I'll get you something for the pain," Cloud said, interrupting Rab's thoughts.

She was still bent over Neila, the little woman's hand clutched in hers.

"No. I don't like the taste of it."

Rab watched as Cloud glanced hopefully over at Fin, seated on another skin bag beside her.

"Just a little, Neila," Fin said.

Rab went to retrieve the small pack Cloud had brought with her, fished around inside it and found the right vial.

"Here it is," he said, taking the vial to Cloud.

Button and Lilly were studying every move Cloud made. What were they thinking? How inconvenient it would be should Neila up and die on them while they were all still trapped underground? Or did they feel some real concern for Fin's wife? It was hard to know. Lilly wasn't the same woman he had once known and he had never really got to know Button at all.

Lifting the vial, Cloud placed the rim to Neila's lips and tapped the side of the vial once, very swiftly, with one finger.

"Now swallow, Neila," Cloud instructed.

Neila's mouth distorted and she shook her head.

"Water will help," Cloud said and blindly grabbed the cup that was sitting on the floor behind her.

"No!" Button jumped quickly to her feet. "That's Lilly's cup," she said, snatching the cup from Cloud's hand. "I'll get her some water."

"That was strange," Cloud said to Rab once Button had walked out of earshot. She was on the other side of the room, siphoning water from a large cask into a different and larger cup. "What difference does it make which cup Neila drinks from?"

Rab turned to Lilly. "Well," he said, "what difference does it make, Lilly?"

But Lilly only shrugged and replied, "That one is mine."

So they had just been informed!

Button stepped up with the new cup. "This one is easier to use," she said, steadily eyeing Rab, and placed the filled cup into Cloud's outstretched hand.

Cloud lifted Neila's head and managed to get her to take a few sips. The cup, when she brought it away, was still almost full.

"Purple mushroom?" Fin asked when Neila's eyes slowly began to close.

Cloud nodded and edged away, grabbing Rab's arm. As he stepped away, Rab had seen pain, like a crippling mist, ebb and then vanish from Neila's face.

Reclaiming her old place, Cloud motioned for Rab to join her. "I hope she can sleep through this noise," she said, glancing as had become their habit towards the low ceiling. "What do you think is happening up there? It sounds bad."

Rab was about to reply when another loud crash sounded and then resounded overhead. Tickie came running up – Rab wasn't sure from where – and launched himself into Cloud's lap.

"It's all right, Tickie," she said, brushing the fresh dusting of grit from his hair. "It'll be over soon and we can all go back up to the surface."

"When?" Tickie pressed her. "I don't like it here."

Me, either, Rab thought, and looked once again towards the ceiling. As he glanced back down his gaze happened to catch Pi'a'weh's. The little Feather hadn't moved from his spot by the stairs for a long time now. Sooner or later they were going to have to eat and Rab wondered if they were supposed to wait for Pi'a'weh to decide when that should happen. Then again, maybe the Feather didn't care one way or the other how much they scavenged among the supplies in his store room. Rab stood, keeping his eye on Pi'a'weh. The Feather's head tilted up just enough for Rab to know that the little Feather was keeping an eye on *him*. Probably had been the whole time. Did he think Rab might try to make it past him? Oh, he'd thought about it, fleetingly, but he'd already made the decision to stay.

"It must be getting dark by now," Rab said. "I'll see about getting us some food."

As he crossed in front of Pi'a'weh, the Feather rose from the step he'd been sitting on. Another bass rumble shook the ceiling and by the time Rab looked back down, Pi'a'weh had slipped past him. Rab found him over by the food bins, already making preparations for their meal.

***

It was the smell of smoke that woke Rab. At least, that's what he assumed it must have been because somehow, amid all the commotion, it seemed he'd fallen asleep. There were no loud noises now, only a kind of low-pitched droning sound – and the smell of fire.

"Get up," Rab shouted.

He wasn't the only one who had fallen asleep.

"What?" Cloud mumbled, lifting her head from a Qworka-skin bag battered shapeless from her restless sleep.

"There's fire somewhere," Rab said, quickly scanning the room, anxious should Tickie have kicked over one of the oil lamps during the night.

But all the lamps were there exactly where he had last seen them, although two of his companions were not. Button and Pi'a'weh were missing.

"What's burning?" Fin rasped as he bent to gather Neila from her makeshift bed.

"It isn't down here," Rab replied in relief. "The settlement must be on fire."

"Then we're getting out of here right now," Cloud announced as she made a grab, first for her little pack, and then for Lilly's left arm. "Come on," she urged, dragging the old woman onto her feet. "We can't afford to be trapped down here. Where's Tickie?" she asked, swinging her head around wildly before pointing with her free hand towards the food bins. "There!"

Rab darted across the room to collect him. "You all right, Fin?" he asked, stopping at the base of the stairs before making the ascent with Tickie in his arms.

"For the moment," Fin called back, "but I'll need help getting Neila up the steps."

"Got to get the trap door open first," Rab sang back then, looking up, realised that the trap door leading to the kitchen above was already open.

A square of red-tinged light filtered down through the opening from the floor above, confirming not only that it was daytime but that the settlement was on fire.

They stopped once they reached the courtyard, partly to allow Neila to rest after the ordeal of being manhandled up the steep and narrow staircase, but mostly, Rab suspected because, like him, they were both desperate and reluctant to discover what lay beyond the high walls of Lilly's quarters. They'd barely started off again when the door leading to the lane burst open and Button was pushed inside. Pi'a'weh stepped in after her, taking pains to close and bolt the door once again from the inside.

The first thing Rab noticed was Button's bound hands. The second was the blood-drained pallor of her face. It was the shock of Button's appearance that had made him slow to notice Pi'a'weh's attire. Before he'd left the safety of Lilly's quarters, Pi'a'weh had taken the time to don his old feather cloak. The last time Rab had seen it was the day they had delivered Pi'a'weh back to his people. The cloak was ragged, tattered, its once fine feathers marred by a large dark stain – Pi'a'weh's long-dried blood.

"Win," Pi'a'weh said, turning from the door to address those gathered in the courtyard. Again he tapped his chest just a fraction above that dark black stain, repeating the gesture he had made down in the cellar.

Rab made to hurry forward but Button raised her bound hands to stop him. "I …" she began, stammering, then her gaze fell on Tickie who was now cradled in Cloud's arms.

"You can't let the boy go out there," she said with an addled shake of her head before she turned to Pi'a'weh and raised her bound hands again, this time directly in front of his face.

Rab watched as Pi'a'weh withdrew something from inside his clothing – a knife that, from a distance, looked like an ordinary kitchen knife – and proceeded to cut though Button's bonds. They fell, forgotten, at her feet. Freed, Button darted across the courtyard, heading for Lilly who, while Rab's attention had been distracted, had come forward to sit on the raised edge of the well.

"Are you all right?"

"Fine," Lilly replied, placing a hand to Button's face when she sat down beside her, "but I'm thirsty."

Rab left Button there, promising to find Lilly something to drink, and struck off to intercept Pi'a'weh. The Feather had begun to cross the courtyard but pulled up swiftly the moment he realised Rab was coming for him.

"Why were Button's hands bound like that?" Rab shouted. "What's really going on out there?"

"Leave him alone!"

Behind Rab, Button's voice rang out in alarm.

"He had to do it, otherwise I wouldn't have been able to go out."

"What are you talking about?" Rab demanded, swinging on Button. "He just said we won."

Button shook her head. "Go out and see for yourself," she said. "Pi'a'weh will take you. It's safe enough for you but not for the little boy."

"Safe enough!" Cloud barked. "How can it possibly be safe? The settlement's on fire!"

"Not anymore," Button replied, grasping Lilly's hand. "It's mostly just smoke now from the ts'uns in the southern ward. The northern and eastern wards were hardly touched."

And the western ward was already in ruins from the recent Top-sider attack. At best, roughly half the settlement was lost.

"Go with Pi'a'weh and see for yourself. The rest of us will stay here to look after Neila and the boy until you come back."

"If Rab's going, I'm going," Cloud said, lowering Tickie to the ground.

Gift began to round the well. "So am I."

Fin was still holding Neila in his arms and now had Tickie tightly clutching his leg. "I'll stay," he said with obvious hesitation.

It was best.

Rab walked, with Gift and Cloud to either side of him, towards Pi'a'weh, but when the little Feather withdrew a long strip of Qworka-sinew twine from his clothing, Gift immediately backed up.

"No," she cried. "I won't go tied. I won't!"

Rab turned in time to see Button rise from the edge of the well.

"Then you'll have to stay here with us," she said.

"What do we do?" Gift asked anxiously.

"Button came back unharmed," Rab replied. "If we're going to find out what's out there, I don't think we have any choice but to do it his way."

"They'll arrest you if you don't," Button called to them from the well. "Trust me. The Feathers out there don't know Pi'a'weh. They won't listen to him. If they think he has captured you, they won't bother to stop you."

"Captured us? That's it," Cloud snapped and stepped deliberately up to Pi'a'weh, hands raised. "I'm going. Tie me up and make it quick. No wait." Slipping the bag of medicine from her shoulder, she held it at arm's-length behind her and called for Fin. "You guard this," she said. "And don't let Tickie get into it."

Fin took the bag and returned to his companions at the well.

"All right," Cloud said, raising her hands in front of Pi'a'weh once more. "Now I'm ready."

***

Rab didn't like it. He didn't like having his hands bound and he didn't like what he saw and heard the moment he stepped into the lane outside Lilly's compound. He didn't like it one bit. Button hadn't lied about the fire. Rab couldn't see anything that was still burning — at least not in the immediate vicinity — although acrid-smelling smoke billowed all around the settlement, taking advantage of every available channel, fouling the air and limiting vision. And Button hadn't lied about the need for their hands to be bound, either. Pi'a'weh wouldn't have been able to take one step down the lane with three unrestrained humans for company. It was now also clear why Pi'a'weh had gone to such lengths to retrieve his old ruined cloak. Although physically there was nothing Rab had yet noticed to distinguish this new race of Feathers from the Kun's people, Pi'a'weh's tattered cloak concealed the plain clothing he was wearing underneath. But the poor little Feather hadn't understood what he was saying earlier. They hadn't won. They'd lost. Lost the fight. Lost the settlement. Lost the little freedom they, as humans here, had. As he looked around, took in the new race of Feathers who were moving unhindered about the settlement and barking orders in a tongue that was at the same time familiar and unfamiliar, Rab couldn't help but wonder who would fare the worst in the end: the Kun's people or his own?

As they passed the Kun's palace, Rab was further troubled at the sight of the deserted platform. The whole front of the palace was broken down. He couldn't see all the way through to the other side but enough of the palace lay in ruins for Rab to realise that, if the Kun hadn't been taken to safety, he was now a captive. Or he was dead. There was little doubt that these ata'iri were superior to the Kun's Feathers in every way that mattered. Their clothes were the finest and sturdiest Rab had ever seen for these Feathers wore breastplates of Qworka-skin that had been so heavily worked and oiled they almost shone and the rims of their boots were trimmed with gleaming metal. The weapons they carried were unmistakeably lethal; to a one, each of these new Feathers went armed with long and many thonged whips that were sheathed together at the handle and equipped with razor sharp projections at the ends. And the number of ata'iri was far greater; for each settlement Feather or human Rab saw being herded away, hands tied and ankles often hobbled, he counted ten or more of the new race of Feather.

"We made a mistake," Cloud whispered as she walked to one side of Rab, stumbling over loose bits of debris littering the laneways. "We should have stayed with the others."

"It wouldn't have mattered," Rab replied. "Sooner or later they'll find them, too. I just wish I knew what they're going to do with us."

"They could have killed us all if they wanted to," Gift observed, voice raspy from smoke.

She was right about that. Instead the new Feathers seemed more intent on rounding up the strays, Feather and human, and gathering them all in one place. As they followed Pi'a'weh unchecked through the lanes, heading towards the southern ward, they passed countless numbers of the settlement's inhabitants being escorted back in the opposite direction. Among them Rab spotted Nat. He'd made it through alive. But either Nat didn't see Rab or chose not to reveal that he had because he just kept walking on, head down, feet shuffling. Rab made no attempt to speak and single out the old man. That probably wouldn't have been a good thing to do. Not a good thing at all.

Gift was walking with her head down now as well, maybe wishing that she'd stayed behind.

Had they made a mistake? If Pi'a'weh intended to lead them to safety, then surely he'd have taken all of them. He seemed genuinely fond of Lilly and Button but it was possible he'd just been deceiving them all along.

Rab took a chance.

"There's nothing but more ts'uns in this ward, Pi'a'weh," he said, pitching his voice low.

Ts'uns that had obviously taken the brunt of the attack. Rab hadn't seen a single ts'un that hadn't been damaged in some way. Nearly all were missing their Qworka-skin roofs. A good many vomited smoke through the narrow entrances. And whatever had been inside those ts'uns was now smouldering. Here and there Rab spotted an injured Feather propped up against the wall of their ruined ts'un. Most were being attended to by other settlement Feathers, overseen by two sometimes three heavily-armed ata'iri. The dead had been left where they had fallen. But not all of them. Rab couldn't imagine that all of this carnage hadn't occasioned a higher mortality. He'd counted only four dead so far – all Feathers – and judging by their simple dress, all settlement Feathers. How ironic if the doq'iri had actually fared better during the attack than their Feather overlords. Perhaps the human dead had simply been the first to be carried away. They'd probably never know.

Pi'a'weh still hadn't answered and Rab was about to prod him again when the little Feather stopped and pointed.

Ahead of them, the inner gateway was jammed with debris and the central and outer defensive walls beyond it lay in complete ruin, stones smashed, broken and shattered. There was only one way out of the settlement now – up and over the long mound of jagged rubble. From beyond the walls came a booming kind of drone – like a persistent rumble of thunder.

Pi'a'weh motioned Rab forward.

"Someone will stop us," Rab warned him. "Everyone is being taken to the northern ward. They'll want to know why you're taking three doq'iri in the wrong direction."

"Qoh," Pi'a'weh said and pointed to the filthy bluish-coloured trim along the neck of his feather cloak. Again he motioned Rab towards the breached perimeter walls.

"What do you think he means?" Cloud asked, stumbling and almost coming to her knees.

"Whatever he means," Gift said before Rab could answer, "it seems to have got us this far. And now that we are this far, I want to know what's on the other side of those walls."

"More of them," Rab said with a jerk of his head, indicating the horde of ata'iri behind him.

"But that isn't all. Look up," Gift suggested. "Into the sky."

Rab did as Gift suggested. At first he interpreted the diffuse dark band he saw over the top of the ruined walls to be the precursor of an oncoming storm. Then he looked more closely. Through the drifting smoke haze, Rab realised that, within that dark band, there was movement. A lot of movement!

"Qworkas!" he said.

"Hundreds of them," Gift replied. "Maybe even thousands. All beating and flapping those big, beautiful wings of theirs and all coming this way."

The ata'iri had already rolled through the roost settlement. Must have since the runner who'd advised the Kun of their approach had reported them advancing in that direction. They could have disturbed the nests and set the Qworkas flying north in a frenzy. But that didn't account for the number of Qworkas darkening the sky. These ata'iri had to be bringing their own flocks – flocks, Rab didn't fail to notice, of singularly *black* Qworkas.

Cloud was the first to start up the ruined inner wall. Even with her hands tied, she was managing better than the rest of them. Pi'a'weh, despite having the use of his hands, struggled the hardest. Even Gift, who was roughly the same size as Pi'a'weh, clawed, stumbled and staggered her way up and over the undulating mounds with greater ease than the little Feather. When they reached the pile of rubble between the breached defensive walls, the noise from outside the settlement became noticeably louder. Rab couldn't pick out individual voices within the incessant chatter or identify exactly what was making the shrill screeching sounds, but when they came down the pile onto the ground outside the perimeter walls, he wasn't surprised by what he saw. Just as the sky was teeming with Qworkas, the ground outside the settlement was teeming with Feathers on the move, weaving between crude and tightly packed shelters and the stockpile on stockpile of tinder offloaded from myriad carts that appeared to have been abandoned wherever there was a scrap of open ground to be had.

Pi'a'weh was the last to come down off the debris and the moment he did, he started straight off into the chaos. Rab hurried after him. As far as Rab could see, there wasn't a single human outside the walls. Pi'a'weh wasn't going to be able to carry off this ruse much longer. They would be spotted and separated with Pi'a'weh likely being led off in one direction while he, Cloud and Gift were led off in another. Perhaps their fates would not be the same, but neither could be good. If Pi'a'weh's intention was to save them, then it would have been better to try and make it up and over the eastern walls of the settlement. As rescues went, Pi'a'weh's was a poor one. The little Feather had to have another motive for leading them directly into the hands of the enemy. Were the three of them only tools to secure his own freedom from the ata'iri?

Evidently Gift was wondering the same thing.

"It's too late to make a run for it now," she said.

"But Button said it would be all right. Why would she lie?" Cloud asked. She sounded more dejected than fearful.

What was the point of fear now that they were coming so close to the end?

"He couldn't have brought her out this far, Cloud. I don't think Button had any idea what Pi'a'weh intended."

At the sound of his name, Pi'a'weh glanced over his shoulder, always an awkward-looking movement for a Feather. He had barely turned back around when a southern Feather stepped directly into his path, halting their progress. Whatever he said, the clipped delivery left Rab in no doubt it was a challenge.

So the moment had come. Rab looked from Gift to Cloud. What better company could he have asked for? When he and Gift had started on their journey together, he had known it would be a long road but never had he dreamed it would be quite so long. He was tired. And there were times, more and more often lately, that he could see that Cloud, too, had grown weary.

Their life together had been hard but, even in this strangest of circumstances, improbably happy. Their time could stop now with nothing left undone. For Gift though, everything was left undone. Perhaps in the end it was a reasonable justice for the one who had wounded Pi'a'weh, for the one who had tried but failed to return him to what he had once been, and for the one who had brought him home, broken, to a life of demeaning servitude.

And Fin? What of Fin, who had fashioned the spear that had wounded Pi'a'weh all those years ago? Even if he had been with them now, he would have struggled to make sense of the words that passed between the two Feathers. It was the first time Rab had heard this new language spoken at any length. To his ear, it was a more pleasing language than the Kun's people used, punctuated with far fewer clicks, although enough for Rab to suspect he stood little chance of mastering it, either. Pi'a'weh, on the other hand, appeared to be well acquainted with it.

Maybe when the three of them failed to return, Fin would realise that Pi'a'weh had deceived them and that he, Neila and Tickie were on their own. Maybe he could think of a way to get his little family out. Rab clung onto that hope and just as he thought he understood what was about to happen, the Feather who had stopped them walked away.

No! Rab had had enough. If this was to be the end of their journey, then he wanted it done. Over with. Now!

"What was all that talk about?" he barked at Pi'a'weh, who had started them off once again.

"Qoh," he replied, raising his hand briefly to the neck of his cloak once again.

"Why does he keep saying that?" Cloud asked, grasping a hold of Rab's sleeve with her bound hands. Her voice sounded strained, brittle. Like him, she was at the point of breaking.

"There's something about that cloak," Gift said so softly she could have been talking to herself.

"Where are you taking us?" Rab demanded.

"Chen'eh," the little Feather replied, clarifying nothing.

Rab thought Pi'a'weh might have used that same word while talking with the Feather who had stopped them.

Pi'a'weh raised a finger to his little beak of a mouth and shook his head. "No doq'iri tork," he said before hurrying them on.

So, the little Feather didn't want to hear any more talk from the thin-skins. Why?

There was *something* about Pi'a'weh's cloak, something that was getting them through. It was ancient. Filthy. Darkened and stiffened to the point of fragility with old dried blood. And there was that blue trim – hardly detectable now without looking closely. Rab tried to think. Had he ever seen trim that colour before on any of the cloaks the Kun's favourites wore? Ridiculous. How could he possibly remember something as trivial as that? Still …

He looked around, tried to take in everything around him. Most particularly he was looking for Feathers wearing cloaks. At first he saw none. There was only Pi'a'weh and that seemed odd in itself. Pi'a'weh, attired in a feather cloak the way no other Feather was, had been able to walk essentially unchallenged through an enemy encampment. That had to mean something.

Rab peered off into the distance – over the heads of a host of Feathers – through the gaps between their makeshift shelters – and found what he'd been looking for. So Pi'a'weh wasn't the only one wearing a cloak. Just a rare one. That had to mean even more.

Rab nudged Cloud's elbow, trying to draw her attention to the Feather in the cloak.

"What?" Cloud whispered.

"Look at the Feather in the cloak. Over there."

"I see him," Cloud said finally. "But what of it?"

"I think I understand," Gift interrupted. "Something about Pi'a'weh's cloak is allowing him to pass."

"And allowing us to pass with him," Rab added.

"That damn blue trim," Cloud said, earning for herself another cautionary glance over the shoulder from their Feather guide.

Chapter 12

"CHEN'EH," Pi'a'weh said, pointing.

Rab looked. He couldn't see anything but more of the same makeshift shelters and more Feathers. Always more Feathers and, overhead, the raucous flock of migrating Qworkas.

He might be taking an enormous risk but if this was the end, what did it matter? Reaching out with his bound hands, he grabbed a hold of Pi'a'weh's once fine cloak and spun him around. The scraps of a few broken feathers floated to the ground.

"We don't understand 'Chen'eh', Pi'a'weh. We don't understand *anything*."

Pi'a'weh's eyes blinked sideways – once – twice in rapid succession, startled.

"Chen'eh," he said, glancing around nervously. "Sist'a."

"Sister! Chen'eh means sister?" Cloud said, looking even more startled than Pi'a'weh.

"I don't think Chen'eh *means* sister," Gift interjected, "I think Chen'eh *is* his sister. Look." Gift nodded towards a nearby rise and the crude shelter erected on top of it.

There was a female Feather standing outside the shelter, looking their way. Without warning, she starting running, making directly for them.

"Chen'eh," Pi'a'weh said, pointing again. "Sist'a."

Instinctively Rab backed up, using his elbows to nudge both Gift and Cloud with him. Then Pi'a'weh started running, too, heading for the female Feather, leaving the three of them behind. Rab couldn't hear a word of the exchange that took place between the two Feathers but they appeared to be talking over the top of one another. If Chen'eh was Pi'a'weh's sister, was this reunion a good or bad thing for them? Seemed they were about to find out because Pi'a'weh turned around excitedly to call them forward.

The female, Chen'eh, eyed each of them as they drew near. She offered no words and, as usual, the expression on her Feather face betrayed nothing. Pi'a'weh led the way up the rise to the shelter and Chen'eh followed behind. At the opening to the shelter, Pi'a'weh stopped and motioned for them to enter. Rab was obliged to stoop, ducking his head low, to step inside.

It was dark there underneath the protection of the Qworka-skin covering and, at first, Rab could see little. His talent for blindsight had left him long ago; he'd had little use for it lately. Once his eyes adjusted, he realised there was little to see. A small pile of tinder. A Qworka-skin bag that looked as though it had been flung with little regard towards the back of the shelter and, coiled-up on top of it, one of those whips he had seen the ata'iri wield inside the settlement.

"Chen'eh tents'un seff," Pi'a'weh said, peeking through the entrance.

"It better be safe," Cloud grumbled softly.

"Wait," Rab called as Pi'a'weh's head disappeared and then quickly reappeared. "Where are you going? And how long are we supposed to wait here?"

"And for *what?*" Cloud added sharply as she dropped to the earthen floor.

Perhaps they'd fired too many questions at Pi'a'weh at once. He seemed not to have understood. Then he spoke.

"This go – *click!* – get Fin, Neeya, Yiri, Putton."

"And Tickie?" Cloud prompted, edging forward. "You'll get Tickie, too?"

"Tek'eh," Pi'a'weh said with one of his stilted Feather nods. "Get Tek'eh." Grabbing the Qworka-skin over his head with both hands, he gave it a mighty shake. "Good tents'un."

With that, he disappeared again. Rab was expecting Chen'eh to enter, but through the narrow opening, heard both of them walking away. They were chattering again, each over the top of the other.

Rab turned to find Gift, seated in the dirt beside Cloud.

"You don't happen to be carrying that cropping knife, do you?"

In the darkness, he could just make out her smile.

"I am," she replied. "Do you want me to cut us free, because I'm not sure that's such a good idea."

Cloud's head snapped around. "You got a better one?"

"Not yet, Gift," Rab said, ignoring Cloud. "For now, I just want to know if you have it."

"Why not cut ourselves free?" Cloud asked. "I mean if we're so safe here, then why didn't Pi'a'weh untie us before he left?"

"Maybe he thought if someone did come in, it would look better if we were tied."

"That's human thinking," Cloud shot back. "Who knows how a Feather thinks."

"He never even asked us if we had any weapons," Rab reminded her.

"Unless he just didn't think to," Gift suggested.

"Now you're saying we should cut ourselves loose?" Cloud complained.

"No," Gift replied. "Just trying to work out what Pi'a'weh is up to."

Rab stretched out his legs in the dirt in front of him, seeking a more comfortable position. "One thing seems to be clear. He belongs to the ata'iri, not the Kun's people."

"I can't see how that's possible," Cloud objected. "We found him with the Kun's people."

"Did we?" Rab asked. "We found him near the Kun's people. Not with them exactly."

"Maybe he was running."

Cloud turned to study Gift's shadowed face. "What?"

"Escaping from them. We thought he was scouting for them. But maybe he wasn't. And when I wounded him, we –"

"Took him back to his enemy," Rab finished for her.

"Oh, no." Cloud brought her bound hands up and kneaded her forehead a moment. "Then that explains it, doesn't it? Why he was Lilly's cook, I mean. Rab, what have we done?"

"And what's he going to do now that he's back with his own people?"

As Rab made to answer Gift, the coiled-up whip lying on the discarded skin bag caught his eye. They'd left that behind, too. Maybe Pi'a'weh hadn't known about Gift's knife but somehow Rab doubted that his sister would have forgotten about her weapon.

"Do you think you can use that thing?" Cloud asked, noticing the direction of his gaze.

"No. Could you?"

"I'd likely take my head off. Or yours."

"Anyway even if one of us could use it, there are too many Feathers out there. We might get by the first, but not a second."

"So we just sit here and wait …" Cloud raised her bound hands once more "… all trussed up like this? I'm not so sure Pi'a'weh is going back to get Fin and the others. If he intended to bring us all here, then why didn't he bring us all here together?"

"One crippled Feather. Eight humans. The numbers don't add up. Not if he was trying to make out like he had us under guard," Gift suggested.

"I don't think it's going to look much better bringing five," Cloud pointed out.

"Except one is old. One is lame and one is only a child."

"I suppose," Cloud conceded. "Maybe his sister went with him."

Rab hadn't really been listening. He was more concerned about Pi'a'weh's motive for bringing them to the encampment rather than how he'd done it.

"What do you think Qoh means?" he asked. "Every time I asked him if we could get through, his only reply was Qoh."

"Could be his family name," Cloud suggested.

"Or a rank," Gift added. "He might have been a soldier. Like a scout for the ata'iri or something. He was by himself when I …" she shrugged instead of finishing what she had started to say.

"Rank," Rab said. "Yes, it could be a rank. Whenever he said Qoh, he did point to the trim on his cloak."

"All we're doing is guessing," Cloud snapped. "If Pi'a'weh brought us here to kill us, then I wish he'd just done it and got it over with. Even if the Kun is still alive, he won't be making any bargain to get us back. And we're of absolutely no use to these Feathers."

"You wouldn't think so, would you," Rab replied thoughtfully.

"You know something," Cloud said accusingly. "Rab, if you know something and you're hiding it like the last time –"

"I don't know anything."

"Then you're thinking something," she said with a hint of suspicion.

"I'm trying to," he conceded.

***

"How long do you think it's been?"

"Too long," Cloud said, answering Rab. "Pi'a'weh has had time to get to the settlement and back by now. Either something has gone wrong or he lied to us."

Gift lifted her head. She'd been sitting still and quiet for such a long time, if he hadn't known better Rab would have thought she was asleep. "Neila and Tickie will hold them up. Maybe that's all it is."

Leaning down, with her head almost level with the ground, Cloud peeked out under the opening of their shelter. "I can't see anything but

Feathers moving around out there and I can't hear anything but those wretched Qworkas flying and flapping overhead. It's driving me crazy. If they're not back by dark," she said, straightening, "then I think we should cut ourselves free, take that whip and make a run for it."

"I agree," Gift said readily.

Rab's hopes were still with Pi'a'weh. Besides even if Fin couldn't understand ata'iri feathertalk, he could press Pi'a'weh about it. Unlike him, Fin couldn't be so easily led into a trap.

"We wait a bit longer," Rab said at last.

"Until dark," Cloud said, glancing at Gift who nodded.

"Until dark," he agreed reluctantly.

He was eyeing that whip, knowing full well that not one of them stood a chance of using it effectively. Over and over again Rab had scanned every dark nook and cranny of the shelter, searching for something – anything – that would serve them better. Beyond the old Qworka-skin bag, which Rab suspected held nothing but food and clothing, and the small mound of tinder, there was nothing. So that was all the weapons they had: Gift's cropping knife; a whip that though lethal enough, none of them was proficient at using; and perhaps a piece of urse wood if they could find one big enough. It didn't amount to much.

"Someone's coming," Gift said.

Rab's attention shot immediately to the entrance.

"I see Tickie," Cloud said, sounding relieved. Her head was pressed against the dirt floor of the shelter again. "They've come."

The little boy was the first to enter. His hands weren't bound but there was a circle of rope about his waist. As he came, tentatively at first, through the entrance, he spotted Cloud. Rab held his breath, willing Tickie not to scream out in delight. Thankfully the boy was content to simply dart for Cloud, trailing a short Qworka-sinew rope behind him.

Fin was the next to enter, hands bound. Behind him came Lilly and Button, also bound. Lilly looked weak and distracted and, as she walked, assisted as well as could be by Button, she stumbled and frequently staggered. Gift scooted aside to free space for Button and the failing Lilly.

"What's wrong with her?" she asked.

Button dismissed Gift's concern. "She's tired," she said, then set about making Lilly comfortable near the rear of the shelter. "It's been a long walk for her. She needs her water."

Rab was about to ask Fin about Neila, when Chen'eh, Pi'a'weh's sister, stooped and entered. She was carrying Neila. Her hands weren't bound but there was a rope tied about her ankles.

"Where's Pi'a'weh?" Rab asked of the featherwoman as, bending, she gently deposited Neila on the ground beside Lilly.

Chen'eh simply raised her eyes and looked blankly at Rab.

"He took off the second we got here," Fin replied. Placing his hands to the small of Neila's back he, with Cloud's help, began manoeuvring her into a more comfortable position. "Went that way," Fin added, nodding in a vaguely southerly direction.

Chen'eh quickly left the shelter but returned almost immediately with two heavy packs. Carrying them to the back of the shelter she placed them in a neat pile beside the coiled-up whip. The packs stowed, she returned to the entrance of the shelter and dropped to the dirt, curling her legs beneath her. When her focus began to shift unhurriedly backward and forward among them, it occurred to Rab that she might be settling herself in for a wait.

"Have you seen what's going on out there?" Fin asked.

Cloud reached for the bag hanging from Fin's shoulder, the one she had given him before they had left the settlement. "We've been in this shelter since we got here. We haven't got any idea." She couldn't get the bag past Fin's bound hands, so simply dumped its contents onto the ground.

"There are shelters going up everywhere," Fin said, glancing quickly at Rab. "Whoever these ata'iri are, it looks like they intend to stay for a while."

"Do you know what happened to the Kun?" Rab asked.

Fin shook his head. "His palace was destroyed."

"Yes, we saw that. Were they still rounding people up when you left?"

"Some," Fin agreed as he gently took a hold of Neila's hand. "People and Feathers – but the lanes were pretty well empty when we passed through. I think they must be holding them in ts'uns somewhere. Those that weren't burned-out."

"Why did it take you so long to get here?" Cloud asked. She was cradling Neila's head in one hand and struggling to hold the little metal vial of purple mushroom extract in the other.

"We packed food and water before we left." Fin nodded towards the packs Chen'eh had brought into the shelter. "And once we left the settlement, we had some trouble getting Neila and Tickie through. We were stopped three or four times along the way. According to Pi'a'weh, they were curious what use he and Chen'eh had for a child and a cripple."

"Suspicious, more likely," Rab suggested.

"What did he tell them?" Gift asked.

"That given the proper incentive, Chen'eh thought a strange thin-skin might make a better servant than a jit'iri and she intended to have Neila for her cook."

A nice touch of irony, Rab thought. But what was a jit'iri?

"Northern people," Fin suggested, answering Rab's question. "The Kun's people, I guess."

Cloud glanced up from her ministrations. "Or backward people."

Jit and backward – they were the same word in Feather. Did the ata'iri, and Pi'a'weh, view the Kun's people as backward?

"Anyway …" Fin took up, "Pi'a'weh told them that Neila kept trying to run away, so Chen'eh tied up her legs. I guess they fell for it because they let us go."

"How did he explain Tickie?" Cloud asked. She was attempting to get Neila to sip from the upturned vial and having a tough time of it with her bound hands.

"He said if you want a good and loyal servant, then you've got to start the training young. The Feathers who stopped us seemed to think that was pretty clever. Seems odd to me though. I mean, if one of the Kun's Feathers had tried to bring in some strange and new looking people, I don't think they'd have got away with it so easily."

"They might have," Rab pointed out, "if they were in a high enough position."

Fin's hand slipped from Neila's. "What are you saying?"

"Gift thinks that the blue trim on Pi'a'weh's cloak might indicate some sort of rank."

"I hadn't thought of that. He did –"

"Can't we undo these ropes now?" Cloud interrupted, clearly frustrated when the vial nearly fell from her grasp.

"Pi'a'weh said not to," Fin told her. "He said it's got to look like we've been taken."

"*Look* like we've been taken?" Cloud objected. "We *have* been taken!"

"I don't suppose he told you how long he intends to keep us here like this?" Rab asked.

"Not long. Before he left, he promised to come back for us soon."

"That's what he said when he went off to get you and the others," Cloud informed him. "But we've been tied up here half the day."

"Oh, that reminds me," Fin said. "Tickie, bring one of those packs here, will you. They're over there – see them?"

Tickie wasn't listening, so Gift rose and went to bring Fin one of the packs.

"There's food and water in here," Fin said, carefully emptying the contents of the pack to the ground.

"Lilly's flask?" Button piped up from the shadows.

She'd been so quiet, Rab had almost forgotten she and Lilly were there.

"Here," Fin said, retrieving a quite ordinary-looking flask from the ground before passing it to Button who, on hands and knees, had shuffled forward. Quietly she slipped back into the shadows.

"This is ridiculous," Gift said suddenly. She'd been watching Fin fumble with the scattered flasks and canisters on the ground. Rising onto her knees again, she made her way to Cloud. "Cut me loose. The knife's inside my coat. Left side."

Cloud didn't require further encouragement. Gently laying Neila's head to the ground, she reached inside Gift's coat and withdrew the well-used cropping knife. Using her teeth, she wrenched the knife free of its sheath.

Chen'eh had to realise what she intended to do, but when Rab glanced at the Feather seated still and silent at the entrance, she showed little reaction beyond a subtle but perceptible widening of her eyes. He'd have said that the featherwoman looked amused.

Cloud passed the knife to Gift, who though encumbered, soon severed Cloud's bonds. Freed, Cloud had an easier time cutting Gift loose. Snatching the knife from Cloud, Gift set about freeing the rest of her companions and, as she cut the rope about Rab's hands, raised her eyes to his, offering a brief and apologetic smile.

If Chen'eh thought Gift's act of defiance amusing, who was he to argue?

No sooner was Rab free than a shadow fell across the entrance. He glanced around and saw Pi'a'weh standing there. The little Feather had made good on his promise to Fin. He hadn't been gone very long at all. But instead of entering as Rab expected, he turned on Chen'eh. Rab had been at the receiving end of enough of Cloud's cool reprimands to take a good guess at what then passed between brother and sister. Maybe he couldn't understand what Chen'eh was saying in her defence, but he thought he got the gist of it. *Don't get yourself all worked up. I've got this under control.*

Whatever Chen'eh had said, Pi'a'weh wasn't buying it. Still he eventually ducked back outside, only to return a moment later, this time with another Feather. By the look of him, this one wasn't just any ata'iri. He wore a cloak, just as Pi'a'weh did, but the cloak was very different. First of all, it was clean, although, looking closely, Rab could see that it wasn't new. There was the odd broken feather here and there and at the bottom of it, where it brushed the ground, enough grime to attest to its age. Compared to the Kun's cloak, it was undeniably less colourful, although the subtle alternation between the green and blue of this Feather's cloak ensured it was just as magnificent. The colours reminded Rab of the pictures he'd seen of the oceans on Earth and left him in no question that this Feather was someone very important. Oddly Chen'eh showed no particular sign of deference as would have been expected among the Kun's people. Instead she simply rose and found herself another spot inside the shelter, freeing up the ground immediately by the entrance.

The new Feather appeared somewhat reluctant to enter at first. Perhaps, like Pi'a'weh, he had been expecting to see the captives still bound – if indeed they *were* captives.

On seeing the Feather's hesitation, Chen'eh spoke a few words, which seemed to reassure the Feather for he soon took up the space she had offered him.

Pi'a'weh made his way into the shelter and stopped directly behind Rab. Cupping his fingers over the top of Rab's head, he spoke one word in this new and strange Feather language and then, turning to Fin, said something in the Kun's language.

"He called you teacher," Fin said for Rab's benefit as Pi'a'weh stepped behind Gift and, cupping his fingers over her head, spoke again in both ata'iri and jit'iri.

"Warrior."

Fin's translation brought an unreadable twitch to Gift's face.

Pi'a'weh motioned for Cloud to approach and once she had kneeled, back towards him, repeated the same odd little ritual.

"Healer," Fin told Rab, but his eyes were on Pi'a'weh as the Feather shuffled across the ground to stand behind him and Neila.

"Friend," Pi'a'weh spoke for himself this time, then pointing towards their remaining companions at the back of the shelter, uttered words in the two Feather languages once again.

"Well?" Rab prompted. "What did he call them?"

"I think he said family," Fin replied hesitantly.

Pi'a'weh started back towards the entrance where he promptly, if awkwardly, seated himself beside the elegantly-clad Feather. Raising his hand, he cupped the Feather's head in the same way and said "Inchtet."

Rab glanced back enquiringly at 'friend' Fin, who just shook his head.

Either Inchtet was the Feather's name or it was his title – maybe both.

When Inchtet began to speak, Rab's hopes shifted to Button, Pi'a'weh's professed 'family', but it was clear that her priority was the old woman. She was only paying the vaguest attention to what was happening on the other side of the shelter; Lilly, none at all.

When he had finished talking, Inchtet turned from Pi'a'weh and settled his focus on Rab.

He could fully understand why Pi'a'weh had referred to Cloud as a healer but by calling him teacher, the little Feather was way off the mark. Was that why they had been brought here? Did Pi'a'weh think there was something Rab could offer the ata'iri? If so, all Rab could do was hope his failure wouldn't ultimately go against them.

The knot in his chest began to tighten when Pi'a'weh also turned to him.

"Inchtet ask how doq'iri come to this p'ace," he said.

It was the same road Rab had already gone down with the Kun and he could offer the ata'iri leader no better explanation.

"To this planet?" Rab asked, hoping that maybe he had got it wrong and the Feather was really asking him something else.

But Pi'a'weh responded with an ungainly Feather nod.

He wasn't going to be able to explain travelling through space any easier than he had before and the Kun, at least, was aware that an old ship was lying out there in a dry river valley somewhere. Likely the ata'iri had no idea.

"I can't answer that," Rab said. "I don't know how it's possible to travel from one planet to another. I only know that it is."

Should he offer Inchtet the same deal he'd offered the Kun? What harm could it do?

"This know that," Pi'a'weh replied. "*Inchtet* ask how."

"Tell …" Rab hesitated and quickly decided against even attempting to pronounce the Feather's name, "… him … that I can show him the ship my people came in long ago but I don't understand how it was done."

As Pi'a'weh translated, Rab sneaked a quick glance at Cloud. She was shaking her head at him.

"Inchtet eye," Pi'a'weh said with an aborted shake of his head. "Ask for more."

Inchtet could ask for more, but Rab had nothing more to give. And what did he mean by saying 'Inchtet eye'? That he'd already seen the ship? That wasn't possible. The ata'iri had come from the south and the ship lay some distance still to the north.

"He saw a ship?" Rab asked, leaning forward. "Where?"

Pi'a'weh pointed south. "Met'al Qworka," he said. "That p'ace."

So that's what Pi'a'weh had meant by metal Qworka. A ship! Of all things: a *ship*! But that couldn't be. Unless …

Rab felt a grip on his arm. Cloud.

"There's another ship to the south?" she whispered.

If a long time ago another ship had landed or crashed in the south, then there were other humans on this planet — humans they had never seen. And that just didn't seem likely. Not likely at all.

"Where *exactly* did he see this ship?" Rab pressed the little Feather.

Pi'a'weh didn't appear to understand.

"Can you explain what I mean to Pi'a'weh?" Rab said, turning to find Fin.

Rab watched the brief exchange between Fin and Pi'a'weh, growing concerned when Fin's speech grew tense.

"He said near the roosts," Fin told Rab. "But that can't be. If there was a ship there, then someone would have seen it before, wouldn't they?"

"He's lying," Cloud said, gripping Rab's forearm even tighter.

That had been Rab's impression, too — at first.

"Maybe," he said and looked back at Pi'a'weh. "Can we see this ship?" he asked. "'Eye' it?"

Rab waited, relieved when the exchange between Pi'a'weh and Inchtet was brief.

"Eye doq'iri," Pi'a'weh said.

To Rab, it sounded like an offer.

***

Chen'eh was taking her time. After Inchtet had spoken to her briefly, she rose and left the shelter. The uncomfortable silence that followed was broken only by Tickie's repeated protests that he was hungry. Button found something for the little boy among the provisions Fin had brought.

By the time Chen'eh appeared in the entrance again, Tickie had had his fill and gone back to sleep.

Chen'eh wasn't alone. Two figures entered behind her – humans bound about the wrists as Rab and his companions had been. One was male, the other female. Rab struggled to guess their age. They weren't as young as Fin and Gift. More his age perhaps. The woman's features were fine; her eyes the cool blue of bitter ice. The man was heavier boned with dark, almost black eyes. And while his skin was the same bronzed colour of a Top-sider, his face was unmarked by the elements or even time, except for a slightly off-centre nose that suggested it might have been broken at some point. Despite their physical differences, both looked fit – very fit. But also very cold. No wonder; their hair was cropped too close to their heads for comfort on the surface. The two were dressed alike in dark grey boots sturdier than anything even the Feathers had, and long coats made of a shiny black material. The coats were heavily padded, concealing their bodies entirely. It was the unusual bulk and texture of those coats that had really captured Rab's attention. These strangers weren't at all accustomed to the cold. Glancing sidelong, he found Cloud staring wide-eyed and bewildered at the strangers.

Chen'eh had the two sit on the ground beside her. She did not, Rab noticed, make any attempt to cut their bonds.

"Doq'iri," Pi'a'weh said, directing his words at Rab. "From met'al Qworka."

"Rab," Cloud leaned in close to Rab's ear. "Those clothes! That hair! I've never seen people like them before."

Nor had the ata'iri he was guessing. Or anyone else! They were sitting on the ground right in front of him and even Rab was struggling to believe his own eyes. Quickly he looked behind, only to be discouraged by Gift's unreadable expression and have his own suspicions heightened by Fin's obvious distrust. He turned back to gaze at the newcomers, as undecided as ever.

They *looked* human, but Rab really had no guarantee that they were. After all, he'd never expected to see anything like the Feather people, either. Had these two really come from a metal Qworka – a ship – that had crashed or landed near the old roosts, like Pi'a'weh claimed? It had been a long time since he'd dreamed of finding a ship that would take him and all his people off this cold hard rock. Sunny had seen to that. She'd shown him the truth and perverted those dreams into hideous nightmares. And now it appeared that a ship had come *to them*. Shouldn't he be feeling something? Joy? Relief? Maybe even a sense of vindication? Anything. If he was dreaming, he surely *would* feel something. He'd been wrenched, shaken and miserable, from bad dreams too often during his life not to finally accept that he wasn't asleep now but awake; this quiet and empty awareness of his own detachment told him so.

The woman looked over at Chen'eh and, receiving no response from the Feather, turned to her male companion. Although Rab caught some of what she said and the words did sound vaguely familiar, he didn't completely understand any of it.

Pi'a'weh pointed to Rab. "Ask how them doq'iri come to this p'ace."

"Pi'a'weh," Rab protested, "even if I can talk to them in the same language, I can't possibly understand *how* they got here, assuming they actually did come in some sort of ship and they're even willing to talk to me about it."

It seemed his argument was too convoluted for Pi'a'weh to absorb. Rab called Fin forward and had him translate for the little Feather, unsure until he started if Fin might not be too awestruck to oblige.

"Ask," Pi'a'weh prompted once Fin had finished talking.

Rab shook his head and turned to the newcomers. "Can you understand me?"

"Of course," the man said so readily, it made Rab jump. "But it can be difficult. Your speech is unusual."

'His' speech was unusual!

Rab had to hang on every word just to make out what the newcomer was saying.

"Then you've come across us before?" Rab said.

"Many times," the woman replied, smiling faintly. "My name is Asher."

"Is that supposed to mean something to us?" Rab asked.

"I'd be very surprised if it did, but for almost a year now, Sevan and I," she glanced towards her companion, "along with twenty others like us have been taking your people to safety."

Although Rab found the woman marginally easier to understand, what she'd just said certainly wasn't.

"Did you just say you've been taking us?" Cloud said, speaking up. "Taking us where?"

With bound wrists, the woman pointed overhead. "To our ship. We've been looking for you for a very long time."

While Cloud had been speaking to the woman, Rab had been watching Pi'a'weh, whose attention was shifting from one human to the other as they spoke. Perhaps he understood something of what was said but even so, it couldn't have meant much to him. It didn't mean all that much to Rab. Inchtet seemed content to allow the exchange to play out without interference. He was exhibiting a patience Rab was starting to find admirable.

"Were we missing?" Gift said, breaking her silence and attracting the woman's attention.

"Indeed you were. Your ship's arrival on this planet was a mistake. They weren't aware it was inhabited," the woman, Asher, said, casting a sly glance towards Inchtet, "or that its climate is so changeable. It was a mistake."

That came across clearly enough to Rab. It had been a mistake all right.

"So now what?" Fin scoffed. Plainly he still wasn't believing any of it. "You just come here and take us all away to somewhere else? That's a fine and fanciful plan!"

"That is the idea," Asher's companion interjected. "But we do appreciate your scepticism. It's been difficult convincing your people to come with us, but most understood in the end. And the plan had been working – until we ran into a problem."

Problem. Rab got that message clearly, too.

"Go on," he prompted evenly.

"We've managed to take most of your people off the planet ..."

Rab noticed Gift lean forward. She looked ... what? ... hopeful? ... apprehensive? He could read Fin easily enough but Rab was still having as hard a time interpreting Gift's reaction as he was interpreting the newcomers' words.

"... but unfortunately our ship developed a mechanical problem and we were unable to avoid being seen by these ... Feathers, we're told you call them."

Fin snarled. He seemed to be picking up on the oddly accented language far easier than Rab, but then he did have a particular talent for it. "What then? You're going to tell us that you're stuck here now, too?"

Rab was only half listening, loosely pondering another matter. If the newcomers were telling the truth, then had they just intended to leave everyone in the settlements behind?

"Us?" It was Sevan's turn now to smile. "Not at all. You misunderstand. By 'our' ship, I mean the small ship we've been using to scout the planet's surface for you. It's just a small transport ship. Another will come from the orbiting ship to pick us up."

"Orbiting ship?" Fin repeated, glancing at Rab. "What's 'orbiting' ship supposed to mean?"

Rab raised his hand and spun it around in a circle. "Orbiting," he said offhandedly. "A ship going around the planet up there." He turned to the woman. "What's the problem?"

"Them," she replied, jerking her head in Chen'eh's direction. "And this." She raised her hands to display her bonds. "I don't suppose there's something you can do to get us free?"

"Now they want us to get them free," Fin said, unnecessarily.

Rab was beginning to understand these newcomers' speech slightly better.

"I'm not sure how you expect us to do that," he replied. "We aren't exactly free here ourselves. And these Feathers here – well – they aren't *our* Feathers. We've actually never seen them before. And, as luck would have it, they just happen to be the enemies of our Feathers."

"So we discovered for ourselves yesterday," Sevan replied. "Can you try?"

"And if I do succeed, your intention is to take us with you?" Rab pressed him.

"That's why we're here."

"Rab, I don't know it's such a good idea to try to help them," Cloud whispered by his ear. "How do we know they aren't lying? Doesn't this all sound a little too good to be true?"

For a long time now, they'd been due something too good to be true, hadn't they? But this? Cloud might just be right.

"They could have been on this planet all along, Rab," she suggested. "Just like the Feathers were."

"Other humans?" That seemed almost as far-fetched as their own kind suddenly coming out of nowhere to rescue them. "In *those* clothes?"

"We don't know they're human," Cloud insisted. "I mean – just because they *look* like us …"

"We vote," Rab said, quickly deciding. "Gift?"

"Yes," she said without hesitation.

Rab turned to Fin. "What about you?"

The younger man faltered, taking a moment to look back at Neila. "I think they're probably lying," he said at last, "but Skylar did say Top-siders were disappearing. So – I guess there's a sure way to find out if they're the reason why. Make them prove it! I vote yes as well."

"I say no," Button called out from the shadows, robbing Rab of the opportunity to ask. At some point, she had started listening to the conversation. "Definitely no," she added more emphatically and reached out to touch Lilly's forearm. "And so does Lilly."

As Rab saw it, Lilly wasn't in a fit state to say anything – or to vote. But he couldn't just ignore her presence.

"Two for. Two against," he said, turning to Cloud. "It's up to Neila and us."

"If I say no, will you simply say no to agree with me?" she asked.

Rab shook his head and tried to smile. "I'm not going to answer that and you know it."

Rab watched as Cloud looked slowly about the shelter, taking in the faces of each of her companions until finally her focus fell on Pi'a'weh. It rested there a long time.

"All right," she said, turning back to Rab. "And we know what your vote is going to be."

"No!" Button shouted. "You can't do this. Let the Feathers deal with them. They're not our problem. If you set them free and they're lying, it might only make matters worse for us."

"And if they aren't lying?" Rab prompted.

"Then how do you know for sure that they can take us off this planet anyway? It isn't up to them." She glanced at Fin, clearly seeking his support. "Is it?"

Button's argument was sound and so Rab waited, but no one spoke up to defend it.

"We try. Have you understood some of this?" he asked Pi'a'weh.

"Some," Pi'a'weh agreed with a nod.

"Then will Inchtet free these doq'iri to prove what they say?"

"This ask," he said and turned to the regal-looking Feather beside him. Their talk was brief – too brief to have played in Rab's favour.

"Why?" Pi'a'weh said simply.

"Tell Inchtet that these doq'iri want to take us off your planet. All of us," Rab said, sincerely hoping, for all their sakes, that he wasn't perpetuating the newcomers' lie. "Tell him that we were never meant to be here."

Pi'a'weh began to say something, then hesitated. Turning to Fin, he launched into a spate of feathertalk.

"They're asking what benefit that would be to them?" Fin told Rab after Pi'a'weh had finished talking. "He said that if the jit'iri found us useful as servants, why shouldn't they?"

"Remind him that the jit'iri are few and they are many. Then tell him that a lot of us have already gone …"

Fin offered Rab a quizzical look. Were most of them gone?

"… there are too few of us left to be of any real use," Rab continued. "We'd be more of a burden than a value."

"You couldn't think of something easier to try to get across?" Fin objected before launching into feathertalk nevertheless.

"They could just kill us, you know," Cloud muttered under her breath while Fin feathertalked with Pi'a'weh. "Those two and us. It's a simpler way to solve that problem."

She was right. Of course, she was right. And when it came down to it, Rab was really relying on just one thing: Pi'a'weh. The odd little Feather he had known only from a distance all these years. The Feather who had every right to hate them – but didn't seem to. The Feather who could have left them as vulnerable as everyone else in the settlement when the ata'iri attacked – but hadn't. He'd called them friends and family. But had he meant it?

"It's the same thing we did for Pi'a'weh," Rab told her.

Pi'a'weh was speaking to Inchtet now and although Fin was obviously listening closely, he didn't appear to glean much from the rapid talk.

"Doesn't look that way to me," Cloud whispered. "Not if you and Gift are right. We let him live – sure – and did everything we could to make certain that he did live – and then took him back to his enemy."

"But we didn't know that, Cloud. And I think Pi'a'weh has been aware all along that it was an innocent mistake."

"Maybe so. Still doesn't mean they'll be inclined to help us."

She was right there, too.

Pi'a'weh's attention turned to Fin and Rab waited for him to finish.

"Well?" he asked when Pi'a'weh stopped talking.

"He asks what guarantee he has that we won't simply take this planet from him," Fin said. "It's a fair argument, Rab." Fin gestured towards the newcomers. "They have that ship – or so they say. And the look of their clothes alone does suggest they're much further advanced than the Feathers. They could have weapons, too. If I can see that –"

"We don't have weapons," Asher interrupted. "And even if we did, this planet's of no use to us. It's unsuitable. You above all should know that. Can't you make them understand?"

"What about their metals," Fin suggested. "You must use metals."

"Copper," Sevan replied. "But there's not a lot of it, and it's too distant from our home worlds to be worth the time and expense to mine. This is a resource-poor planet. Your Feathers are welcome to it."

"All we want is to take our people and go. Try to explain that to them," the woman said. "I don't think it will go well if you don't."

"Just what do you mean by that?" Gift asked.

"We may not have weapons," Asher replied, "but there's a ship up there that can make them. The two of us are missing and our shipmates will come looking for us. The Feathers either let us go or face the consequences."

"That sounds like a threat to me," Rab said, growing increasingly more uneasy.

"Not a threat," the woman said. "Just a fact. We don't want confrontation with these Feathers of yours. From the start we've tried to rescue your people – our people – without their knowledge. We've tried to stay out of their way."

That, at least, did have the ring of truth about it.

"If our ship hadn't run into trouble, our two cultures would never have met."

Rock that was only good for building walls and houses. A few pitiful oil seeps. Qworkas too temperamental to tame. And subsistence food, a good part of which was incompatible with the human body. That was really all the Feathers had. About that, these newcomers were speaking the truth – perhaps more than they even knew.

"Tell Pi'a'weh," Rab said to Fin, "that this planet is no good for us. Tell Pi'a'weh how many of our women die in childbirth. Tell Pi'a'weh how too few of our people reach old age and how the ones that do die from the cold. Ask him to tell Inchtet what he has seen with his own eyes. How the wrong kind of food here kills our children – and us." Rab wrenched up his sleeve and exposed the bare flesh of his arms. "They call us doq'iri, thin-skins, so ask Inchtet to take a look at my skin – a really good look – and compare it with his own. This planet is no good for us. We don't want it. We never wanted it. We were never meant to be here."

It was a lot to ask of Fin who obviously struggled through the translation. Only Cloud and Gift had really been close enough to hear what he had asked Fin to do. Judging by their dour expressions, neither seemed confident of success. Had Button heard what Rab had told Fin, she would probably have interfered. It was well that she was preoccupied with Lilly who seemed to be failing more and more each moment. Neila remained silent, half-sitting, half-reclining at the back of the shelter with Tickie lying curled up in her lap. She was straining to listen though; Rab could see and sense that clearly.

"It's done," Fin said.

And so Rab prepared for the wait and when finally, without any warning at all, Inchtet reached out and took hold of his arm, he actually flinched. The Feather twisted his arm, not cruelly, first one way and then the other, prodding and poking the skin almost gently with the fingers of his other hand. Releasing Rab's arm, he turned to Asher and motioned for her to approach.

She hesitated for a moment, then moved to kneel in front of Inchtet.

"Show him your arm," Rab told her.

"What?" she said, glancing at Rab.

"Your arm. Show him your arm. He wants to see if we're the same."

So did Rab.

Asher thrust her arms out in front of the Feather. He took one of her arms as kindly as he had taken Rab's, drew her sleeve up above her bonds, and began to poke and prod her skin in much the same way. Releasing it, he turned to Pi'a'weh. His words were few and, when he then rose and quit the shelter, hope seemed to leave with him.

Had their request simply been dismissed?

"Well?" Rab asked, glancing apprehensively at Pi'a'weh, who had made no move to follow the Feather leader.

"Inchtet think now," Pi'a'weh replied, then rose and made his way past Rab and Fin towards Lilly at the back of the shelter.

Chapter 13

THAT evening they were moved to a larger tents'un on the fringe of the ata'iri encampment. No sooner had they started to settle in than Pi'a'weh appeared at the opening.

"He's got a message from Inchtet," Fin explained after exchanging a few words with the Feather. "We'll be allowed to return to the Kun's settlement soon, but for now ..." He spread his hands, indicating their current quarters, then turned when Pi'a'weh briefly spoke again before leaving.

"Well?" Cloud prompted. She was on her hands and knees, attempting to make Lilly comfortable.

Fin shrugged a shoulder. "He's says he's going to be gone for a few days. Inchtet's got him escorting Asher and Sevan back to their ship."

"Alone?" Rab asked, surprised.

Fin shook his head. "Chen'eh's going with him. Some of Inchtet's advisers, too."

The leader of the ata'iri was not entirely trustful and Rab couldn't blame him for he found himself feeling the same way.

It became an anxious three-day wait for the return of Pi'a'weh and his sister, three days during which Lilly's condition began to markedly deteriorate and both Cloud and Button grew progressively more concerned. Rarely did any of them venture outside their assigned shelter. Food and water were brought on a daily basis by the same two members of Inchtet's clan, a male and a female, who silently came and went.

Fin was the first to spot the returning Feathers and his call brought Rab from the tents'un with Gift and Cloud close on his heels. Chen'eh was making directly for them, striding lithely through the scatter of tents'uns, cooking fires and industrious ata'iri while Pi'a'weh trudged a crooked path behind her.

Even before she arrived, Chen'eh was clicking and chattering at them with Pi'a'weh frequently jabbering over the top of her. Their excitement was overwhelming and Rab failed to gather anything intelligible from the overstruck feathertalk. Struggling to be heard, Fin finally managed to coax both Chen'eh and Pi'a'weh inside where Button, Neila and Tickie were sheltering and eventually teased out something useful. It seemed they'd delivered Asher and Sevan as instructed, then stayed to listen while the newcomers 'sky-talked' to their comrades circling overhead. 'Sky-talked'! That was the best Fin could do to translate Pi'a'weh's words and Rab took the gist of it. They'd waited to witness the landing of the rescue ship and it was that, more so than seeing the disabled ship or watching the newcomers sky-talk, that seemed to be the source of both Chen'eh's and Pi'a'weh's excitement. Rab could understand. A ship, strange though it may be, sitting crippled on the ground; talk aimed skyward towards an invisible comrade – until the rescue ship appeared in the sky, it could just have been some elaborate deception.

Only a small part of Rab wished he had been there to see it. There was a time when it was all he would ever have wanted. Times had changed. He had changed. The years had had their way.

Sitting wordlessly by Cloud's side, he listened as, through Fin, she showered Pi'a'weh with questions. Evidently the metallic Qworka-like ships were only scouting vessels and the newcomers had been systematically removing the planet's misplanted human population by way of a larger transport ship, accounting for the gouges they had seen in the ground when they'd been searching top-side for Fin and the boys. Although Rab occasionally caught Gift's eye across the floor of the tents'un, he could read nothing in her expression. Pi'a'weh's and Chen'eh's exhilaration had become infectious and most of her time was spent shielding Neila from her lively young son.

True to his word, the next day Inchtet allowed them to return to the Kun's settlement. The ts'uns and the lanes in the western and southern wards were badly scarred. Although Cloud clearly struggled to see Button lead Lilly away, Rab knew, just as she did, that Lilly would fare much better under Button's care in her own quarters. They arrived in their own ward to find their ts'uns in intact and it was an unspoken decision that saw Gift go with Fin to help with the care of Neila and Tickie.

Early that evening, the first of the ships came. The ground to the south of the settlement was congested with ata'iri tents'uns, making it an unsuitable location for landings, so a large area had been set aside outside the northern walls of the settlement for the exodus that was to come. Judging by the number of ata'iri guards stationed there, it was very clear that Inchtet intended to take personal control of the comings and goings.

A sound like strong wind driving through tall *ungtilis* brought humans and Feathers running. Hand in hand, Rab and Cloud sped down wrecked lanes, past smashed inner walls towards the northern field, tracking the flight of the vessel overhead. As he ran, Rab looked for Fin and Gift but failed to spot either in the throng running along beside them.

The northern walls had been hardly damaged during the siege but Inchtet hadn't wasted a moment. Circling the outer wall, they disturbed a small team of jit'iri prisoners at work on some minor repairs. For a moment Rab thought he spotted the Kun himself among them, but no, the Feather he had noticed was too young. Besides the Kun was probably dead – buried anonymously with the lost from both sides in the graveyard on the eastern side of the settlement.

It was a small ship, likely the scouting ship that belonged to Asher and Sevan. With the ata'iri guards holding everyone back, Rab and Cloud found themselves pressed against the northern wall with the rest of the spectators. Finally it appeared one of the guards recognised him and Rab, drawing Cloud in his wake, managed to force his way to the front of the crowd.

The ship had already landed by the time they were in a position to see it clearly. Crouched there in the churned up dust, it looked deceptively fragile. Only large enough to hold its two passengers and whatever machinery allowed the thing to fly, it would have to be cramped quarters inside. Standing beside the ship was Asher and Sevan, along with Pi'a'weh, six of his fellow ata'iri – and Fin!

"What's Fin doing out there?" Cloud barely managed to make herself heard over the noise of the crowd behind them.

"He must be translating," Rab called back to her after a moment's thought. Fin could speak to Asher, Sevan and Pi'a'weh while Pi'a'weh could speak to Fin and the ata'iri.

"He could have told us," Cloud complained.

"Perhaps he didn't get the chance."

When a Feather beckoned, a human jumped and quickly; it mattered very little if that Feather was jit' or ata'iri.

A weak ray of evening light caught the skip's outer skin and Cloud shouted at him again. "Well, I can see why the Feathers thought these ships were big metal Qworkas."

Rab could, too. But they were yet to see a big transport ship and Rab couldn't help but wonder what the Feathers would have thought of those ships if they'd ever had the chance to glimpse one.

Cloud tugged on his hand, attempting to encourage him closer. Rab pulled her back. There was little to gain by antagonising the guards and besides, Rab could see all he needed to see from where he was. It was only a guess, but he was fairly certain that Inchtet had sent Pi'a'weh and Fin out with a declaration of terms.

The excitement of the crowd was beginning to ebb and it appeared as though the discussion out by the ship was going to be brief. While Pi'a'weh's fellow ata'iri remained by the ship, he and Fin began to move away, leading Asher and Sevan in the direction of the ata'iri encampment.

"What's happening now?" Cloud asked impatiently. She was balancing on the tips of her toes as though that might help her hear better.

"I guess Inchtet has a few words of his own," Rab replied. "Come on." He nudged Cloud's shoulder. "We should go. There'll be other ships and we should think about packing for the ride."

Together they passed by the jit'iri prisoners who were already back at work on the walls, tapping the last of the dying light. On the way to their ts'un, Rab stopped to check on Neila and discovered Gift. She'd remained inside with Fin's wife and son the whole time.

It hadn't taken Rab long to realise there was little they could pack, little they had that would be of any value on their new world. A few clothes to see them through the first few days of the journey until they were provided with more appropriate clothes onboard. And after Fin's return from Inchtet's encampment later that evening, every human in the settlement was probably coming to the same realisation.

Some would die on the way to the new world. That had probably been the hardest reality for any of them to face. Rab should have guessed from the start that the journey to the new world would take a long time but he hadn't stopped to consider that — at least not while he'd sat waiting, uncertain of Inchtet's decision, inside the ata'iri encampment. It hadn't been his biggest concern.

Seven years! Seven years in space!

That was the news Fin had brought back from the meeting between Inchtet, Asher and Sevan and it had spread throughout the settlement faster than the Top-siders' fire. By the next morning, there were few, if any, who didn't know. And as more scouting ships flew overhead throughout the following day, and rumours began surfacing that the big transport ship would soon arrive, the agonising debate had gone on. In the end, only Button had remained adamant that she and Lilly would not go. The others were prepared to take their chances at making it to a new world where there would be sunshine and food and freedom – if not for them, then at least for their children. Without Pi'a'weh's intervention, Rab wondered if Button and Lilly would have been allowed to stay.

A sound foreign to anything he'd ever heard woke Rab from a light slumber early the next morning. Cloud was usually the one to hear things in the night but she'd slept right through it. He dressed quickly and, not wanting to wake her, carried his boots outside to put them on. A wash of a watery-pink sky was just visible low on the horizon and the lanes were empty, so he walked towards the landing field alone. There were ata'iri guards standing sentinel just as they'd stood since the field had been cleared. One guard glanced Rab's way when, finding a place against the northern wall, he lowered himself to the ground. But that one glance was all he garnered.

The larger ship didn't whistle the way the smaller scouting ships did, it moaned. And as the moan grew louder and louder, baser and baser, Rab turned his eyes to the sky. Soon others from the settlement would come out to the field to watch, while those who had been scheduled to depart today on the first wave of the evacuation would be making their final preparations, having passed, perhaps, the most-sleep deprived night of their lives. Rab could only imagine what they might be thinking ... how they might be feeling. His and Cloud's turn was yet to come. Along with Gift and Fin's small family, they'd been assigned to the very last wave of the evacuation and Rab was content to have it that way.

Out in the field, the ata'iri guards were on the move. A feeble early morning shadow touched the ground in front of him and glancing over his shoulder, Rab got his first look at the ship as it glided over the ts'uns behind him. Outwardly, there was some resemblance to the wrecked ship he'd seen out in the dry river bed all those years ago, but Rab expected that inside, it would look very different. The years had marched on and the descendants of those who had survived the flight from old Earth had marched on with them. They knew more. They'd ventured further and their technology now would make the technologies of their forebears seem as crude as that of the Feathers.

Rab watched as the ship coasted out to the west, wheeled once as it descended, then came to rest in the large field in front of him, leaving an eerie kind of silence behind when its powerful engines went still. From the corner of his eye, he caught sight of the first group of spectators coming out from the settlement. Rising, he cast one last look towards the ship before starting back for home. There was time left for them on this planet still, some things yet to do, and Cloud would be angry that he'd gone off to watch the big ship's arrival without her.

That afternoon, Rab had made a hasty excuse not to go with Cloud to witness the first departure. Conceding the same ploy wouldn't work twice, when the transport came again the next day Rab grudgingly agreed to go with her to the northern field. Dawn had barely broken but the second evacuation was already well underway. It was a slow process as now and then someone jumped out of line to speak to one of those scheduled to leave on the next and final wave. If all went to plan, they'd meet up again that evening, but it seemed that despite the first successful transfer to the orbiting ship, the spectre of uncertainty lived on among those left behind.

Finally the last of the travellers was aboard, the hatch was closed and the transport began to lift gracefully, noiselessly at first, into the clouds. As it picked up speed, it began to generate that same odd and distinctive moan that had woken Rab the day before. Trailing in its wake was a long white ribbon of vapour that looked very much like smoke. If Cloud hadn't seen that same white trail when it had left yesterday, and thought to warn him, he'd have feared the ship had caught fire.

Although the ship was beginning to edge from sight far above the ata'iri encampment, Rab fully expected Cloud to wait and watch for a while, to delay that walk home for what would now be the final time. People – *their* people up there among the clouds. It was a difficult thing to accept. And their turn was next.

Instead Cloud hurried him away.

On their way back, Rab stopped by Fin's ts'un to help pack the family's meagre belongings. It occupied his mind. There were few of his own things left to pack. Most of what remained could be distributed as the Feathers chose, but Fin's spear, he'd give to Pi'a'weh. By Feather standards, it was a pitiful weapon, but on this planet there was no such thing as waste; Pi'a'weh could find some use for it.

Returning to his ts'un, he found Cloud at work sorting her medicines. The stack of canisters on the left, those that contained the medicines she was taking, was very small. Sometimes a canister that had made its way to the left eventually was consigned to the right; never the other way around. He watched her work for a while longer, then moved to stand by the doorway so he might look into the lane outside.

"I know why Button won't go," Cloud said, breaking the long silence.

There were times when Rab was certain she could see inside his head. Right at that very moment, he sincerely hoped that she really couldn't. She wouldn't like what she saw. Those feelings of detachment that had descended on him inside Chen'eh's tents'un were still with him. He couldn't explain it. Couldn't bring himself to talk to Cloud about it. The only person he could think of who might understand was Gift. And Cloud certainly wouldn't have been pleased to discover him thinking something like that.

"Why?" Rab asked, glancing over his shoulder.

"Because of Lilly."

Rab abandoned his daydreaming and joined Cloud at the bench. He picked up the last canister she had moved to the right. "That's obvious," he said, popping the lid to sniff the contents. Green-weed. "She thinks Lilly might die on the way."

"That isn't it," Cloud said, taking the canister from Rab and resealing it. "Didn't you think it odd how concerned Button always was about Lilly's water? And why she was so particular about Lilly's cup?" She returned the canister to the stack of discarded medicines.

"I noticed," Rab agreed, looking directly into his wife's face, "but I never really thought that much about it. Why?"

"Because what she was giving Lilly wasn't water. It was some concoction she'd made from o'epu root."

"But that's poisonous to humans, isn't it?"

"Eventually. But boiled down – and in small enough doses – it has a beneficial effect."

"Like purple mushroom extract?"

"Not quite. O'epu is infinitely more lethal if you get it wrong."

"Huh," Rab mused. "But what has that got to do with Button's decision?"

"Without o'epu, Lilly will revert to the way she used to be. And each day it's requiring more and more o'epu to stop it."

"Then that explains –"

"What happened to her at the ata'iri encampment," Cloud interrupted. "She might not look it but Lilly is one of the strong ones. Her body can go on for years yet. Her mind can't … not without o'epu."

"So Button is prepared to sacrifice herself to stay? All for Lilly?"

Cloud nodded. "I finally got her to confess everything this morning."

"I didn't know you went out again this morning."

Cloud shifted another canister to the right. "After the transport left … while you were helping Fin. I had to try one more time to convince her to leave with us. I guess I wore her down so much, she finally had to give me the explanation."

That was believable. Cloud did have a certain talent for wearing someone down.

"But … I don't know," Cloud continued. "I think it's more than that. I think she might be scared to leave."

Cloud stopped fussing with her collection of medicines to give Rab her full attention. "Aren't you? A little scared to leave, I mean."

Rab stopped to think about that for a moment.

"I'm not sure I'd say I was scared," he replied at last. "Not exactly. I can't say I don't have any concerns though."

"About what?" Cloud prompted him.

Everything was moving so fast, Rab hadn't really had the time to fully grasp all his concerns himself. How could he put them into words for someone else?

"I wouldn't know where to begin," he confessed with a small smile.

"Try," Cloud pressed him. "It's important."

The last person who'd said something like that to him was Button, when she'd tried to coerce him to look through the books the Kun had taken from the tunnels. He'd said the same thing then, too – that he wouldn't know where to begin. And it turned out that just as Button had said, there was more than the Kun's idle curiosity involved. Just like now. Cloud wasn't asking about his fears out of idle curiosity; for some reason she needed to know.

"I suppose firstly because we've placed an awful lot of faith in people we've never seen before."

"You still think they could be lying?"

"No. I don't really think so. They've made good on their word and if they didn't come here only to rescue us, then why come here at all? It's a long way to come for nothing."

"There could be something on this planet that's useful to them, Rab. Just because they said there isn't, doesn't mean it's true."

"If there is something especially useful, we haven't found it. And nor have the Feathers. No. I think they're telling the truth about the planet and why they came here. But they could have just forgotten all about us. Considered us lost. They've gone to an awful lot of effort to save us and, let's face it, that's a little unusual for our kind."

"You did it."

"I did what?"

"You went to a lot of effort to find Gift. To return Pi'a'weh. Fin, too. He went after Tickie. Even Sunny did it in her own way."

"I suppose," Rab agreed, although he wasn't so sure about Sunny. He'd never be so sure about Sunny.

"Go on. What else?" Cloud prompted, leaning against the edge of the bench.

"I suspect we've all thought about it but no one has mentioned what's going to happen to us after we get there. We're uneducated –"

Cloud waved her hand to interrupt. "They promised to teach us during the journey. Have you forgotten?"

"No. But we're starting a long way behind."

Cloud shrugged. "In some respects," she said. "What else?"

"How well we'll fit in there. What they'll think of us. How they'll treat us."

"All those things must have been considered before they came to get us, Rab. Is that all?"

"Isn't that enough?"

"Well, yes, but I guess what I'm really asking is if you have absolutely no reservations at all about leaving? If there's nothing about this planet that you'll miss?"

"Miss? You've been sniffing too many of your canisters. What's there to miss?"

"Lilly. Button. *And* Pi'a'weh. I feel guilty about leaving them, Rab."

Rab didn't reply.

"And …"

"Yes," Rab prompted.

"Oh, I don't know … it just seems to me that we haven't given much thought to what we'll leave behind. It's like we've just dismissed every human who lived here and decided that everything they ever did counted for nothing. Like we're admitting we're just a bunch of ignorant orphans who *need* to be educated in these newcomers' ways."

"I hope it won't be that way, Cloud, but that's the risk we just have to take."

"I suppose," she said at last, offering him a thin smile. "Do you think it will be a busy place? With a lot of noise and people?"

"Maybe."

"Then I think I might miss the quiet here, too."

"What exactly are you trying to say?"

"I …" Cloud began but didn't get to finish what she had started to say because Fin appeared at the entrance to their ts'un.

"Could you come to my ts'un, Abby?" he asked. "A doctor has come to get Neila ready for the journey and I'd like you to watch what he's doing."

Cloud pushed off from the bench. "Don't you trust them?"

"It's not that – but – well, I'd feel better if you were there, too."

And so it began … this reserved and uneasy kind of trust that would follow them to the new world.

The doctor was standing by Neila's bed when they walked through the open doorway. He was dressed in the same heavily padded style of clothes that Sevan and Asher wore. His hair, too, was cropped in a manner totally unsuitable to living on this world. After briefly introducing herself, Cloud quickly had the doctor engaged in conversation, something about the treatment she had already given Neila. Catching Fin's attention, Rab motioned him aside.

"Where's Gift?" he asked.

"She took Tickie out while we got Neila ready. I think she intended to show him the palace now that we can get in there. It'll be his only chance, although he probably won't remember anything about it."

Rab, himself, hadn't bothered to investigate the rest of the palace. The bit he'd seen during his interview with the Kun had been enough.

"I'll see if I can find her. Tell Cloud where I've gone," he said and, turning, headed out into the lane.

The settlement was still a busy place although many of the humans had already left. Those waiting on the final transport were passing the time scavenging anything that could be of value – pitiful reminders of the years they had already lived. Like his and Cloud's mementos, they wouldn't count for much. The ata'iri were out and about, too, as well as those jit'iri who had survived the raid. While Inchtet's Feathers supervised, the Kun's Feathers saw to cleaning up the settlement. A few of the newcomer humans, those allowed by Inchtet, were moving about the settlement as well. Not many – only enough to help with the evacuation. Like the doctor who was now seeing to Neila, they were easy to spot.

The simultaneous arrival of the ata'iri and the newcomers had brought about a strange and dual reversal of fortunes. If the ata'iri had never stumbled on the newcomers, Rab wondered what the fate of the humans in the Kun's settlement might have been. It didn't bear thinking about, he supposed. The ata'iri *had* stumbled upon the newcomers and that was that. Now the doq'iri walked about free in the settlement, while the Kun's Feathers were the slaves.

He found Gift seated on the steps of the ruined palace. Pi'a'weh was sitting beside her and, on the platform behind them, Tickie was making a game of stacking pieces of rubble into an unstable tower. Rab took up a spot beside Gift.

"Fin told me you'd be here," he said and then peered around Gift so he could speak to Pi'a'weh. "What are you going to do?" he asked. "Now that you're free."

"Go jit," Pi'a'weh answered.

North?

"I thought the ata'iri were staying here."

"Some," Pi'a'weh agreed. "Some go jit."

"Inchtet?" Rab prompted and Pi'a'weh clumsily shook his head.

"Who are you, Pi'a'weh?" Rab asked after a moment. "I mean – really."

"Cook for Yiri," he replied.

The little Feather was making a joke.

"He's Inchtet's nephew," Gift explained. "And since Inchtet has no sons or daughters, he or Chen'eh are the next in line for their ..." she faltered, "... throne, I guess. Whatever they call it."

"How do you know that?" He wasn't sure he believed it.

"He just told me." Gift smiled. "In a kind of roundabout way. I didn't believe it myself at first but when you think about it, it makes sense."

Rab supposed it did. Pi'a'weh and Chen'eh did seem to have something of a privileged position with Inchtet.

Tickie came running up, pieces of rubble in hand. With exaggerated formality, he handed each of them a small shard before he scurried back to his wobbly tower. Rab rolled the shard over and over in the palm of his hand.

"Why north? Jit?" he asked, turning again to Pi'a'weh. "Is it better jit?"

Pi'a'weh shrugged, one of those disconcertingly human like gestures of his. "Wat'a. Many wat'a," he said, making a sweeping gesture with his hands.

An ocean? Was he describing an ocean? Well, why not?

"Many ts'uns. Proken now," Pi'a'weh added.

Broken. It sounded to Rab as though he was talking about an old settlement, one that had long been abandoned.

"Good p'ace."

"An old settlement by the water?" Rab asked.

Pi'a'weh offered a jerky nod.

Beside him, Gift began to laugh softly. "A city in the north," she said. "Haven't I heard about some place like that before?"

"I'm betting this one doesn't have a launch pad though," Rab replied.

"I'm sure it doesn't. It's a shame I won't be able to let you know."

"What are you talking about?"

"Is it true that they've taken all our people from the mine?" she asked instead of answering Rab's question.

"So I heard. From the other settlements, too."

"And the Feathers who were there?"

"The jit'iri? Scattered. Gift, stop avoiding my question."

"I'm going with Pi'a'weh," she replied. "I've decided."

Although he hadn't consciously come seeking Gift with the intention of confiding anything about his lingering sense of detachment, the notion had been at the back of his mind. It was done with now though. Out of the corner of his eye, Rab noticed Pi'a'weh rise and begin to mount the steps, making for Tickie.

"Why?" he asked. "Because they're heading to an old settlement? That's not much of a reason."

Gift waved his protest aside. "It's got nothing to do with any settlement. I didn't know anything about that. I was going anyway."

"Why?" Rab pressed her again. "Gift, they're going to find Sunny and the rest of the Top-siders. They've been looking for them."

"I know that. I've seen some of the scouting ships go west."

Perhaps Pi'a'weh had said something – something that had changed her mind.

"You voted to leave when we were in Chen'eh's tents'un," he reminded her.

"No," Gift replied, glancing quickly over her shoulder to check on the whereabouts of Tickie.

The boy was occupied with his tower of rubble, adding broken stones to the base of it, constructing a perimeter skirt while Pi'a'weh, bent to his knees, added a little turret.

"I voted for you to approach Inchtet on the newcomers' behalf," Gift said.

"Are you saying you'd already decided then that you wouldn't go?"

"I hadn't decided anything. I hadn't had a chance to think about it."

"But why, Gift. Did Pi'a'weh have something to do with it?"

Gift smiled. "Pi'a'weh? No. Not at all. Do you remember what I said to you down in the tunnels? About being moved somewhere else and then somewhere else again?"

"I remember," Rab replied.

"Well, nothing has changed. I'm still tired of living that way. But now — for the first time in my life, I get to choose. And when Pi'a'weh and some of the ata'iri start to move north, my choice is to go with them."

"Sunny will be on that ship, Gift. And she'll be on the new world, too," he told her.

"More reason to stay on this one," she replied easily and, reaching out took a hold of his hand. "I thought you'd be the last person to argue with me about choices, Rab. You've made your own before — years ago, when you decided to leave our village. Now it's my turn." Slowly, she shook her head. "I suppose my life would be longer and easier on that new world, but it wouldn't be happier. So you go to this new world and when you get there, don't waste a moment worrying about me. This is where I want to be."

***

He'd felt guilty enough leaving Button and Lilly behind, now was his conscience to be plagued by what he could only see as another abandonment of Gift as well? Cloud had little to say about Gift's decision when he told her, but Fin reacted with a shock that shifted gradually to surprise that Inchtet would allow another of the humans to stay. Rab thought he might understand. An old woman and a carer, whose only concern was the welfare of her charge. And now a lone and prematurely ageing woman bent on passing her abbreviated life wandering the surface of their hostile planet. How could Inchtet seriously regard them as any kind of threat?

The last evacuation was to take place around nightfall, so Rab left Fin to his final preparations. Standing in the doorway to his ts'un, looking out once more into the laneway, Rab noticed Gift returning with Tickie. Fin might try to persuade her to go with them. But he wouldn't succeed.

"Rab," Cloud said, snatching his attention. "Do you think the new-comers will ever come back here? Sometime in the future I mean. Long after we're gone."

Rab turned around to face Cloud. She was seated on their bed and there were two small packs at her feet.

"I suppose they could stumble on it sometime. Maybe even some race from another planet might eventually come here. Why?" he moved to join her on the bed.

"Do you think the Feathers might ever go looking for them?"

"Through space? I doubt it. It'll will be hundreds, maybe even thousands of years before they advance as far as the newcomers and by then —" he shrugged "— all of us will have been forgotten."

"I'm not sure the Feathers can last thousands more years on this planet," Cloud said thoughtfully.

Rab didn't reply.

She was silent for a while before she spoke again. "You know what I said before? About being scared? Well, I'm not scared anymore."

"No?" Rab prompted.

"You don't think I've noticed but I have. You keep standing in the doorway, staring out into the lane. You're thinking that maybe you won't even make it to the new world. You're thinking that maybe you shouldn't even try." She raised her hand when Rab made to interrupt. "Don't try to tell me that isn't true. I know it is because I've been thinking the same thing. After all we're getting old."

Rab's face crumpled into a frown.

"But we are. Old for this world and leaving it can't undo that."

"You're not much older than Fin," he reminded her.

She raised her hand again. "If Fin doesn't make it to the new world, there's Tickie."

"You're regretting we didn't have children," he said after a moment.

She shook her head. "Never. You and me ... we have other things."

"I think you mean *had*," Rab said pensively.

"No, Rab." Her arm came around his shoulder while her focus shifted. "I don't."

Rab followed her gaze towards the abandoned canisters on their old battered bench and something in his expression must have told her that he was finally beginning to understand.

"We'd better find Pi'a'weh." She stood up from the bed. "The ship will be leaving soon."

***

"The ata'iri are murderers and they're going to keep on being murderers. They'll move on and one by one take the jit'iri settlements. The ata'iri's weapons are better. There's more of them. And that seems to make them think they have the right to just take whatever they want."

"I'm not sure there are any jit'iri settlements *left* to take," Rab replied, answering Fin. "Besides, Cloud and I won't be going with them. We're staying here."

"What difference does that make?" Fin shot back.

Rab cast a sly glance towards Neila, propped up alert in her bed. The bandages on her legs looked different. "I wouldn't have thought you felt any sympathy for the Kun's people."

"I don't," Fin snapped. "But that doesn't change what the ata'iri are."

"Maybe they are murderers. Or maybe there's a reason they consider the jit'iri their enemy. Unless Inchtet told you and I doubt it, you don't really know, Fin. And nor do I. Perhaps someday I will."

He'd attracted Cloud's undivided attention. Until then she'd been content to let him speak for them. He'd just had enough time to rush back from his interview with Inchtet and hadn't had the opportunity to tell Cloud anything yet, but she was more than curious now.

"Besides," Rab continued. "I'm not so sure they're all that different from us. There's a lot in Earth's history we can't be proud of."

"How would you – oh, the books! It's always those books with you, isn't it? That's finished. Over with, Rab. It's got nothing to do with us and it shouldn't have anything to do with your decision now. You think that by staying here in the settlement, you and Cloud are distancing yourself from it. But what about Gift? She says she's going with them. Pi'a'weh calling her a warrior must have gone to her head."

Gift spoke up. "I'm going with *Pi'a'weh*," she reminded Fin, setting Tickie on the bed by his mother. "And Pi'a'weh is no warrior. If he was, he wouldn't have been down with us in the cellar, would he? And we're going north, Fin. North. There are no jit'iri settlements there and you're forgetting," she added, glancing at Rab for confirmation, "that even the mine has been abandoned."

Fin's argument began to crumble. "Then how are you even going to speak to these Feathers? Without Pi'a'weh, there's no one –"

"Pi'a'weh isn't the only one who can speak jit'iri and ata'iri," Gift replied evenly. "He says that the languages aren't all that dissimilar. They're basically the same. It's like the newcomers' language and ours. They're almost the same, just sound different when you first hear them."

"You can't rely on Lilly to learn the difference and even if she could, she won't be able to speak for you forever."

"There's Button," Cloud suggested.

"I think you're all mad. Why would you want to stay here? Isn't the ship that's waiting for us out there what you were looking for all along?"

"Once," Rab conceded. "But that was a long time ago."

"Well, I can't stay. Even if I wanted to. I've got to think of Neila and Tickie."

At the mention of his name Tickie looked up, clearly picking up on the tension inside the ts'un.

"Of course you can't stay. It's right you should go. But it isn't right for Cloud and me. That's all."

"And Gift?"

"Rab had nothing to do with that, Fin," Gift said. "And my decision has nothing to do with theirs. We're staying for very different reasons."

"And I can't understand either of them."

"Nor can I," Neila interjected. "Won't you change your mind?" she pleaded with Gift, then shifted her attention to Rab. "All of you?"

Cloud slipped away from Rab and walked to Neila's bedside. "You don't need to understand our reasons, Neila. Just accept them. Please. I don't want you to leave angry at us."

"It doesn't seem we have much choice but to accept them," Fin replied, giving Neila no opportunity to speak. Rab watched as, instead, Neila reached out to take Cloud's hand. He thought she might be crying.

Outside the last of the humans were on the move. Rab could hear them as they headed down the lanes. There was little talk, mostly just the persistent crunch, crunch, crunch of their passage. The sound was starting to wear on his nerves. Soon they'd be making their way out through the walls of the settlement. It would be for the last time. The transport was ready and waiting for them on the northern side of the settlement. There'd been no word on the scouting ships that had gone in search of Skylar and his band.

"Come on," Fin said, breaking the awkward silence. "You can help us take our things to the ship."

Fin went to lift Neila from the bed while Cloud gathered one of the packs. Gift carried Tickie, leaving Rab to shoulder the two remaining packs filled with the couple's scant belongings.

The lane outside was abandoned now, Fin and his small family being among the last of the humans to make their way towards the ship. As they walked past the shabby ts'uns and pitiful patches of garden, it occurred to Rab that in the future his and Cloud's neighbours would be ata'iri, for surely they'd be taking over the abandoned ts'uns.

A group of ata'iri were gathered by the northern wall of the settlement watching the ship slowly swallowing up Rab's people. Singly and in groups they disappeared. How would they react when they discovered that he and Cloud weren't among them?

Lilly was nowhere to be seen, but Pi'a'weh and Button were standing among the gathering of Feathers. Rab started towards them until Fin stopped him.

"There's time," he said. "You can still come with us."

Cloud, too, halted and crouching to her haunches, began to say her goodbye to Tickie when Gift lowered him from her arms. The little boy couldn't possibly understand that he was about to take his final walk on the surface of this planet and Rab suspected that, in the years to come, though he might recall the journey to his new world, he would have little memory of those he left behind on this one.

Rab glanced away to look at Fin. "We've made our decision, Fin. We're happy with it."

"I wish you'd never talked to Inchtet," Fin replied.

Strictly speaking, Rab hadn't. Pi'a'weh had done all the talking for him. As he had hurried along with Pi'a'weh out of the settlement earlier that day, through the tightly packed tents'uns in search of Inchtet, Rab had been plagued by misgivings. Were they making a mistake? Would Inchtet even agree to let them stay? But the Feather leader had seen the worth in what, through Pi'a'weh, Rab had proposed and as he had returned to Cloud, Rab had come to a quiet peace with their decision. He hoped that, some day, Fin would, too.

Rab placed the packs he was carrying to the ground and out of the corner of his eye saw the newcomer doctor approach.

"Go," Cloud said sharply, distracting Rab as she rose from the ground. "Go," she said again and gave Tickie a shove towards the doctor.

The doctor took Tickie's hand and bent to collect the small packs Rab and Cloud had left on the ground.

As he walked away, Tickie called to Cloud over his shoulder.

But Cloud wasn't looking.

"You get yourself well," she said brusquely to Neila. "That boy's a handful and Fin needs all the help he can get." Raising her hand she touched Neila's cheek, then did the same to Fin.

Neither Fin nor Neila were given the chance to reply. Cloud struck off quickly, heading for Pi'a'weh and Button.

Gift stepped up to take her place beside Rab. "If you ever meet up with Sunny on this new world of yours," she said to Fin, "promise me you won't tell her about me." Fin nodded, unable to reply.

"I'll miss you, Fin. I missed you all those years I lived with the Topsiders and I miss you now already. But I'm glad to see you go – you, Neila and Tickie. It'll be a better place for you. I know it will be."

She slipped away then as swiftly as Cloud had done, leaving Rab with Fin and Neila.

Fin was beginning to struggle – to hold Neila – to hold his tears – to hold on to his conviction to leave.

"Time to go, Fin. Neila is tired," Rab said and bent to kiss the small and fragile woman, tasting the salt of her silent tears. She grabbed onto his hand and continued to clutch it as Rab lifted his eyes to Fin.

Fin.

Not the boy he had constantly argued with and shouted at for so many years. Not the boy who had derived so much pleasure in defying him. Not the young man who had stood sullen and mute across from him as they had buried his brother, either. Fin was all grown up now and had the care of a child to consider, a responsibility that had only ever been thrust upon Rab. He'd probably failed more times than satisfied that responsibility but he had tried. Stitch was dead; Gift had effectively left him a long time ago; and now he would let Fin go.

"Tickie will be frightened on that ship all alone."

Fin glanced towards the quickly filling ship, then turned back to Rab.

"I don't know how many times in the past I'd expected us to part company," he said.

Rab cut him off. "Or wished we had," he suggested with a smile.

"That, too," Fin agreed. "But I never thought it would be like this."

Whoever would have?

"No regrets," Rab said, slipping his hand from Neila's.

"No regrets," Fin replied and, turning, began to walk away.

Alone, Rab watched them go. Along with his wife and son and the few possessions he had, Fin was taking a little piece of Rab to the new world –

a piece that was all used up now, a piece that had once been a part of who he had been, but could never be a part of who he would be from this day on.

Before Fin was halfway to the ship, Pi'a'weh stepped away from the gathering of Feathers and intercepted him. He passed something to Neila, but Rab couldn't see what it was. By the time Rab had joined Button, Cloud, and Gift among the remaining Feathers, Pi'a'weh was making his way back.

"What did he give them?" Rab asked, speaking to Button.

"A vial of soil from this planet."

"Why?" Cloud asked.

"So they would never forget where they came from."

Or who they had left behind.

"Is Lilly all right?" he asked of Button.

"She's resting," Button replied. "She's been aware of what is happening, if that's what you're asking. But I didn't tell her the last evacuation was today."

Just as well. If Lilly were fully aware of things, then she could very well have insisted that Button leave with the others. It was a confrontation Button was understandably keen to avoid.

Fin and Neila were among the last to enter the ship. Behind them came a few lone stragglers, including Nat. The old man didn't notice Rab and his companions standing with the Feathers and Rab was just as glad that he didn't. He'd said too many goodbyes in his life time and it was likely that Nat wouldn't make it to the new world. He'd die in space and probably knew it.

Once the last of his neighbours had disappeared inside the ship, Rab had expected that the big heavy hatch would be closed. It was a sound he'd been dreading to hear. Instead one of the newcomers stepped down through the hatch and began making his way towards the gathering of Feathers. He was carrying something in his hands, a large shiny crate of some kind. Rab stepped out to meet him and, drawing closer, recognised Sevan, the man whose release they had secured from Inchtet.

"Fin tells me you intend to stay," Sevan said when Rab stopped in front of him. "Are you certain of your decision? You and the others?"

In Sevan's dark eyes, Rab plainly sensed genuine concern.

"We won't be coming back. There'll be no more chances."

"We're certain," Rab replied.

"Then this is for you," Sevan said. "We'd intended to give it to the Feathers, but I think it might be better left in your wife's hands. Seeds," he explained as Rab was about to ask. "Different varieties of foods. They germinate for us in space and perhaps they will here, too, if you care for them well enough."

Rab took the crate with muted thanks. It was heavier than he expected.

"But is there *nothing* else we can give you before we leave?"

Clearly Sevan thought they were insane.

"Nothing," Rab said, then suddenly changed his mind. "Wait. There is something. You can give us some information. Did you find our people to the west?"

"Early last night. We picked up a small group. About thirty or so."

"Was there a boy and girl with them?"

Sevan smiled. "*Two* boys and a girl and it took a lot of persuading to get the older ones onboard. Why do you ask?"

"It's not important," Rab replied.

"Well, they're on the mothership now. Are they the last?"

"Perhaps," Rab replied. "Probably. At least I don't know of any others." He hefted the crate in his hands. "Cloud *will* care for these."

Sevan looked around and found Cloud among the gathering. "So Fin has assured me." He thrust out his hand. "I suppose this is goodbye then. Thank you for helping us back there –" he jerked his head in the direction of Inchtet's encampment.

For a moment Rab was uncertain what to do, then realised he was expected to take the newcomer's hand. Sevan held his hand briefly, then turned and walked away. As Rab looked past him towards the ship, he noticed a lone figure standing just inside the still open hatch. It occurred to him it might be Speth Asher, the woman they had first met in Chen'eh's shelter. When the woman raised her hand in a kind of salute above her head, he laid the crate on the ground for the moment it took to return a wave and no sooner had he lowered his hand than she was gone.

He walked back to join the others and although Cloud glanced at the crate in his hands, she asked him nothing about it when he placed it on the ground by his feet.

The sound Rab had been dreading happened an instant after Sevan stepped up into the ship. There was an awful finality about that sound – an ending – but when Cloud moved her hand to cup his shoulder, he knew that it was also a beginning.

Cloud's hand tightened on his shoulder as the ship began to rise. Her eyes never wavered from the ship, which hovered in air for a moment, kicking up dust. Rab shielded his eyes as the dust drifted in their direction. Then the ship began to move – slowly – picking up height as it went. The ship nudged south into the coming darkness, so high overhead that Rab could barely see it anymore. And then the speck was gone and only the long trail lingered until it, too, turned to a broad band of white blemishing the grey clouds of evening, then to a wisp and then to nothing at all.

Rab finally lowered his eyes and, as he did, saw a Feather, barely visible, standing by himself on a small rise to the north. Inchtet. He elbowed Cloud, drawing her attention to the Feather leader.

"He's worried," she said. "That they'll come back."

"They won't."

Rab and Cloud were the last to head back towards the settlement.

"There goes a strange pair," Cloud said softly as they followed behind Pi'a'weh and Gift who walked, side by side, through the entrance to the outer wall.

"Not sure I'd call them a pair," Rab replied.

"You know what I mean. Will you try to talk her into staying with us in the settlement?"

"No," Rab said with conviction. He had a suspicion his wife might have smiled.

"So are you ever going to tell me? Or am I just going to have to wait to find out?"

"Tell you what?"

She tapped the crate Rab was carrying. "What's in there for one thing?"

"Seeds. A present for you from Sevan," he told her, buoyed by the flicker of excitement he caught in her eyes.

"What about the arrangement you made with Inchtet?" she asked more hesitantly. "I know you're not going to be content to spend the rest of your life here watching me plant crops and tend to the odd Feather ailment. You've got a plan."

"It came to me when Pi'a'weh and I were rushing to see Inchtet. No ..." he hesitated, "... that's not quite true. I half had it before we even found Pi'a'weh."

"And?" she pressed him impatiently.

"Inchtet's seen our books," Rab said, almost as an aside.

"So?"

"I'm going to teach the ata'iri how to read."

Cloud's eyes widened in surprise. "Our books?"

"Them, too. But mostly I'm going to help them write their own books in Feather. We can use thin strips of Qworka-skin or maybe make a kind of paper from *ungtilis* or some other …"

"You're going to write feathertalk using our – our –"

"Alphabet," Rab suggested.

"Yes. Our alphabet."

"I can't very well use any other, can I?"

"Well, that'll cause some confusion."

"To who?"

"Anyone who might find it after all the Feathers are gone."

"Not my problem," Rab said.

"But why, Rab?"

"Why did Inchtet agree or why did I offer to do it?"

"Both, I guess."

"It was you who gave me the idea. Inchtet isn't stupid. The Feathers' time is limited. You said it yourself. And the way it is now, when they're gone, there'll be nothing but ruins to show that they were here. Who they were. What they did. It will all be lost. Recording it was something that needed to be done and I seem to be the only one on this planet who can get it started."

"And *our* story?" she asked after a brief hesitation. "Will you write that, too?"

"Of course," he answered. "We're part of the Feathers' story, aren't we? And they're part of ours."

That seemed to please her as much as Sevan's gift.

"These Feathers," he said, "aren't really so different from us. When it comes down to it."

"I suppose," Cloud said pensively, "but it never occurred to me that even powerful Feathers like the Kun and Inchtet might be afraid of being forgotten."

THE END

Thank you for reading THE UNFORGOTTEN.

We hope you enjoyed it.

If you would like to be kept informed of further
releases from Hague Publishing, why not subscribe to our newsletter at:

www.HaguePublishing.com/subscribe.php

And if you loved the book and have a moment to spare we would
really appreciate a short review. Your help in spreading the word is
gratefully received.

About The Author

SHAUNE Lafferty Webb was born in Brisbane, Australia. Her father was an amateur astronomer and her eldest brother, an avid science fiction reader, so perhaps it was inevitable that she developed an early enthusiasm for writing speculative fiction.

After obtaining a degree in geology from the University of Queensland, Shaune subsequently worked in geochemical laboratories, exploration companies, and, while living in the United States, at a multinational scientific institute involved in exploration beneath the ocean floors.

Her short stories have appeared in AntipodeanSF, The Nautilus Engine, Blue Crow Magazine, and The Vandal and her novels, 'Bus Stop on a Strange Loop' and 'Balanced in An Angel's Eye', were released by Winterbourne Publishing in 2011 and 2012, respectively.

Commencing in May 2015, 'Cold Faith', 'Faithless', and 'The Unforgotten', which together make up 'The Safe Harbour Chronicle' series, were published by Hague Publishing.

'Once a Dog', an anthropomorphic novel, was released in May 2018 by Jaffa Books; the novel was nominated for the 2018 Ursa Major Award in the category of Best Novel and ultimately ranked first runner-up in the awards ceremony held at Columbus, Ohio, 26 May 2019.

Shaune lives in Brisbane with her husband, a research scientist, and when not writing, she is kept busy pandering to a pair of wayward canine companions.

Hague

Publishing

www.HaguePublishing.com

PO Box 451 Bassendean
Western Australia 6934